MW01527666

New Beginnings
Mary Metcalfe

ALSO BY MARY METCALFE:

"WINDS OF CHANGE"
"ROAD TO TOMORROW"

Copyright © 2012 by Mary Metcalfe

First Edition – October 2012

ISBN

978-0-9879300-4-0 (Paperback)
978-0-9879300-5-7 (eBook)

All rights reserved.

This is a work of fiction. All names, places, characters, and events in this book are fictitious. Any resemblance to actual persons, living or dead, events, or locales is purely coincidental. No part of this publication may be reproduced in any form, or by any means, electronic or mechanical, including photocopying, recording, or any information browsing, storage, or retrieval system, without permission in writing from the publisher.

Published by:

Laskin Publishing
54 impasse Roy
St-Emile-de-Suffolk, QC
Canada
J0V 1Y0

www.lakefrontmuse.ca

Distributed to the trade by The Ingram Book Company

Acknowledgements

Thanks as always to my wonderfully supportive husband, Jacques Chenail, who cheers me on daily and helps me brainstorm on my stories. I'm grateful for the advice and corrections of editors Cara Lockwood and Warren Layberry.

Dedication

Dedicated with love to our daughter, Danielle Metcalfe-Chenail, and son-in-law, Doug Pagnutti, whose new beginnings started with the birth of our grandson, Andre Barrett Pagnutti, on April 17, 2012.

Chapter One

"DAMN. I DON'T HAVE TIME FOR THIS." Carol Brock stared down at her electric-blue BMW in dismay and growing anger. She'd been completely boxed in by a SUV on one side and a glossy black pickup on the other. Not a chance she could get in either the driver or passenger doors. *I'm supposed to show a house in thirty minutes, half way across town. I don't need this.* Then she saw her driver's side mirror and gasped. It was dangling on a couple of wires.

"What the hell?" Taking out her phone, she pressed on the camera app and started shooting. "Think you can get away with this? Think again."

She snapped the scene, the vehicles, and their license plates and sent the photos to someone she knew in the Boston Police, with the message: "Guzzo, you're my witness. I'm having the pickup towed out so I can get in my car."

As she called for roadside assistance, Carol stamped her feet to try and warm them. It was another cold, wet, gray November day. Gone were the sweet smells and vibrant colors of early fall. While her soft leather boots were beautiful and comfortable to walk in, they were not meant to stand around in. *I should call the Fowlers and let them know I'll be a bit late,* she thought and keyed in another number. *I can blame it on the traffic.*

The tow truck arrived. Within a few minutes, the driver had hitched up the gleaming black pickup and was pulling it onto the truck bed when a loud voice yelled over the grinding whine of the hydraulics.

"Whoa. Wait a minute. What do you think you're doing? Stop."

Carol turned to see a very tall, well-dressed man running across the parking lot. She stood her ground and watched his approach, with a smirk on her glossed lips.

Great eye candy, but boy, does he look angry. I might enjoy venting on such a magnificent male. If you're going to have a good mad on, might as well be mad at someone good looking.

As he drew up beside her, Carol looked up into molten hazel eyes that were flashing with anger. She felt a small frisson of fear but brushed it aside. She already had a business card in her hand. Before he could say a word, she held it out to him.

"You ripped off my side mirror. Here's my card. I'd appreciate yours if you have one. You owe me for the mirror." She could almost feel the heat of his anger and swallowed a bit nervously. But adrenaline was coursing through her veins. Her emerald green eyes stared straight into his.

"My God, woman." He looked at her card. "Carol Brock, real estate agent. Well, you're a real piece of work, Ms. Brock, let me tell you. What gives you the right to move my truck? I could have you charged with theft."

"Go ahead and try. I've already sent photos to the police. I can prove you boxed me in and ripped off my mirror. I'm sure I can have you charged with something too."

"Well, I'll be damned. You don't miss a beat. Photos to the police already."

Carol watched in amazement as the flashing fire of anger was completely extinguished and replaced with mirth. She was sure the color of his eyes had changed in an instant. Now the brazen man was smiling and laughing at her. Her temper seethed as she fixed him with a look that only a mother could muster.

"I hardly think this is anything to laugh about." Her voice dripped with disdain as she fixed him with a steely gaze. "I have a full day ahead. You've thrown my entire schedule off, and you've damaged my car. I'm going to lose valuable time getting it fixed."

"Okay, Ms. Brock, mea culpa. I did park badly, but I didn't realize

I'd damaged your car. Now I see that I have, and I'm making you late for your next appointment. Can't argue with you on any of those points. My name is Devin, Devin Elliott." He held out his hand, which now held a business card.

Carol took the card but refused the offer of a handshake. She couldn't argue with him. She swallowed her temper reluctantly.

"Devin Elliott, the architect." Carol knew the name. Anyone in Boston real estate circles knew Elliott and Co., Restoration Specialists. "Well then, at least I know you can afford to pay for the mirror. That honking big truck of yours was a pretty obvious clue, too. The mirror will cost at least eight hundred dollars. It's articulated, electronic, and heated." She looked at her phone. "Damn. I really am going to be late. I need to get going."

"Excuse me?" They both looked over as the tow truck driver leaned his head out of his window. "Where do you want the pickup, sir?"

"Just put it over there, please." Devin pointed towards the entrance of the lot and then turned back to Carol. "What do you say we get the tow truck to take your car to your dealership? I'll drive you to your next appointment if they don't have a loaner for you."

Carol snorted and put a hand up to smooth her coppery auburn waves. "I do not need a ride, and I am perfectly capable of handling this situation. You've been quite enough help already." She pulled up to her full height. Even with towering heels she couldn't look him straight in the eye. She thrust her chin up stubbornly.

He smiled down at her. "After seeing you in action just now, I'm quite convinced you can take care of just about anyone or anything. But I don't think your day will get any better driving around with your side mirror hanging off." Devin continued his delicate negotiations. "You'll just get stopped by the police, ticketed, and pulled off the road. Then you'll be calling for the tow guy again. He's already here. Why not take advantage of it and save some of that valuable time you just mentioned? Plus, we can get the estimate, and I can pay for it right then and there."

His small jab of sarcasm was not lost on her, but he did have a good point. "Oh, all right. I accept your offer." The driver agreed to switch the vehicles.

Devin walked over to the tow truck. Reaching into his pocket, he took out a thick wad of bills, peeled off a twenty, and handed it up to the surprised driver. "Thanks for taking care of this." He walked back to where Carol was stamping her feet again.

"This way, madam." He opened the passenger door of the pickup. "I still don't know how I managed to rip off your mirror without feeling or hearing anything. And I can't see any damage to my truck."

As they got in and buckled up, he turned the key in the ignition. The truck cab was immediately rocked with Aerosmith at a decibel level normally reserved for a concert hall. Devin winced and quickly turned it off. "Guess I know why now." He grinned sheepishly.

"Thanks for turning it off." Carol wasn't ready for loud music or conversation. "Just drive, please. I need to call my client, re-schedule our meeting, and probably several more."

After programming his GPS, Devin pulled into the steady stream of traffic and headed towards Carol's dealership.

She made a number of quick calls to rearrange her schedule and confirm a loaner. After making a couple of call-backs, she closed the phone and gazed around her, somewhat more confident about the day ahead. The truck smelled new but with another very faint scent. It wasn't a perfume smell. It was more a slight musk. It made her think of the horses and riding stables, where she'd spent many happy Saturdays as a teen. Looking at his expensive tailored clothes, she found it hard to imagine him mucking about in a stable. But then people probably wouldn't imagine it of her either.

"Devin, first an apology and then my thanks for your offer. I was seeing red when I couldn't get into the car. When I saw the mirror, I was totally pissed off." She looked over at her chauffeur, noting his chiseled jaw line and what she could only describe as sculpted ears. "I don't usually have such a wicked temper."

"Could've fooled me." Devin drawled out the statement while signaling a lane change. "From what I saw, you've had some practice I'd say."

"I've been told I have a few control issues." Carol pursed her lips and smiled faintly. "Okay, maybe more than a few." Being driven around by someone else was a whole new sensation. She always drove herself and almost never took a taxi. She felt herself relaxing even as she wondered how she was going to get everything done for today.

"Feel free to put Aerosmith back on. I'm pretty partial to *Dream On.*"

"I'd rather talk to you. By the way, are you free for dinner tonight? It's the least I can do after throwing your whole day out of whack." Devin smiled and glanced sideways at her.

"Thanks for the invitation, but I have a class I don't want to miss this evening."

"Some other time, then. I'd like to make it up to you other than just paying for the mirror. You have lost valuable time. I know how I would feel."

"It's really not necessary." Carol felt her good angel warning her not to fall for yet another good-looking man. She wanted to swat her away but remembered her promise to herself. "I appreciate you taking me to the dealership and agreeing to pay for the mirror. That'll be fine."

"I'm crushed." Devin hung his head down in a gesture of dejection, but he was still smiling. "I don't often get turned down for dinner by beautiful women."

Carol smiled and looked again at his handsome profile. "There's a lot going on in my life right now. Let's leave it at that." She turned to look out the passenger window. Damn the good angel. She wouldn't shut up.

"I was only talking about a simple meal. No big deal." Devin shrugged and drove on in silence. He signaled his turn to the exit nearest the dealership.

Carol went to register for the mirror replacement. She wasn't surprised when the clerk estimated over a thousand dollars with the labor. What did surprise her was her reaction. *It's just a damn mirror,* she thought. *When did I start to need a car with thousand dollar mirrors?* She shook her head to clear it.

Carol watched as Devin pulled out a charge card and chatted with the parts clerk as she processed his payment. She smiled sardonically as the young woman blushed prettily when Devin complimented her on her earrings. *What a shameless flirt,* she thought. *Why do men like him feel this need to hit on every good-looking woman they see?* She let go an exasperated sigh and wandered into the showroom.

"It's all paid for." Devin came up behind her. "Carol, I really hope you'll reconsider my dinner invitation. I do feel badly about the damage."

She turned to face him, her face a neutral mask. Now that she'd put him in the player category, she really didn't want to bother with dinner no matter how handsome he might be. She knew his type. He was nothing but trouble. "As I said, it's really not necessary. It was nice meeting you, in an awkward kind of way. I'd better get going. Take care." Carol put out her hand. She was all business. After a quick handshake, she turned and walked back to the service area.

CAROL PLOWED THROUGH THE REST OF HER DAY with a zeal that surprised even her. Despite the morning debacle with her car, she managed three showings and helped two other clients put together offers of purchase. By six o'clock, she was primed for her yoga class, ready to call it a day.

"Have you heard of Devin Elliott, the architect who restores old heritage properties?" Carol stood next to her friend Jennifer and stretched gratefully as they finished their session. The tension had drained from her body even as her muscles received a powerful workout.

"Actually, I have. His firm handled one of the houses down the street from me. Brought the house back up to code, re-did a roofline, and found replicas of the antique windows to replace the originals. Everyone in the neighborhood was impressed. You met him?"

"In a manner of speaking. He parked too close beside me at the bank and tore my mirror off. I couldn't get into the Bimmer, so I had him towed out. He ended up driving me to the dealership. Long story short, he paid over a thousand dollars." Carol took a long drink from her water bottle.

"Sounds like he did the right thing all around. What did you think of him?"

"He asked me out for dinner, but I said no. My attractive-man-meter hit the top with a major whammy. I don't need another entanglement with a cute guy. I'm still trying to sort out the mess Michel left me in. My reputation took a huge hit when the con story and trial hit the news." Carol shook her head and took a deep, slow breath. "Several clients demanded I be taken off their listing."

"I remember that very well." Jennifer picked up her mat. "But Devin Elliott is well-known and respected."

"I know, but you know my track record with handsome charming men."

"So you attracted Lance the leech and Michel the con artist. You're a high-profile, successful professional who happens to be quite good-looking. It was probably just a matter of time until some criminal tried to profit from your contacts and clients. With social media, you're very visible. Maybe too visible?"

Carol loosened her pony tail and fluffed out her hair, preening just slightly at Jennifer's compliment. "That visibility is important to my work. Being a successful agent is all about networking and visibility. I suppose you're right about Devin being well-known and respected professionally. But he's still a flirt. He had the clerk at the dealership blushing. I'm not ready to get involved with a man with major magnetism, who clearly knows how to use it.

"Besides, I've gotten used to being alone this past year. There's no drama. Other than spending time, when I can, with Ash and Jim, I've pretty much kept to myself. A lot of people I thought were my friends disappeared after the art theft story broke."

"Well, you've still got Ben and I. Speaking of which, we've finally set a date for the double wedding. Lana didn't want to get married while she was pregnant. You need to keep next May twenty-fifth open. We want you to be our witness."

"That's wonderful news!" Carol gave Jennifer a warm hug. "Let me book it in right now." Carol fished her tablet out of her bag and blocked off the full day and the day before. "My personal wedding gift to you—the day before the ceremony we get our hair done and have a manicure, pedicure, and facial. What do you say? My treat. Get you all primed for a wild wedding night with your husband." Carol cocked her eyebrows as a wicked grin played across her lips.

"That's no cheap gift, Carol. Are you sure?"

"It's my way of saying thanks for not calling me the matron of honor. I'm not ready to see myself as a matron, even if my kids are in their twenties."

"We thought witness was more contemporary." Jennifer chuckled. "And no, I could never see you as a matron. Many other things, but never a matron."

"And what other things would those be?"

"Sexy cougar, for one."

"A few months ago, yes, for sure. Now, no." Carol tossed her water bottle into a turquoise blue tote as they prepared to head back to Jennifer's for dinner. "Now I'm focusing on being a good mother. Jim and Ashley still aren't sure if I'm sincere about being interested in their lives. I got pretty wrapped up in my career and a parade of men during their later teen years."

"And got them both to college. They can depend on you a lot more than their deadbeat dad."

"That's for sure. Did I tell you he completely forgot to send even a check to Ash or Jim for their birthdays? I couldn't believe it. He has a wife. He has assistants and a private secretary. What does it take to put the date in your agenda?"

"What was his excuse?"

"Said he forgot. That with the new baby, he and Charlene don't have a routine. Yadda, yadda, yadda." As they strolled across the parking lot, Carol tried mightily to retain the Zen feeling from yoga. It was fizzling fast thinking of her ex.

"I almost feel sorry for Charlene. Gord hasn't changed his stripes one bit. He was like this during our entire marriage. Funny thing? When he was courting, he didn't forget anything. That razor-sharp lawyer mind retained it all. First date, first kiss, first roll in the hay. He remembered the day, date, time, and year. Forget something? Not Gordon Brock. Mind like a steel trap."

As they reached their cars, a bitter cold drizzle had started. "Let's go get some warm food and a glass of wine. Ben is organizing dinner."

"Sounds wonderful. I'll follow you." Carol threw her bag and mat into the back seat, got in, and started the loaner.

"WE'RE HOME." They came in through Jennifer's back patio door to the kitchen, which was redolent with fragrant aromas. A flurry of excited dog came scrabbling across the ceramic floor to greet them.

"Hey Charlie." Jennifer scratched the dog's ears before walking to the counter where Ben stood making a salad. "I thought we were having leftovers."

"Hi sweetie. Thought I'd surprise you with a Ben Powell special." He leaned down and planted a loud kiss on Jennifer's head. "Hi Carol. Let's get you two ladies a glass of wine. It's pretty cold and damp out there. I'm sure you need some fortification."

Ben poured each a generous glass as they took off their outer wear. Carol wandered over to the stove, lifted the lid off one pot, and rolled her eyes in ecstasy.

"Oh my. That smells absolutely heavenly."

"It's my Vietnamese green curry. The vegetables are about to go in. Have a seat, and we can talk while I prepare."

Carol and Jennifer sat at the kitchen table to keep Ben company and stay close to the aromatic smells. Looking into the dining room, Carol saw the table was set with a damask tablecloth, tall candles, water glasses, and shining cutlery. "This sure beats the heck out of going back to my condo to eat takeout at my kitchen counter."

"Carol had a little run-in with Devin Elliott this morning." Jennifer sipped her wine appreciatively. "He's the architect who oversaw the remodeling at Gerry and Ellen's old place."

"Run-in?" Ben drained the steamed vegetables and added them to the curry.

"I'll let Carol tell you. It gets better with the telling." Jennifer grinned devilishly. "We can embellish this to the point where he totaled the Bimmer. Just need to work on it a bit more. Over to you, Carol."

Carol filled him in with delight. "I have to admit, I was so totally pissed off at the situation I let him have it. I gave him the look, too."

"Not The Look?" Jennifer's eyes widened. "That poor man. I'm surprised he wasn't reduced to a smoldering puddle on the ground."

"No, he was actually laughing at me, which just made me angrier."

"He laughed at you? Poor guy." Ben rolled his eyes as a smile played around his lips.

"Then he admitted it was all his fault, that I was right, and he would pay for everything. Took the wind out of my temper sails. What a frustrating man." Carol smiled just slightly as she remembered being bested in the fair fight department.

"He asked her out for dinner, and she said no." Jennifer breathed in the fragrant scents in her kitchen. "She actually turned down one of the most eligible bachelors in Boston. I don't think he's ever been married. I seem to recall he was engaged."

"I remember now. His fiancée was found murdered. That was years ago. She was an up-and-coming lawyer." Carol said. "That must have been so heartbreaking for him."

"Okay ladies, let's move to the dining room. Dinner is ready."

Carol and Jennifer strolled, arm in arm, into the dining room and got comfortable as Ben served. Both men were forgotten as they tasted the silky green curry that was now swimming with tofu, broccoli, cauliflower, bamboo shoots, red pepper, celery, and baby corn on a bed of Jasmine rice. Ben produced a fine Pinot Grigio, and the three friends tucked in to their meal.

"Thanks so much for a very, very fine dinner, Ben." Carol slipped one arm into her leather jacket as Ben held it for her. "After the car issue this morning, I figured my whole day would go to hell in a hand basket. But it's turned out to be a great day, capped off by your sublime curry. I don't think I've ever tasted better. Would you consider catering a dinner party for me?"

"Don't think I want to get into catering, Carol. But thanks for the vote. I'm really into my memoir writing now. Cooking is a way for me to take a break and let my mind work on remembering some of my journalistic escapades over the past three decades."

Carol checked herself in the hall mirror, gave a little extra tilt to her hat, and hugged Jennifer and Ben. "Great evening, you two. Next time, it's my treat."

"What restaurant did you have in mind?" Jennifer smiled indulgently at the offer.

"Okay. Maybe, I could just order in at my place."

"Maybe, you could just come here again. Bring Ashley or Jim, the next time one or both are in town."

"Which would just confirm to both of them that I'm not much of a cook." Carol laughed merrily. "Thanks for your help there, Jen."

"We'll figure out some way to rehabilitate you as a mother figure." Jennifer was enjoying seeing Carol returning to her motherly ways. It was a far cry from the friend she had known even just a year ago.

"I sure need all the help I can get. Must tell you, today, when they gave me that thousand dollar plus estimate for a bloody side mirror, I found myself wondering why I even drive a car that expensive. Can you believe it? I'm actually questioning my—dare I say it— extravagant lifestyle. Tell me I'm sane and not going through a midlife crisis."

"Carol, what you're going through is a re-evaluation of what's important in life." Ben put a hand on her shoulder. "I went through it last year, big time. After decades of jet-setting around the world, chasing the latest headlines, I finally realized that knowing my son and being part of his life was way more important than making big bucks and trying to figure out where to spend them. If that's a midlife crisis, then we all need one. Right, Jennifer?"

She smiled and nodded. "Carol, what I see now is a woman who's facing her demons head-on and trying her very best to make amends to her daughter and son. You're absolutely sane, my friend. And I love you for it." Jennifer put her hands on Carol's shoulders. "You're doing what you need to do to get your kids back and get your life back. Just keep on."

It wasn't the wine, but Carol found her eyes welling with tears. These were her real friends. She was determined to get a real life back, including her wonderful daughter and son.

"Thank you, Jennifer, and you too, Ben. I don't know where I'd be without you two." Carol walked out to the loaner, shivering slightly in the damp, cold air.

While the car was warming up, she retrieved a text message from Ashley confirming her arrival time at the airport and smiled. *I'm so glad she's coming home for Thanksgiving. I need to think of something to make Christmas memorable this year,* she mused. *We need to build some new family traditions that get beyond splashing money around and eating in restaurants.*

As she drove home, she turned over different ideas. *Maybe I could book a ski holiday in Vermont. I don't ski but there must be other things I could do. Or a cruise. Never been on one of those.* Then it hit her. *About time I worked on some of my control issues,* she realized. *Maybe I should just ask Ash and Jim what they'd like to do for Christmas. They're both adults.*

She arrived home a few minutes later and texted her kids as she walked into the living room and turned up the lights. "Hi guys. Need to get a plan together for Christmas. What do you say we get out of Boston? Any ideas?"

There, I did it. I didn't go into control mode. Good girl, she thought, looking out over Boston's sparkling nightscape. *I'm sure there's hope for me yet.*

Chapter Two

CAROL HAD BOOKED BACK TO BACK OPEN HOUSES on both Saturday and Sunday, morning and afternoon. She knew from visits to her listing site that there was plenty of interest. There was good buzz on all four properties, particularly the old Victorian in Dorchester.

"You're crazy to do all that in one weekend," Jennifer chided her friend gently as they left their yoga class. "At least come over for dinner on Sunday. You'll be exhausted by then, I'm sure."

"Thanks. I'll be there by five at the latest. I don't usually book that much into a weekend but next weekend is Thanksgiving, and I want at least two full days with Ash. Jim can't come. Some project is due, so it's a girls' weekend, which she and I really need."

"Well, you and Ashley come here for Thanksgiving dinner. I haven't seen her since she left for Syracuse. She's in her third year now, right?"

"Third year and loving it. She's doing really well."

"Does she know I'm engaged to Ben?"

"I told her about Ben uncovering Michel's scam of posing as a corporate pilot looking to move to a new city. I can't get over how he managed to con so many agents, let alone how much art he stole. She'll be really excited to have dinner with such a famous Syracuse alumnus."

"Mark, Lana, and the kids will be here, too. I've ordered a monster turkey that could feed the whole neighborhood."

"Thank you for the invite. Ash is going to want to bake something. She always does, whenever she's home." Carol walked towards her shiny car that now sported a new side mirror. "We'll bring a dessert of some kind."

She was just pulling out of her parking spot when her phone

chirped. She looked at the number display but didn't recognize it. She touched the screen. "Carol Brock here."

"Hello, Carol Brock. Devin Elliott here."

Carol instantly felt exposed and a little bit jumpy. Her stomach pitched. She couldn't tell if she was nervous or annoyed that Devin was calling. "Hello, Devin. What's up?" She pulled into the lighter traffic of a November evening.

"I'd like to see that property in Dorchester. The old Victorian."

"I'm doing an open house there on Sunday from one to four. Come by any time."

"I'd like to see it sooner if we can arrange it."

"Sorry, no can do. The owner's daughter stipulated no showings this weekend except for the open house." Carol signaled her turn as the GPS guided her towards a property she was about to list.

"All right then. I'll be there before one so I can be first in line. I take it you're only letting one visitor through at a time?"

"That's right. I keep a close eye on the visitors and the client's property. Plus, the owner's daughter insisted on it." Carol figured most of Boston knew about Michel's con. She didn't bother raising it with Devin. The real estate world was very small when it came to the latest gossip flying around.

"See you Sunday."

As Carol pulled onto the street early Sunday afternoon, she stopped at the corner and put out an Open House sign with an arrow pointing down the street. Driving up to the stately Victorian, she admired the building's lines, yet again. It was late nineteenth century with some visible upgrades, including a new roof. Looking up at the turret, she well remembered the striking living room with its five sun-drenched windows overlooking the street. The nine-foot ceilings gave each room an elegant air. She could almost imagine couples in evening attire sipping before-dinner drinks while a maid passed around canapés.

She parked her car, took out another Open House sign, and put it on the faded patch of lawn. Then she drove down the street and parked about half a block from the house to leave space for the visitors. *I shouldn't have any problem getting full asking on this place*, she thought with a smile. *I'd be surprised if I don't have an offer within a day.* She walked up the wide verandah steps and approached a solid wood door with a frosted oval window in the middle.

She had barely reached out to press the door chime, when the heavy wooden door swung inwards.

"Hello, Carol. Good to see you again." A tall woman with short dark hair invited her in. Stepping into a small tile-covered foyer, Carol glimpsed the warm sheen of the hardwood floors beyond it. She realized the house no longer had the smell of a home inhabited. No one had cooked here in weeks. But she did catch a whiff of something unsavory and pungent, like a litter box that needed emptying. She wasn't sure she could do anything to overcome the smell before the open house and shook her head ruefully.

"Good to see you too, Allison. How's your mother?" She tried to remember where the litter box was.

"She can't communicate at all. The stroke was so severe she'll probably never walk again."

"I'm sorry to hear that. You must be very worried about her." Carol stepped into the hall and moved towards the kitchen. "I'm expecting a good turnout. There's been a lot of traffic to my web listing and quite a few re-tweets. Where's the litter box?"

"It's down in the basement. I really just want to get this over and done with and get on with my life."

"Let's do a little tour then and make sure everything is ready." *I'll empty the litter box when I'm down there*, she thought.

"You should know I've already put away everything of any value." Allison's eyes were hard.

"If you're referring to the con artist, he's now in prison for what he did." Carol smiled thinly. Allison hadn't even attempted to veil her snide comment. Most people weren't so blunt. "I'm sure the house is

in showcase condition, but let's go have a quick look. It'll remind me
of the features I want to play up." As Carol strode away, she didn't see
Allison's piercing stare.

Within minutes, they had checked each room and were standing
in the sun-filled living room. Carol shook her head. The litter box she
had emptied hadn't been emptied in days. An acrid smell hung in the
air. The cat was nowhere to be found.

The elegantly-styled room she was standing in held only a frayed
couch and some chairs that had seen better days, along with an old
television on a metal stand. Between the smell and the worn furnishings,
she'd need to get into her best selling gear to get people to see beyond it.

"The new owners will have a major redecorating project on their
hands. I see some cars parked out front. Let's let the first visitor in."
Time to get going, she thought, looking at her watch.

As she opened the front door, she saw Devin Elliot striding up the
walk. *Of course, he'd be the first to arrive.*

She had opted for mid-height heels, knowing she'd be on her feet
virtually the entire day. Without her highest heels, Devin towered over her.

"Hello, Devin. Figured you'd be first."

"Hello, Carol. I need to warn you about something. This house
and I have some history. If Allison Wendover is here, it could get ugly."

"She's here. Should I call the police?"

"It won't get that ugly but—"

"What are you doing here, Devin?" Allison had come to the door
and stood, legs akimbo, with her hands on her narrow hips. Carol
glanced between the two of them, thinking she wasn't the only one
who'd managed to get on Allison's bad side. She couldn't help but
wonder what Devin had done.

"I'm here to see your mother's house, of course. It's a free world last
time I checked."

"You are not welcome here." Allison's eyes blazed with anger.

"I don't have to be welcome. My money's as good as the
next person's."

Carol watched in some alarm as the two titans suddenly squared off. "Allison, please step back and let Devin in. I don't think we want an audience."

"He is not coming into my house."

"Last I heard it's your mother's house." Devin's voice was cold.

"Devin. Allison. Can we please take this inside?" Carol could feel the electricity arcing off the two adversaries. *Like Gord and I back in the old days.* Three couples on the sidewalk were watching the altercation with interest.

"He is not coming into this house."

"I most certainly am. I will simply call the police if you don't let me in to view this publicly advertised Open House."

Carol recognized the molten color of Devin's eyes. He was angry. Very angry. "Allison, you don't have a legal right to bar him from seeing the house. As your agent, I must ask you to step aside, let him in, and we'll go from there." Carol thanked the gods as Allison stood down and moved away. "I suggest you go and get a cup of coffee. I'll take it from here."

When Allison moved to object, Carol cut her off. "Are we clear on this? There are other prospective buyers waiting outside in the cold."

Allison's mutinous look was evident but she stormed off to the kitchen. Much noise could be heard as she slammed and banged her way around getting the fixings for her coffee.

"Thanks for the warning. What's that all about?"

"Allison is an ex-girlfriend. Her mother Clara and I are very close. She knew I loved this old house just as much as she did. We talked about me buying it if she ever had to sell. When I broke it off with Allison, I stayed in close touch with Clara. I'm the one who found her and got her to the hospital a few weeks ago."

Devin gazed lovingly at the staircase they were climbing. The sunlight pouring through a large stained glass window bathed the broad stairwell in soft colors, setting the yellow walls aglow. The dark oak spindle railings were straight out of the Victorian era. Their glossy patina further reflected the sunlight. There was a soft smell of age and gentility that even the absence of the owner had not erased, nor a dirty litter box.

"Look at this window. It's such a classic. You can't find these anymore." Devin's comment made Carol look at the simple but striking design in a new light. "This may have been done by John LaFarge. I always meant to check. He did quite a few windows throughout New England in the eighteen hundreds. His specialty was opaque stained glass."

Carol could sense his reverence for the house. "Allison told me this house has been in her family for over fifty years."

"Her mother raised a family of three in this house. Two boys in that left bedroom and Allison on the right. Allison is the youngest; the spoiled baby." Devin looked over the bathroom as Carol stood in the doorway. "She has no real feelings for either her mother or this house."

Given what Carol knew about Allison, she believed it. Allison had all but said she didn't care about the house. Carol was startled as a large calico cat brushed by her legs and went straight to Devin's feet purring loudly.

"Well, hello, Pasha. How's my girl?" Devin reached down to pick up the furry creature and scratch its ears. "This poor cat has been here alone for weeks. I hope Allison is taking care of her properly."

"She's been feeding her if the overflowing litter box I found is any indication." Carol felt sorry for the cat. "Why doesn't she want you to buy this house?"

"It's revenge. I dumped her. She wanted to marry me. More accurately, she wanted to marry my money and standing in Boston society." Back in the hall, Devin put the cat down and again ran his hands over the smooth wood railings. The weak November sun warmed the landing.

"Her first husband left her, too, thankfully before they had any children. She's completely shallow. Lots of beauty and charm she can turn on when it suits her, but no depth. We lasted about a year. By then, I had become very fond of her mother and this house." They were now standing in the main bedroom, with the soft November sun streaming in the windows. The cat had jumped on the bed and was studiously cleaning herself in the middle of it. Carol was pretty sure Allison couldn't hear their conversation. She could still hear faint noises from the kitchen.

"Carol, I want to put in an offer she can't refuse. I know you can get full asking for this place. You priced it perfectly. But I also know Mrs. Wendover still has a mortgage and MassHealth won't be covering everything. Her bills must be piling up. Allison is going to want to get this done quickly."

"Very true, she's made that clear. She has no emotional attachment or involvement in any of this."

Devin and Carol looked around the spacious bedroom. It was as cozy and bright as the living room below it. The oak hardwood floors gleamed. "I'm thinking twenty-five thousand above asking should block any and all competition, and I get the furnishings. What do you think?"

"I can't divulge anything, but I do know you will well exceed her bottom line price. And I know she's concerned about having to empty the house." Carol realized with a start that this was the first time in her entire career she had seen someone buy a house because they needed to own it. Devin was motivated because he loved the elderly woman who had lived in this house. He respected her wish to see it preserved.

"Clara worried about this house as if it were one of her children." Devin rubbed a finger along his earlobe. Carol noticed he had a faint scar along his jaw line. "After Allison and I broke up, she called me and got me to promise to buy the house if anything happened to her. That was last year. I wonder if she had a premonition. She isn't seventy yet."

"Let me get through the rest of the open house and we'll work on it from there. I doubt she'll refuse an unconditional offer so far above asking."

"When can we write it up?" They were still standing in the middle of the master bedroom. The cat had gone to sleep in a shaft of sunlight. "I'm going to a friend's for dinner at five. Want to meet me about eight o'clock at my office? You have my cell number."

"Sounds good."

"YOU SHOULD'VE SEEN THAT WOMAN. She has a hate on Devin so nasty I thought we'd have to call the police. You know me, I'm not easily intimidated, but she looked like she was ready to scratch his eyes out." Carol forked up some fluffy mashed potatoes and sighed. "Thanks so much for the dinner invite. I would've been eating out of cardboard after this weekend. I'm bushed, and my day isn't even over."

"Nothing like a nice Sunday pot roast on a cold November evening. This house smelled wonderful all day long while it was slow cooking." Jennifer offered Carol some more wine.

"No thanks. I'm meeting Devin at eight to draw up his offer. He wants to sign it tonight, before Allison can even think of looking at another one. So far, no one else is ready to make an offer. They all want an inspection. Devin knows the house and knows exactly what's needed to get it up to code again."

Carol set her cutlery on the plate. Her only regret was leaving this table and house and going back to work on a Sunday evening. But it was part of her profession. You traded your weekends and evenings to show and sell houses when most other people were with their families.

"Sorry to eat and run, but I must get going. I'm meeting Devin in twenty minutes." Carol had a last small sip of wine and set her glass aside. "I know you probably have a sinful dessert, but I'll pass. Next time."

As Carol settled into her car, she looked back at Jennifer's home, which glowed comfortably from its many windows. *There was a time I had a home like that*, she thought, with an inevitable stab of regret. *When the kids were young I made our house a home. I could have ignored Gord's infidelities. Many wives do.* Carol couldn't remember exactly why she snapped and broke up their lives over Gord's final fling. But she did snap and, in the process, overturned their lives, most especially Ashley's and Jim's.

They were just children and had no control, she reflected. *At least Ashley is coming home for Thanksgiving.* Carol pulled into her parking spot at the agency just as Devlin pulled up. He opened his window and leaned out.

"Hey, Carol. Good timing. Look, I haven't eaten yet. Would you mind coming with me and hitting a diner or something? I haven't eaten since breakfast. We can take my truck."

Carol tried not to appear flustered. He had boxed her in again. It wasn't a date. It wasn't a mutual dinner. It was business, and she couldn't refuse.

"Let's go then. But I can't stay long. I have an early morning ahead."

Devin took them to a trendy bistro near the harbor. On this Sunday night, the place was winding down. Carol set up her laptop and opened a blank Offer to Purchase and started entering the main data as Devin explored the menu. *This is a business dinner, nothing more,* she thought, *even if he is the most handsome man in the room.*

"Can I offer you folks a drink?" A waitress set down glasses of water.

"Thanks, I'll have a soda with lemon please." Carol noted with satisfaction that the bistro had Wi-Fi.

"I'll have a Heineken."

"So, you want to offer twenty-five thousand above asking with the furnishings included?"

"Yes. And I want to include a proviso that if a family member wishes to purchase anything it will be done at fair market value. Oh, and please let Allison know I could take the cat off her hands. She's allergic to it. It was one of her excuses for not visiting her mother very often."

"It's so sad to see a daughter almost abandoning her aging mother like this. I've been in the real estate business for years, and I'm still surprised when I see it happening. It's abuse by neglect."

"Allison's mother lost her husband almost twenty years ago. She was only in her late forties and had never worked outside the home. Allison was still a teenager. Her mother finished raising the children alone by doling out her husband's life insurance and cleaning houses. She saw them all off, one by one, and put two through college. By the time they were all gone, she had just enough money left to pay her bills and little more. Not one of her children stepped up to help her, although they could have afforded to. You saw how empty the bedrooms are?"

"Yes. I thought… I don't know what I thought. I just figured she had given stuff away because she didn't need all those rooms to live in."

"She rented out the rooms to students. At some point she started giving the furnishings to the students when they left to get their own apartments. She was hoping to buy some newer furniture but never had the money."

Their conversation turned to business matters, as Carol began filling in the offer to purchase using the online form.

Minutes later, Devin tucked into the burger platter that arrived as Carol saved the file and set the laptop aside so she could eat.

"When I realized how little support she was getting from the family, I had to help. Got her set up with the Boston Food Bank for a monthly grocery supplement. Bought food for Pasha. I just couldn't, in good conscience, let Mrs. Wendover end her years without dignity. It's a blessing she doesn't know what's happening now."

Carol sipped her soda pensively. She couldn't help but worry that some day the same thing might happen to her. *Would Ash or Jim ever do this to me?* The ugly thought wormed its way into her thinking. She thought not, of course, she bet Mrs. Wendover didn't see this coming, either.

"I'll write up this offer so tight they won't get a trash bag out of there for free. You have my word." She was surprised at the intensity of her feelings.

Her own parents had lavished her with love and support over the years, especially after she and Gord split. Over the past several years, she had been giving back whenever she found a way. She couldn't imagine them being left in the situation of Mrs. Wendover, living at the whim of her daughter, and all but ignored by her sons.

Did Mrs. Wendover ever do anything that would make her children so uncaring? I completely uprooted my children when my marriage fell apart. Clara Wendover held her family together and kept them in their home. Of anyone, she deserved better than this, Carol reflected.

I kicked their father out, sold our family home, bought a condo, and moved the kids to a new neighborhood and school at the start of their teens. I threw the lives of my son and daughter into a complete tailspin and then complicated it by bringing home strange men who were never around long enough to get to know them. Carol cringed slightly at the thought.

I did it with the best of intentions. I didn't want them to settle for a mate who wasn't faithful. But somewhere along the line, that message seems to have become lost in translation.

"Carol. Hello? Are you with me?" Devin was peering at her over his beer.

"Sorry. I got lost in my thoughts. Where were we?"

"You said something about me having to keep the trash, your offer will be so tight." Devin smiled over at her. Carol sat up and willed herself to focus on the business at hand. Suddenly, she felt bone-tired.

"I've done four open houses in two days. I'm completely whacked. I need to get home and get to bed."

"It's only nine o'clock."

"Sorry." Behind her hand, Carol yawned widely and shut down her laptop. "Could we finish this tomorrow?"

"You really are exhausted." Devin popped another fry into his mouth and waved for the bill. "I'll drive you home. You can cab to your office in the morning. It should be safe enough there for the night."

"I'm fine. I'm not leaving a BMW down here for the night. You finish your dinner. I'll catch a cab back." With that, Carol stood up, smoothed her coat, put the laptop in her tote and made ready to leave.

"Just give me a few minutes. I'll take you back."

"Thanks, Devin. I just want to get home and get some sleep. Be at my office at eight, and we'll move it through. Good night." Carol turned and walked away before he could stand up or shake her hand.

CAROL PADDED INTO HER LIVING ROOM in her stocking feet with a glass of wine and looked around with new eyes. For one thing, there was no sign anywhere that she had children. There were no photos on display. *That's going to change before next weekend,* she promised herself as she sipped the crisp Chablis. She also realized there were almost no decorations. The tables were bare, apart from a lamp here and there. The Wendover home was just that, a *real* home, with family photos on display and wonderful knick-knacks on tables and the decorative shelves.

This place needs a makeover, she decided. *No more designer chairs for me. That time in my life is over now. It's time to make a home that Ashley and Jim will want to visit.*

Walking into her bedroom, she put the wine glass down and took off her earrings. As she put them away, she shook her head at the sheer volume of jewelry in front of her. Easily half of it she hadn't worn in so long she couldn't remember. Picking up a favorite strand of grey pearls she thought, *I wear these all the time. Why am I keeping all this other bling? Just so someone like Michel can steal it?* She blushed as she remembered how easily she had succumbed to his charms.

She started taking her clothes off, hanging her soft wool jacket up and folding her skirt over a chair. She stretched her arms over her head before slipping into a floor-length emerald-green dressing gown that matched her eyes. She smoothed the soft material lovingly. *There are many things I can and will give up,* she thought, *but silk is not one of them.* Picking up her glass, she walked back to the living room and opened up her computer to do a last check on her site listings.

It wasn't long before she was closing down the laptop, turning down the lights and heading for bed. Her last thought before she fell asleep was that Ashley and Jim would love the old Wendover place.

Chapter Three

"JENNIFER. I NEED YOUR HELP. Are you free this afternoon for a couple of hours?" Carol had finalized Devin's offer and presented it to Allison by mid-morning. She had almost smelled the woman's smoldering fury when she realized she'd been given an unconditional offer well above asking. It made Carol's skin crawl just being in the room with her, knowing the way she had treated her mother.

There was something almost sinister in the way the woman clenched her jaw as she obsessed over every item in the offer, looking for a way to refuse it. Ultimately, she refused to sign, saying she needed more time to consider it. Now, Carol was back at her office and had more important people on her mind.

"Ashley will be here on Friday. I really need help with some shopping."

"Since when do you need help with shopping? I can carry your bags of course, but—"

"Jennifer, I saw the condo last night for what it really is. It needs warm touches and family photos. I want Ashley to realize I'm really sincere about mending fences with her and Jim, and part of that is making the condo more inviting. It needs to be more about them and less about me." Carol looked up as the sales manager poked his head into her office. She waved him in.

"I have to go now. Can you meet me here at two? Great! I'll drive. Thanks, Jennifer." Carol put the phone down and looked up at Colin Carmichael and saw a distinct scowl on his normally jovial face.

"What's up, Colin?"

"I've just had a disturbing call about the Victorian in Dorchester."
"What's the problem? I brought in an unconditional offer at twenty-five thousand over asking." Carol knew who had called him. "I went over the offer in detail with Allison Wendover not an hour ago. She hasn't signed but she has twenty-four hours to consider it. There are no other offers pending that I'm aware of. What's her problem?"

"She says you're the problem. She believes you colluded with Devin Elliott so he could see the house before anyone else. And then told him about her concerns about selling or disposing of the contents, so he offered to buy them. She's very suspicious because he didn't ask for an inspection." Colin smoothed his tie. "Given the age of that house, I'm more than surprised that he didn't either. So, you tell me."

Carol listened to Colin and felt her blood begin to simmer. The crazy bitch wasn't going to smear her reputation just to get revenge on her ex-boyfriend. She rose up from her desk, squared her shoulders, and looked Colin straight in the eye.

"Before this gets out of hand, Colin, you need to know a few facts. First off, I met Devin Elliott not seventy-two hours ago when he backed up his truck and ripped off the side mirror on my car in a parking lot." Carol warmed to her anger. "Secondly, I learned yesterday at one o'clock that Allison Wendover is Devin Elliot's spurned lover. She hates him with a passion. And thirdly, and most importantly, Allison Wendover has been neglecting her mother for years. Devin arranges for food bank support for Mrs. Wendover, and he's the one who found her after her stroke and called the ambulance.

"It so happens Devin knows the house very well. He visited it every week despite no longer going out with Ms. Wendover. He's offered her twenty-five thousand above asking and plans to fix up the place. How can she possibly say I'm causing problems? I'd call it the perfect solution for Ms. Wendover."

Colin shook his head. "I hate when we get one of these," he sighed. "They're as bad as the divorce cases. I know you've made plans to meet someone at two. Leave this with me. She's demanding to file a formal complaint."

Carol came around her desk and picked up her coat. "I have the contact information for the three couples who were waiting to see the house after Devin. They were witnesses to her public temper tantrum."

"Good thinking, Carol. Maybe if we counter her demand with proof of her personal animosity she'll back off."

"Somehow I doubt it, Colin. I don't think she has any intention of signing Devin's offer and every intention of causing trouble. Do me a favor and don't put anything I've said in writing. I don't need a lawsuit."

"Remember when I told you about the run-in Devin had with Allison Wendover yesterday?" Carol waited for Jennifer to buckle up her seatbelt before pulling onto the busy street. "She called to file a formal complaint against me. Said I colluded with Devin to make sure he got first dibs on Mrs. Wendover's home."

"Where'd she get that idea from?" Jennifer shook her head. "You barely know the man."

"She made it sound like Devin had never seen the house before but was willing to buy it without an inspection. She implied that the only reason he made the offer was that we conspired together to fix the price."

"And did you? I mean, was anything you discussed about the price unethical?"

"Absolutely not. I was very clear to him that I couldn't discuss specifics about her target price. And, anyway, he's offering twenty-five thousand above asking. That's more than the property is appraised at!"

"You don't need another public scandal, Carol. This is awful. What're you going to do?" Jennifer glanced out the window. "Take the next left." She guided them to a store known for its casual decorating accessories.

"Fortunately, there were three couples who saw Allison's behavior yesterday afternoon. I've left messages asking if they would be witnesses in the event Allison pursues this further. I'm hoping that will stop her.

Here we are. Let's hope for a parking spot."

Jennifer and Carol soon found themselves exploring a store brimming with colorful rows of home accessories. "You've seen my place. I need to warm it up quick without it looking like it was professionally staged. If Ashley even suspects that, it will flop."

"I would suggest three things. One, I buy you one centerpiece item as a gift. Then, you can honestly say it came from me. Second, we keep everything small. Some candles. Three or four picture frames of different sizes to hold family photos. A vase or two with branches and twigs. And third, one gorgeous afghan throw in a color you both like. What do you think?"

"You forgot one thing." Carol was beaming.

"What's that?"

"There's one other thing I want to get. Tell me if you think it's too much too fast." Carol picked up a textured throw pillow in shades of turquoise and chocolate brown. "I want to get a set of everyday dishes. Mine are all gold-plated. You can't put them in a microwave. I know that's always been one of Ashley's bugbears."

"That sounds like a great idea. Do you have room for a set?"

"I'll just get four place settings for now. And yes, I can move a few things into a box and put it in my storage locker."

The two friends spent over an hour trolling the aisles. By the time they reached the cash, Carol had a lovely collection they both agreed would add warmth and charm to the condo, including a few colorful throw pillows and a turquoise blue afghan that would drape elegantly off the end of one white leather couch. Carol paid for her purchases as Jennifer piled the bags into the basket to bring to the car.

Then it was Jennifer's turn to pay. She had found a lovely glass vase with a variety of smooth stones and four large live bamboo shoots. "You only have to rinse it out with tap water once a week. Tell me you can manage that."

Carol laughed. "There's a reason I don't have any plants you know. I can't even keep a bunch of cut flowers going for more than a few days. I forget. They dry out. They die. But I will do my best. And thanks. Ashley would know I'd never buy this on my own. I think this will work."

When they arrived back at her office, Carol hugged her friend. "Thanks for your help. See you at yoga on Thursday." She watched as she climbed into her car. "Give my love to Ben. We need to start thinking about the weddings soon."

"Let's get through Thanksgiving and Christmas first." Jennifer chuckled. "We've booked the florist, also known as my future son-in-law; the location, the gardens at Brentwood Manor; and the caterer, Brentwood's chef."

"Wow, you've been busy."

"Lana did it. We're keeping it very simple and informal." Jennifer waved and drove off.

Simple and informal. That sounds like a recipe for the rest of my life. Carol sighed happily and went back to her office to wrap up some paper work and prepare for her evening showings.

She was taking her coat off when Colin strode into her office.

"This Allison Wendover has friends in high places. I've had a call from no less than a senior board member from the Greater Boston Real Estate Board wanting to know what's going on. Fortunately, I know him well enough that I was able to defuse the situation somewhat when I told him a few of the facts you shared. This isn't going away, Carol."

"I never believed for a moment that it would." Carol's happiness was quickly dampened. "We'd better bring in one of our lawyers with an ethics specialty. I have two showings tonight." She perused her agenda. "I could be available tomorrow morning after ten o'clock. Let's call now."

Within minutes, she had a call-back from one of the lawyers who had advised her after Michel's arrest and arraignment. With the phone on speaker, Carol and Colin outlined the situation. They made an appointment for the following morning to discuss options.

"I've left messages for the couples who saw what happened yesterday.

I can't believe it was just yesterday." Carol shook her head. "If I'd never met Devin Elliot, none of this would have happened."

She really was beginning to wish he'd never crashed into her life.

AFTER UNLOADING ALL HER PURCHASES onto her granite counter top, Carol went to change out of her business clothes. She left her phone on the counter. She'd reached two of the open house couples, and both shared their alarm over Allison Wendover's behavior. She'd left a message for the third couple, telling them she could be reached until ten o'clock.

She changed into her silk lounger, padded out to the kitchen and poured herself a generous glass of Shiraz. Pulling out scissors, she began snipping off price tags. First out was the turquoise afghan. *I don't know why I didn't get myself one of these years ago. Actually, I do,* she realized. *I never spend time lounging around in the evening. It's always been about doing up offers, preparing listings, organizing open houses. I can't even think of the last time I read a book.*

As she looked at the three picture frames, she realized she had no photos of either Ashley or Jim since high school graduation. *I'm going to put them out and just guilt the two of them into giving me newer ones. It's partly my fault for not taking more pictures when we're together.*

Carol spent the next hour organizing her new treasures. She placed Jennifer's vase of bamboo on a table near her floor to ceiling windows that overlooked the harbor. The willowy green fronds added a warm touch of living color against the sparkling nighttime backdrop. Next, a decorative copper plate became home to a large vanilla candle surrounded by smooth pebbles. A terra cotta vase with a profusion of silky imitation orchids was placed under a glass-topped table. The throw pillows went on the couch with the afghan draped at the end. She set the other candles out.

She stepped back to admire her handiwork when the phone chirped. Without looking, she picked up.

A voice hissed into her ear. "Devin Elliott will never get my mother's

31

house." Carol nearly dropped the phone in shock. Allison's venomous tone reverberated in her ear. "If you persist in aiding and abetting him, you will regret it. His offer expires tomorrow at ten o'clock. I will not sign."

As the line went dead, Carol put the phone down. Her hand was shaking. She tried to pick up her glass of wine and sip it. It didn't work. Wine slopped onto the counter. She quickly put it back down with a wobbly hand. *This woman invaded my home through the phone,* she realized. For the first time, Carol felt exposed. Looking at the nighttime vista of Boston outside her windows, she wished she had drapes.

"Devin. It's Carol. Sorry about the hour." Carol felt her hands still shaking. "Your lovely Allison just called and threatened me." She heard his sharp intake of breath.

"What the hell? I know she's spiteful, but I had no idea she would take it this far. What happened?"

Carol told him about the complaint, about the real estate board member's call to the sales manager, and about the personal call. "Why does she hate you so much?"

"I'm not sure what motivates her. She's a chameleon. One minute she's smiling and charming, smooth as butter. Next she's livid with barely contained rage. And she is completely unpredictable. She's very intelligent and interesting to talk to, but I couldn't handle her mood changes and temper tantrums. I don't need that in my life."

Carol heard the weariness in his voice.

"Well, I don't need it in mine, either. My senior broker and I are meeting with one of our lawyers at ten o'clock tomorrow. Could you join us? Between your knowledge of Allison and her history, on top of the witnesses who were on the sidewalk yesterday, I know we can get her complaint set aside. Hopefully, before it gets to the media."

"Tell me where, and I'll be there. I am so sorry, Carol. If you hadn't met me this wouldn't have happened."

She smiled slightly. "Well, maybe. But it is my listing so we would have met each other regardless."

"Now I really owe you a dinner, and this time you cannot say no."

"You get Allison out of my life, and I will buy *you* dinner." A small laugh bubbled up in her throat. "Devin, thanks for helping me get a perspective on this. You just saved me a bundle of money."

"What do you mean?"

"Buying drapes for this place would cost me thousands, and I live on the fifteenth floor, so I really don't need them."

"I'm not going to pretend to understand what you mean, but I'll take your word for it. See you in the morning."

Carol picked up her glass of wine and topped it up. *I'm just going to chill here for a few minutes.* She went into her email and saw one from Jim.

Hey Mom –

Ash and I think we should all take up snowshoeing. You game? There's a place in northern Massachusetts we could stay that supplies everything. We could go up after Christmas and stay for three or four days. We both agree with you, we need to get out of Boston and explore.

Love, Jim

Carol's eyes misted. This was the most positive email she'd seen from Jim in a couple of years. The fact that he'd reached out for both himself and Ash meant the world to her. *He's trying,* she thought. *That's my boy.*

She took her glass over to the couch and set it on the side table. After finding some matches deep in the corner of a kitchen drawer, she went around and lit some of her new candles. Sitting on the couch, she spread the soft afghan over her legs. She looked around and approved the softer touches she'd added. *My girl is coming home. My son is engaging in the Christmas plans. Allison Wendover can just go to hell. I will not let her into my life. My family comes first.* She sipped at her wine and gazed calmly at the twinkling lights surrounding the harbor.

Chapter Four

"Colin, I'd like you to meet Devin Elliott."

Colin stepped forward to shake hands. "We've met. Good to see you again, Devin. Unfortunate circumstances, though."

"Devin. This is Avery Hutchinson, one of our lawyers." Carol made the introductions.

When everyone had their coffee, Avery took the lead. "Let's walk through this step by step. As Colin and I discussed just before you got here, Carol, we want to nip this in the bud before it reaches the media." The lawyer cleared her throat. "After the Demercado case, the media would hang you out to dry without waiting for the facts."

"And Ms. Wendover would be hit with a lawsuit so fast it would make her head spin." After a good night's sleep, Carol was in fighting form. "That woman is not going to interfere with either my career or my life. You can place bets on that." Avery recorded the discussion and also took notes on her tablet.

They were just wrapping up the deposition when Colin's secretary knocked and came in. "Hi everyone. Colin, sorry to interrupt, but you'll want to take this call. It's Ellis Fielding from the board. It's about Carol."

"I'll speak to him." Avery picked up her tablet and followed Colin back to his office.

"The timing couldn't be better." Carol brought out her phone to check for messages. "By the time Avery has her say, Fielding will know this is a trumped up charge."

"I agree. I'm sure this won't go any further now that we're all getting onto the same page." Devin stood up and took his mug over to the side table. "I think we're finished here, and I need to get going. Let me know what happens about this and about the offer. And let me know if there's another offer pending?"

"Will do." Carol closed her tablet and stood up. As she turned, she came face to face with Devin. Looking into his soft hazel eyes, she felt their warm regard. When she went to move past him, he put a hand on her arm.

"Carol, have dinner with me."

She swallowed down a lump in her suddenly-dry throat. Her good angel warned her against saying yes. *He's a ladies man. He's already caused you a heap of trouble, and you're not even dating.* Carol smiled at Devin as she tucked her good angel away and let the naughty one out for some air. "I'd like that."

"Are you free Thursday evening?"

"I have yoga at six. Is seven thirty too late?"

"I'll make a reservation. What's your favorite restaurant?"

"How about that bistro we went to on Sunday? That burger platter looked really good."

Devin grinned. "Oh, come on. You can do better than that. Don't you want a place with linen tablecloths and a maître d?"

"Y'know? I don't. Something simple and informal is just fine with me."

"Then the bistro it is. Meet you there?"

"Sounds good. See you then." Carol was smiling as she walked back to her office. *Simple and informal feels better and better,* she mused. *Just because I've agreed to dinner doesn't mean anything more has to happen. But I'm sure it would be fun if it did.* Her naughty angel flexed her wings.

She checked her emails, pleased to find no less than six new clients for her online private client services. *I'm getting better and better at the online marketing,* she thought, mentally patting herself on the back for diving into social media and internet marketing for her listings.

She was just about to go out to do exterior photographs for a new listing when Colin called. "What's up?"

"I'm not sure. Ms. Wendover appears to be a good friend of Myra."

"Shit. Shit. Shit." Myra was the regional vice-president of the company. "She wasn't my biggest fan when Michel was arrested. Wanted me to take a leave of absence. I can just imagine how she'll feel about this, whether it's true or not. I really don't need this."

"Avery strongly recommends we send a legal notice on her firm's letterhead to Wendover advising her that she is leaving herself open to a slander suit. If it gets to that, the company will pay all your costs. Myra may not like it, but there's nothing she can do. It's company policy."

"Let's do it then." Carol pulled a hand through her hair. The movement calmed her, if only momentarily. "Let me know if there's anything I need to do."

"As a matter of fact, yes. Avery strongly suggests you keep a very low profile for the next while until Wendover has received the letter and responded to it officially. The letter will specifically require her to retract her accusation in writing, remind her she can't refuse to let in a reasonable person who comes to an advertised open house, and demand that she let you do your job without further interference."

"Let's go ahead with the notice, but let's transfer the listing to another associate. I can't work with her any more."

"I'll switch her to Steve. They can take turns powering up the charm-o-meter."

Carol finally laughed. "Great idea! Steve will make her feel like a queen in no time."

As they parted ways, Colin called out to her. "Go get 'em tiger."

"Stand back. I'm on a roll."

"I'M HAVING SUPPER WITH DEVIN." Carol tried not to sound excited as she relayed her news to Jennifer. "He says he owes it to me for what Allison has done."

"There's more?" The two women stretched during the cool down after their yoga class.

"She called me late Monday night and told me I'd regret it if I, quote, aided and abetted Devin on the house purchase. She sounded absolutely furious. She was seething. Like a volcano ready to erupt."

"How long has it been since Devin broke it off?"

"A few years, I gather. The way Devin talks about his friendship with Allison's mother, it must be at least five years or so."

"It sounds like Allison is seriously obsessed. Normally, someone would move on within a few months. I'm not a psychologist, but in my line of work, this kind of angry obsession is definitely not normal. Not after this length of time and never with this level of animosity. You need to be careful. Devin, too."

"I hadn't really thought of it that way. I've only met her a few times: to take the listing, organize the video shoot for the web listing, and then do the open house. She seemed quite friendly until Sunday."

"Psychopaths can be very charming when it suits them. And potentially deadly when they feel they've been crossed. If Allison has been harboring obsessive anger over her break-up with Devin for all these years, she could be very dangerous."

"Psychopath? Isn't that a bit extreme?" Carol took a long drink of water as she toweled her forehead.

"They're more common than you think."

"Well, the agency brought in one of our lawyers to serve her with a warning that she's facing a slander suit if she doesn't back off. I'm hoping that will get her to leave me alone. We're also transferring her to another agent. He should help divert Allison away from me. At least that's my hope."

"Don't count on it. I don't have direct experience, but my gut tells me this woman is out for revenge in a way that has nothing to do with logic or present circumstances. It sounds like she's locked into a delusion that their breakup happened just yesterday. For everyone else, it was years ago. There's a real disconnect, and that disconnect could be a major problem."

"I wish this had never happened. I just want to focus on Ash and Jim and getting them back into my life. I don't need more complications."

"You're still in touch with Detective Guzzo, right?"

Carol felt a chill down her spine. "You think it's that serious?"

"I do. We're talking about a woman who was dumped by one of Boston's most illustrious and eligible bachelors. Five years later, she's still so angry, she phones you and threatens you. And phones her top gun buddies to try and smear your reputation. Do you think she's going to stop because of a lawyer's letter?"

"Jennifer, you're scaring me, and I don't scare easily."

"I know. You need to take this very, very seriously. Call Guzzo. Trust me."

Carol stared at Jennifer and paled. "You're totally serious."

"I am. I've seen enough case studies and files to know that this lady is not having temper tantrums or simple mood swings. You're dealing with someone who is seriously mentally ill. In her mental state, you can't expect her to react logically. And she won't feel any empathy with you whatsoever. She has a very personal agenda, and right now, it's to do whatever it takes to keep Devin from getting her mother's house."

"Guess I have something to talk to Devin about over dinner other than the weather." Carol was shaking as she changed out of her yoga pants and shoes and donned street clothes. "You're sure about this, Jen?"

"I'm beyond sure. You need to call Guzzo and bring him up to speed."

"Hɪ Devɪɴ." Carol reached the table after Devin waved her over. "Hope you're up for a serious discussion. My closest friend Jennifer is a social worker, and she thinks we're in real trouble over Allison."

"Before we get talking about Allison, please sit down. Relax a bit. Let's order a drink and then go from there. How was your day?"

"Nice try, Devin, but we have a real problem on our hands if Jennifer's assessment is correct. When did you and Allison break up?" Carol had her questions ready.

"About six years or so, give or take. What's the problem?" Devin ordered them a bottle of Shiraz as they both put in orders for medium rare steaks.

"And what has Allison done over those years to let you know she's still really pissed off about that break-up?"

"Geez. Hadn't really thought of it. When we first broke up, she still had a key to my condo. I came home one day and found my place trashed. Slashed would be a better word. My pillows, couches and mattress were destroyed. She wrote 'burn in hell' on my bathroom mirror in bright red lipstick. I figured she was just taking our breakup really badly. I had the lock changed."

"Anything else?"

Devin became pensive. "Nothing I could ever prove, but now that you mention it, there've been some incidents that I just put down to random vandalism."

"Such as?" Carol took a sip of wine and watched the emotions playing over Devin's expressive face. *He's just realizing Allison is still obsessed with him,* she thought.

"A few years ago my new car was badly scratched all along the driver's side within days of coming off the lot. A few months later, a can of paint was thrown at it in a lot. Just mine though; no one else's."

They watched as the restaurant filled. Carol's phone chirped. She looked at Devin apologetically and took the call, finishing just as their food arrived. "Sorry about that. I meant to put it on silent and forgot. This looks delicious. Has anything else happened?"

Devin speared up a hunk of steak and chewed thoughtfully. "There have been some other incidents. Always at night. I was at a community fundraiser a few years ago. Allison was there with friends I knew. I stopped by to say hello to them all and could see Allison was rigid with anger."

He stopped to take a sip of wine and then shook his head slowly. "When I went to my car later, I had a flat tire. I didn't think of it until just now, but I haven't had a flat tire in more years than I can remember. But the one night I saw Allison, I ended up with a flat in a closed garage."

"It's all pretty petty stuff, but it's obvious she hasn't given up her anger about the big one that got away." Carol looked into his eyes and saw a flicker of confusion. "Jennifer said something that really caught my attention. To you and I, you breaking up with her is all in the past. It's over and done with and life goes on." Carol forked up some stir-fried vegetables. "To a psychopath, the memory and the feelings that go with it remain vivid. To Allison, it's as if you two just broke up yesterday or last week."

"I find that hard to believe." Devin set aside his empty plate and twisted the wine glass between his hands. "It's been six years. She should have moved on by now."

"Exactly my point. But she hasn't, and now you're trying to buy the house she was raised in. In her mind, it must be the ultimate humiliation. First, you break up with her, and then you buy her mother's house for all the world to see?" Carol set down her knife and fork. Without thinking, she reached across and put a hand on Devin's.

"You saw how she was on Sunday. Can you imagine how angry she must be? Jennifer told me in no uncertain terms to bring this to the police."

"I can't imagine it's that serious. Anything she may have done, and I can't prove any of it, has been petty and annoying. Nuisance things. Sorry, but I think your friend Jennifer is reading too much into this. Besides, what I really want to talk about is you. Not her."

"You're right. Sorry to let an ex-girlfriend who isn't even here, hijack our meal together." Carol smiled up at the waitress who came by to clear their table. "But let's talk about you, instead. What's your favorite project these days?"

"A couple of years ago I took over my parent's hobby farm, a couple of hours northeast of here. I've been doing major renovations and upgrades. I spend most of my weekends and any weekday I can putting the finishing touches on it." Devin smiled and leaned forward in the chair. "You should see it. I have fifty acres of rolling countryside. Can't see my neighbors. I look out the kitchen window and watch my horses grazing. It's heaven."

"Sounds wonderful. You said it belonged to your family?" Carol smiled at the mention of horses and imagined a large house with a wraparound porch and white wicker chairs. She felt his enthusiasm.

"It originally belonged to my grandparents and was passed down to my father. I spent all my summers there, right through college. My parents are getting too old to manage more than one property. And to me, it's my real home."

After ordering coffee, Devin stretched back. "How about you Carol? I checked you out online. I can see you're active in the community. What about family?"

"I have a daughter, Ashley. She's studying journalism at Syracuse University. My son, Jim, is in second year mechanical engineering in the Thayer School of Engineering at Dartmouth."

"Thayer. That's a very prestigious school. You must be very proud of him. And Syracuse is a top school as well. Way to go, Mom."

Carol smiled brightly. "I'm very proud of both of them. Ashley's coming home for Thanksgiving. I'm really looking forward to spending some quality girl time together."

"Where's their dad? I know you're not married. That con artist media frenzy kinda laid out your personal life for all to see."

"He's just a deadbeat dad who forgets their birthdays."

"Sounds like a wonderful guy. A real saint."

Carol laughed lightheartedly at his deadpan voice. "He's a total cad. I'm perfectly happy to be rid of him." She looked at her watch. "Oh my. It's getting late for me. I lost track of the time."

"Me too. Guess we better get you home. Ashley's arriving tomorrow, I take it?"

"Yes. I'm picking her up at the airport at noon."

As they walked to their cars, both shivered in the damp cold air. It was almost freezing, a stark contrast to the cozy restaurant.

"I'm heading up to the farm for the weekend and coming back Tuesday morning. You have my cell number. If anything stirs about the

Dorchester house, you'll let me know?" They were standing by her car.

"I asked to be taken off the listing. I'll give your number to the agent. His name is Steve. Thanks for dinner. It was great." Carol opened her door.

"Carol, I'm sorry you lost the listing and commission."

"It was my decision. I don't want to be around Allison ever again. No commission is worth having to deal with her."

"Will you still have dinner with me again sometime?" Devin grinned boyishly.

"I think that would be very nice." She was smiling as she got in the car and drove away.

DEVIN TURNED AND WALK TOWARDS HIS TRUCK. As he got in and looked out the windshield, he realized it was shattered into a spider web of cracks. It looked like someone had taken a baseball bat to it. Getting out of the truck, he took out his phone to call the police and towing. While he was waiting, he walked around and looked at the other vehicles. There weren't many left in the lot, but even in the dim light, he could clearly see not one of them had even one crack in its windshield.

Chapter Five

CAROL SMILED AS SHE CAUGHT A GLIMPSE OF HER TALL, WILLOWY DAUGHTER striding up the ramp. She was a head taller than almost everyone else in the crowded Arrivals area. *I'll give Gord and I credit for one thing,* she mused, *we produced two very fine children together.* She chuckled as some young men ogled her daughter as she sauntered by.

"You naughty girl." Carol wagged a finger at Ashley as she came up to give her a hug. "Those young men you just sashayed by are still recovering. Look at the poor guys."

Ashley laughed, looked back and waved to them. In unison, all three waved back. "The middle one is cute. We talked on the plane. We're all at Syracuse. We're going back on the same flight, too."

"No luggage?"

"Nope, just me and my backpack. I travel light." They headed towards the short-term parking.

"Good practice for being a reporter from what Ben said. Speaking of whom, we're having Thanksgiving dinner with Ben and Jennifer on Monday."

Ashley gave a little whoop of joy. "No way! My friends will be so jealous. He's a legend at Newhouse."

"Well, the legend can cook up a storm, too. I can hardly wait to see what they'll have laid out. Lana, Mark, and the kids will be there. I haven't had one of Lana's desserts in a long time."

"What're we bringing?" Ashley hooked her arm through Carol's as they walked along.

Carol mentally hugged herself. She and Ashley hadn't walked arm in arm in years. "I was hoping you might make one of your favorites to bring along. Your cookbook is still up on the shelf."

Ashley laughed. "I haven't used an actual cookbook in ages. I find my recipes on the internet, but I'll have a look. Maybe some peanut butter cookies for Danny. He loves them."

"It's so good to have you home for a few days. I've been really looking forward to seeing you." They reached the car. "Want to drive?"

"Sure. I'm a bit out of practice, but I'm sure Bimmi will remember me." Ashley tossed her backpack on the back seat and climbed in the driver's side. "Where to?"

"Had any lunch?" Carol felt herself relaxing. This was a much more mature Ashley. She realized they were relating as adults. Her sullen teen had blossomed into a lovely young woman without her even realizing it.

"No, and I know exactly where to go." Ashley drove away from the airport. The noon traffic was heavy, so it was over half an hour before she was looking for a parking spot on Harvard St. "There's nothing like Rubin's near me. I missed their corned beef sandwiches so much. Mind if we pick up some corned beef and pumpernickel for lunch tomorrow too?"

"I was thinking we might want to do a bit of shopping and go somewhere for lunch."

"We could do that. I can always make the cookies on Sunday. You have flour, butter, peanut butter, and eggs right?"

"We should pick up some peanut butter. Ours is pretty old. I never eat it myself."

"You don't know what you're missing, Mom." They found a parking spot almost a block away and strolled casually towards the restaurant. "I like Syracuse, but I love Boston. It's good to be home."

"I'm glad to hear you call it home. Time was you couldn't wait to get away." Carol glanced sideways and noted her daughter's fine features and smooth cream colored skin. She wore no makeup and only a small pair of earrings. Carol knew she was lucky. Many mothers had to deal with nose rings, lip rings and tattoos. "I'm curious. Do you have any tattoos?"

Ashley laughed. "No, and I'm not planning to. It's not my style." They walked into the busy deli.

Carol smiled with relief.

"Can I offer you ladies a menu to look over while you're waiting?"

"Only if you've run out of corned beef platters." Ashley smiled brightly at the young man, who promptly blushed.

"You have quite the effect on the young men." Carol smiled.

"Must be genetic."

"Ouch."

"I meant it as a compliment, Mom."

Carol laughed. "I thought you were referring to Lance the leech. It took me months to realize he was just a boy toy living off my money."

"Still feeling guilty about him?"

"Less and less as time goes by. He and Michel were life lessons I badly needed to learn." They were jostled a bit as a boisterous group of patrons filed out the door. The blushing maitre d' escorted them to a table that had just been set up. Menus and water arrived in quick succession as they settled in. Both declined the menu and ordered the house specialty.

"I've really missed you, Ash. I'm so glad you're back, even just for a long weekend." Carol fingered her gray pearl necklace. She was wearing it over a white cashmere turtleneck that made her feel cozy and warm.

"It's good to be back and just take a break. It's been a crazy busy semester. I need some downtime."

"I haven't planned anything except Thanksgiving dinner. We'll do whatever you like or nothing if you feel like it. I'm booked off until Tuesday. My first weekend off in months." Carol was startled to realize she hadn't taken a week off since sometime in the spring. *Note to self... take one weekend off a month.* They chatted happily as the wait staff bustled between the tables and the kitchen churned out the orders.

"Oh, goodie. Here comes the food." Ashley watched hungrily as the waitress brought the platters over and gazed wide-eyed as they were set in front of them. "I could get religious over this, it smells so heavenly."

They both tucked in.

"How's the new apartment set-up working out?" Carol forked up some potato salad.

"So far so good, although Sarah isn't very good at picking up after herself. I have to read the riot act at least once a week. And Melissa hogs the bathroom every morning. I get up at six just to get in ahead of her."

"I'm guessing you're playing den mother then?" Carol smiled.

"Someone has to, and neither of them is mature enough, that's for sure." The crowd was thinning out as they finished their meal.

"Room for dessert?" Carol was stuffed, and her plate wasn't even empty. Ashley's was cleaned.

"Nah, I'll pass. I'll have a coffee though." Ashley smiled at the waitress who cleared their table. "What's the plan for the afternoon?"

"You tell me."

"I'd like to go for a run later, after I digest some of this food. Maybe we could do groceries and I could make dinner for us. How does broiled salmon with baby potatoes, asparagus, and a salad sound?"

"I can't even think of my next meal when I'm still stuffed with this one. But it does sound wonderful. Maybe a movie later? I haven't seen a good chick flick in awhile. We can download something."

"Sounds like a plan. And before I forget, thanks so much for offering to pay my flights. I could've paid myself, but it's nice to have a bit of fun money left."

"I've been really impressed with your budgeting and sharing an apartment instead of insisting on being on your own. I have no problem putting in some extra here and there. You're doing really well. I'm proud of you." They strolled arm in arm back to the car. Ashley elected to drive.

"Thanks, Mom. I know we had a really bumpy road to get to where we are today. I needed some life lessons myself, including just growing up." She pulled out onto the street. "I didn't really appreciate what I had until I moved out and everything became my responsibility, including setting up accounts, paying bills, getting groceries, cooking meals, doing laundry, plus classes and assignments. You had everything so well organized. And even when you weren't home, we were never alone."

"But I wasn't home enough. I realize that now. I can't give you back those years, but I hope you believe me that I want to be a consistent presence in your life from now on."

"I do believe you, Mom. This past year I've watched you change. There's a softer, warmer side to you now that wasn't there for years after you kicked Dad out. He really broke your heart, didn't he?"

"Yes, he did. And I built a wall around it so high and thick that no-one could get through, including you and Jim. And then I turned into a control freak."

"And you were extremely good at it too." Ashley spied a parking spot near their neighborhood grocery store and made for it. "That was the hardest part of living with you after Dad was gone. It was also the most predictable. If there was a way to control it you did, right down to what time I had to be home to start my homework."

"I looked at it as structure. When your dad left, we had to build a family life that was shared with him. You two would go off and spend two weeks with him where there was no structure and come back to me and chafe at the boundaries I set."

"I know now that you were doing the right thing. When I see how my little apartment family functions or doesn't function, it helps me appreciate what you did for us. We've talked about it, and I know Jim feels the same way."

"So you still love me?" Carol smiled hopefully.

"We've always loved you. You're our mom. There was a time we didn't like what you were doing to yourself with all the men hanging around, but we never stopped loving you. And don't forget, we were teenagers then, who believed parents had no brains and we knew everything better than anyone."

Carol laughed. "And then you grew up, thank goodness."

"It was really rough being a teenager with a control freak mother."

Ashley led the way into the busy store and made straight for the produce section. "I just wanted to be treated like a grown-up, even though I wasn't one. It was so frustrating."

"Tell me about it." Carol found the asparagus and added it to their cart. Some romaine lettuce soon joined it, followed by kiwi and apples. "There were many days that condo couldn't contain all your teenage angst. Poor Jim. Between the two of us screaming at each other, he must have hearing loss."

"He's fine. He had ear plugs." They both laughed as they went to the checkout.

As they brought their groceries into the condo, Ashley put her two bags on the counter and looked around. Without speaking, she went back to the front door and looked at the number on the plate.

"What's wrong, Ash?"

"I'm just checking that we're in the right unit." Ashley grinned at her. "When I saw that living green plant over by the window, I was sure we were in the wrong place. You bought a plant?"

"It was a gift from Jennifer. She's promised me I can't kill it even if I forget to put new water in about once a week. Think I can handle it?"

"Wait 'til I tell Jim you have a plant. He won't believe me. And what's this?" Ashley walked over and picked up the afghan and rubbed her face into it. "What a gorgeous color. And you put out pictures of us. How old are they?"

"Old enough that I need to replace them." Carol chuckled. "I tried copying and printing some of your Facebook photos, but the quality isn't good enough. I'll take some this weekend."

"I have some on my phone I can download for you."

The two women chatted amiably as they put the groceries away.

"I'm going to get changed and go for a run."

"Hellooo! I'm back." Ashley called out as she stepped into the entry, set down an envelope and removed her running shoes. "There was a woman waiting outside when I came back. She wanted me to let her in but I didn't feel comfortable doing that. I don't know. Something about her. Anyway, she asked if I knew you and could give you this envelope. I told her I'm your daughter and would bring it right up."

Carol took the large brown envelope and looked it over. There was no writing on it anywhere. Not even her name. Mystified, she opened it and peered inside. And gasped. She dropped the envelope on the counter and stepped away from it like it was crawling with scorpions.

Ashley picked up the envelope, looked inside and then emptied the contents on the counter. Apart from one banner of paper that read Offer to Purchase Real Estate, the rest of the paper had been hand cut into pieces not much bigger than confetti.

"What's this about, Mom? A shredder couldn't have done a better job." Ashley looked at her mother and saw her ashen face. "Oh my God, are you all right?"

"The woman you saw, what did she look like?"

"She was a bit shorter than me, late thirties, short black hair and had these dark, piercing eyes. Even when she smiled, it never reached her eyes. That's why I wouldn't let her in."

"That's what I was afraid of." Carol went to her small desk and pulled out a business card. "Ashley, call this number and ask for Detective Guzzo, please." Carol willed herself to try and breathe normally as she gripped the desk with both hands. "I hope he's on today and can come over here right now."

"Okay, Mom, I'm on it. Go sit down. I'll bring you a glass of water." She watched as her mother made her way woodenly to a large chair by the window. Ashley had never seen her mother so shaken. She quickly dialed the number. She looked back at the pile of paper on the counter while the call was put through.

"Detective Guzzo? This is Ashley Brock, Carol Brock's daughter." Ashley looked over at her mother's white face. "Yes, sir. There is a problem. My mother is hoping you could come to see her right away… No, I don't believe it has anything to do with the Demercado case."

She looked over at her mother, who weakly shook her head. "No, it has nothing to do with it… good… see you in fifteen minutes. Thank you, sir."

She hung up then looked at her mother with concern. "What's going on?"

"That woman you saw is one of my clients, and she is mentally ill. Jennifer warned me just yesterday to get the police involved in case she goes over the edge. I think she's dangerously close now." Carol massaged her forehead. "I can't imagine how she found out where I live. I guard my privacy carefully."

"So why did she slice and dice this Offer to Purchase?"

"It's a long story. Do you mind making a pot of coffee, dear?" Carol leaned her head back on the chair. "I'm so sorry this happened. I was looking forward to a relaxing weekend with you."

"I'm just glad I'm here to help." Ashley looked away from the envelope and paper. "One pot of coffee coming up."

It wasn't long before they heard the chime. "Detective Guzzo? I'll buzz you in." Ashley waited by the door to let him in. "Good to meet you, sir. I've heard all about you."

"Good to meet you, too." They shook hands. "Is that fresh coffee I smell?"

"It is. How do you take it?"

"Black is good."

"Mom, you want a mug?" Ashley asked. Carol nodded. "Okay, three coffees coming right up."

"Thanks for coming over so quickly, Len. It seems I have a very mentally ill client who may be about to go over the edge and do something violent. I was warned by Jennifer Barrett—you've met her— that you need to know what's been happening this past week." Carol gratefully accepted the steaming cup and set it beside the bamboo arrangement. It soothed her to think of her friend and her gift.

Carol outlined the unfolding saga, leaving nothing out. "Devin Elliott has had a lot of strange things happen in the six years since he broke off with Allison Wendover, but when he put in the offer to purchase her mother's home she went ballistic and told me I'd regret it if I helped him. But I'm just doing my job."

Guzzo took detailed notes as she spoke. "I'm going to open a case file on this, Carol. As you both probably realize, Wendover hasn't done anything illegal that can be proven." Setting down his notepad, he took a large plastic ziplock out of his satchel and pulled on a glove. "I'll take the envelope and the contents and dust it for prints. Carol, I know yours are on file from the Demercado case. Ashley, I'll need your prints to eliminate them. I'm going to talk to our psych people. See what kind of take they have on all this. But in my experience, it doesn't look good."

"Whatever you can do to make her stop. I really appreciate this, Guzzo." Carol stood up on still wobbly legs. "Will you be contacting Devin Elliott?"

"You have his number handy? I'll call him now."

Carol read the number to him from her phone. "Call him from here. We aren't going anywhere. Oh yes, I have Ashley's finger prints in my safe. I had them done when she was little in case she got lost or was kidnapped."

Guzzo nodded and keyed in Devin's number and waited. "Devin Elliot? Detective Len Guzzo from the Boston Police. I'm with Carol Brock. I hear you've been having some difficulties with a Ms. Allison Wendover." Guzzo listened and then looked at the two women.

"No, I'm not calling about last night. What happened?" His bushy eyebrows went up a few degrees. "Would you be available to speak with me in the next hour? Where could I meet you?" He paused. "Let me ask...

"He's about ten minutes from here," Guzzo said. "Do you mind if he comes here?"

Carol made a split second decision. "By all means, please give him the address. Looks like we'll need more coffee, Ash. Better make it decaf though."

He closed the phone and looked somberly at both women. "When Mr. Elliot went back to his truck after having dinner with you last night, Carol, someone had smashed in his windshield. Not one other car in the lot had any damage. I think we can add stalking and vandalism to Ms. Wendover's MO."

Chapter Six

By the time Devin arrived, Carol had regained her balance. She was a mama bear now, and someone was threatening her and her cub. And that someone was not going to get away with it.

"Devin. Funny way to wrangle an invite to my place." Carol smiled warmly at him and took his coat. "Detective Guzzo, meet Devin Elliott. Devin, this is my daughter Ashley."

Devin shook Guzzo's hand and then turned to Ashley. "You are the spitting image of your mother. If I'd met her at your age, I would've married for sure. Alas, I didn't and have remained a lonely bachelor all these many years."

Carol laughed in relief. "Thank you, Devin. You just made my day, my week, and the month." She ushered them all into the living room. "Ash, can you take the coffee orders please? I'll get something to snack on. I think we're all a bit hungry at this hour."

Guzzo started asking Devin questions and noting his answers in his old-fashioned paper notebook. "So you split up with Ms. Wendover exactly when?"

"If memory serves, it was in June 2006. I couldn't see myself going through another summer with her. She was getting very clingy and manipulative and needed to know where I was every minute of the day. She was planning our life and future together without ever asking if it was what I wanted." Devin spoke as he watched Carol and Ashley organizing some hors d'oeuvres. He looked back at the detective.

"You told Carol that Allison trashed your condo just after you broke up. Tell me about that."

"Now that I think about it, it was cold and calculating. She knew I was out of town. She had called my office on the pretext she needed to reach me. They thought I was still going out with her and told her where I was." Devin took a cracker with smoked salmon and cream cheese from the plate Ashley set on the coffee table. "When I got back, my place was a disaster. Insurance covered most of it, but it was weeks before I could even live in the place. She had unplugged my fridge, opened the door and turned up the baseboard heaters full blast. The place reeked."

"How do you know it was her?"

"She was the only person in Boston, other than a good neighbor, with a key. Also, there was no sign at all of forced entry."

"Did you report it to the police?"

"I did. Some cop came over, took down the particulars and left. No-one ever came to dust for prints. I guess he figured, same old, same old." Devin reached for another cracker. "Relationship gone bad and ex-girlfriend takes it out on the couch with a large knife. I finally got a case number when my insurance company pushed it."

"Do you remember the officer's name?"

"No. It was over six years ago."

"Okay. Let's go to last Sunday at the open house."

Carol relived that day as Devin outlined Allison's fury at his presence. Ashley looked at her mother with wide eyes as the story unfolded.

"You must have been blindsided, Mom," she whispered. "Why didn't you call the police after she called?"

Detective Guzzo looked at them both. "Good question, Ashley. Why didn't you?"

"Devin and I thought she was just blowing off old steam. Jennifer had warned me otherwise but we convinced ourselves she would just go away when presented with the facts and a legal notice. Apparently, she's delusional. She never moved on."

"I don't need a psych evaluation to tell you this: you all need to stay well under her radar until we can figure out next steps. She knows your cars and knows where you live. My experience and that butchered offer tells me she's capable of physical violence, and it sounds like she's escalating her behavior. We've seen too many cases like this. We can't ignore these signs. Is there anywhere you could go for a few days until I can make a case and have her brought in?"

Carol, Devin, and Ashley all looked at each other. Devin spoke up.

"We could go to my farm upstate. The trick is to get out of town without her being able to follow us. She knows about the farm, but she doesn't know exactly where it is. She was too much of a city girl, and my parents weren't particularly fond of her. She was never invited."

"I have an idea. Let's cab to the airport and pick up a rental there. We can bring it back on Tuesday morning when Ashley catches her flight." Carol sipped her coffee. "Even if Allison is out there somewhere and manages to follow the taxi to the airport, she'll never be able to keep track of us once we're there."

"Good plan, Carol." Devin looked over at Guzzo who nodded in agreement.

"Okay, people, let's get organized." Carol was all business now. "Detective Guzzo, would it be possible to get a couple of patrol cars into the area? If Allison is hanging about she might leave if there's a visible police presence."

"I'm on it." Guzzo called in to the precinct.

"Ashley, can you start packing up the food please?" She looked over at Devin. "I hope you didn't shop for groceries today because we're about to empty our fridge into yours. Ash and I had already planned some meals."

"If two beautiful women want to cook for me, you won't get any arguments from me. Bring it on."

"All right then. Let me call Jennifer. We were supposed to have Thanksgiving dinner with her and her family. Her partner is Ben Powell, the former journalist."

"Remember him well. He would be one interesting guy to share a beer with. Why don't you invite them to the farm? I have plenty of space, lots of dishes, and a couple of farm managers who would be absolutely thrilled if I brought a passel of people home for Thanksgiving." Devin stood up and stretched. "They're always on at me to entertain now that I've done so many renovations."

"You sure? We're talking four adults and three children, including twin babies."

"I haven't had a full house in more years than I can remember. It's a five-bedroom house. Why don't you invite them up for brunch tomorrow and make it a little getaway weekend? I have a couple of horses and a pony. It will all help us forget Allison for the weekend."

"You are one special person, Devin Elliott." Carol looked at him in a new light.

"You are too, Carol Brock. Let's combine forces against Allison and see where it takes us. What do you say?"

"Bring it on." Carol and Devin exchanged smiles.

"Then let's go, girl. We are going to whup that bitch's ass."

"Mr. Elliott! Your language, sir."

"What part of whup ass didn't you agree with?"

"You forgot the word damn."

"I stand corrected. We are going to whup that damn bitch's ass."

"That's better." Carol laughed as he winked at her.

JENNIFER LISTENED IN AMAZEMENT as Carol told her the recent developments. "Why didn't you call Guzzo right after we spoke?"

"Devin convinced me it wasn't as bad as you made out. Now he knows differently. We all do. The police are taking this very seriously. But the bad news is we can't be in Boston over the weekend. How would you feel about moving the dinner to Devin's farm? It's about an hour and a half from your place. You're invited to stay for the weekend. Devin would really like to meet Ben."

"Oh my! What a gracious offer. Let me check with Ben, Lana, and Mark. It sounds very inviting."

"Devin has two horses and a pony named Pablo. I bet Danny would just love to ride one of them."

"If Devin has horses, Ben and I would love it too. Are you sure about this? We're talking about transferring the entire Thanksgiving dinner to a home owned by someone we barely know."

"You're the one who said he's well known and respected in Boston society."

"I did say that, didn't I?" Jennifer chuckled. "Okay, let me check with everyone, and I'll get back to you. But if it's a farm with animals, I'm pretty sure I know what the answer will be."

Carol closed the phone and looked around. "I need to go and pack a bag. I don't have much that will work on a farm, but I can sacrifice my gym sneakers."

"I'm sure we can find you some rubber boots." Devin picked up dishes and cups and brought them to the sink and rinsed them. Turning to the counter, he peered into the bags Ashley had filled. "I have a feeling we're going to need some long country walks if we're going to eat all this."

Carol laughed. "You haven't seen Ashley's appetite. She's a real athlete. We may need to re-stock by Sunday."

"I heard that." Ashley called out from her room. "The bagels are mine."

The detective was wrapping up with a couple more questions when his phone rang. "Guzzo. What's up?" He nodded. "It sure sounds like her. Right height, hair, and clothing. Thanks for the heads up."

He looked at them. "She's across the street, hanging around near your truck, Devin. We could pick her up now, but she'd be out the minute her lawyer arrived. We can't prove anything yet that would allow us to hold her in custody."

"Let's just get away for the weekend and de-stress. I'm not about to let her ruin my first weekend off in six months. Do you agree, Devin?"

"You've got my vote. Ashley?"

"To paraphrase the Three Musketeers, only a fool would try to attack us twice in the same day, but I vote to go."

"Unfortunately, we're dealing with someone who is no fool but mentally ill, which is worse. Let's get out of Dodge." Devin started moving bags to the front entrance.

Carol called for a taxi, telling the dispatcher to send the driver to the back entrance to her building. "Len, can you ask the patrol car to swing by Devin's truck in about fifteen minutes? It should distract Allison when we leave."

"I'll go down myself and get the blue and white to stop for a chat. That should scare her off."

"Thanks. I think we'll all feel a little bit more in control now." Carol walked him to the door. She closed it slowly and then walked towards her bedroom. "I'll be ready in five minutes or so."

Ashley doubled over laughing. "This I have to see. My mother packed for a long weekend away in five minutes?" She pulled out an imaginary stopwatch. "I'm timing you!"

DEVIN CLOSED HIS PHONE. "I've booked a full-sized van. Anything in those bags we can eat now? Those crackers didn't go far."

"I'm hungry, too." Ashley was sitting in the back seat with Carol and a couple of the food bags. "Let's see what's in here. How about an apple and a granola bar?"

She pulled out both and passed them to Devin in the front seat of the taxi. "Mom and I had the corned beef platter at Rubin's for lunch."

"That's right. Hand me an apple, and then tell me about what a great meal you had." Devin took a large bite. "It makes my stomach grumble just to hear about it."

"Wasn't the potato salad divine, Mom?"

"Oh yes, and the sandwich. There must have been half a pound of meat. I couldn't even finish mine." Carol was enjoying their easy camaraderie. She'd never seen Ashley friendly with any of her gentlemen friends before. Of course, Devin wasn't exactly a gentleman friend. They had just banded together for self-protection for the weekend until the police could make a solid move.

"Too bad you didn't ask for a doggie bag." Devin ripped open the granola bar wrapper with his teeth. "I'm hitting the food court before we get on the road. A man cannot live on itty bitty snacks. I need man food."

CAROL'S PHONE CHIRPED just as they got to the airport food court. "Hi Jen. We're at the airport getting ready to pick up a rental for the weekend. What's the plan?"

"As I expected, everyone is very excited about spending Thanksgiving at Devin's farm. Lana says Danny couldn't stop doing a happy dance. You can count us all in. Can we bring Charlie?"

"Let me check." Carol looked for Devin. His tall, lanky frame wasn't hard to spot. She walked over to him. "Jennifer and the family would be delighted to come for the weekend. Do you mind if she brings her dog?"

"Not at all. It'll be good for a city dog to get out to the country."

"Thanks, Devin." She smiled at him warmly and put the phone back to her ear. "Bring Charlie too, Jen. We'll see you in time for lunch?" She nodded and closed the phone.

Devin was next in line. "I'm getting a fajita chicken wrap. What can I get you?"

"I'm not sure if I want to eat anything. I'm still pretty rattled about Allison coming to where I live. I'm still mystified how she found it."

Devin placed an order for two wraps and a couple of coffees for the road. "Whatever you can't eat, I'm sure I can take care of it. You say your home address isn't listed anywhere accessible to the public?"

"I stopped using a land phone a few years ago. I'm purely on mobile." They caught up with Ashley, who was clutching a large bag from Burger King. "What'd you get, Ash?"

"Burger, fries, and milkshake. I'll run extra miles tomorrow." She grinned a bit sheepishly.

"Guard those fries. I may need some to go with my wrap." Devin guided them towards the rental counter as Ashley reached in the bag for one, waggled it in front of Devin's nose and then popped it in her mouth.

"Your daughter is a devil, Carol." Devin grinned.

"You should have seen her at Arrivals this morning. She had three young men swooning as she passed by."

"Ah, she probably had fries stuffed in her pockets."

Ashley punched him lightly in the arm and then laughingly dashed behind her mother for protection and pulled out another fry.

"Okay, children. Everyone behave or there'll be no dessert." Their antics were helping Carol put Allison to the back of her mind. *I have to be in the here and now,* she reminded herself. *Ash and I need to make more good memories from now on.*

They loaded their gear into the roomy van. Ashley settled herself in the back seat with her food and mobile. "I'm texting Jim about our weekend plans. Any message you want me to pass on?"

"Tell him what a great time he's going to miss. And let him know I love him." Carol smelled the fragrant wrap on the console and reached for one. "Thanks for getting this, Devin. I'm actually a bit hungry now." As Devin drove them away from the airport, Carol opened up the paper a bit and handed it to him, then opened the other one for herself.

"Some real food, at last. Lunch was a long time ago." Devin took a large bite as Carol nibbled at hers. The van filled up with the smell of the burger and fries as Ashley tucked into her dinner. "This is good. I don't often buy food at the airport."

"Do you travel often?" Carol looked out at the busy highway. The main rush hour was long over but the traffic was still heavy.

"Not as much as I used to. I tend to fly out for a few days at the beginning of a project, set up the specs and then have one of the mid-level people shepherd it through, with me at the other end of a phone or on Skype. It's way more efficient." The traffic was thinning noticeably. "Pretty soon we'll be back out in the country. Wait until you see all the stars. You can't see half as many in town."

Carol's phone chirped. She unlocked it and put it to her ear. "Carol Brock."

"You're conspiring against me, to take my home. Well, you won't get it. I won't allow it. You will all burn in hell first."

Carol shut her phone and quickly turned it off. "Oh my God. It was her. I forgot to block her number."

"What did she say?"

Carol didn't see Devin's face go pale as she repeated it to him. "It's what she wrote on my bathroom mirror six years ago. Talk about being caught in a time warp."

"There was a steely control in her voice this time. It was almost emotionless." Carol felt rolling nausea build as her stomach roiled. She touched Devin's arm. "Pull over quick. I need to throw up."

"Mom, you okay?" Ashley was rubbing Carol's shoulders as they stood at the side of the road.

"Getting better. Do we have any water?"

Ashley went to retrieve her bottle and brought it back to her mother, who was shivering in the freezing night air. "Get back in the van, Mom. Let's get going."

Carol settled back into the van and took sips of the cold water. "Think we should call Guzzo now or wait until morning?"

"Your call, Carol. Will you be able to sleep if you don't call him?"

"I guess not. I'll call it in now."

By the time they turned up Devin's laneway, twenty minutes later, Carol was fully in control of her swirling emotions. Someone in Guzzo's office had taken down her information and promised to add it to her file. She could see the outline of the large house glowing with lights at the top of a small hill. As they drew up to the side of the house, she smiled. They had just passed the wraparound front verandah she had imagined.

"It's beautiful, Devin. So warm and inviting."

"Wait until you see inside." He clicked buttons and both van doors slid open. Ashley climbed out, stretched, and looked up.

"Nice place, Devin. And you're right about the stars. This is amazing." Above them, the inky black sky was sparkling with millions of rough cut diamonds. It seemed the crisp night air brought them out in even sharper detail.

"Brother Devin, you handsome rogue. Welcome home." A tall, slim man came out the side door and walked gracefully down the stairs. "And who are these darling creatures?"

"I'm Carol Brock. This is my daughter Ashley. And you are…?"

"My name is Flynn. I'm the partner of the farm manager, Gregory." He shook hands with both women. "Devin, you told me you were bringing a couple of guests but you didn't say they had such exquisite taste. I'd recognize a suede Burberry anywhere."

"Hi Flynn. It's been quite a wild day. Did Gregory tell you we have more guests coming tomorrow?" The two men shook hands and then hugged.

"He did mention the house would be full. I gather we're hosting a full-scale Thanksgiving weekend."

"We are indeed. Let's get all this stuff inside and show the ladies to their rooms. I need a very cold beer, and I suspect both these ladies would enjoy a glass of wine." Devin followed Ashley into the house as Carol and Flynn brought up the rear.

"This place is wicked!" Ashley set some bags and her backpack on the floor to take off her boots. They were in a brightly-lit mud room full of coats, boots, hats, and a large antique bench. Through the doorway, a spacious modern country kitchen could be seen. Ashley and Devin went in first.

"Glad you like it. It's been in my family for three generations."

"This kitchen is amazing."

"This place should be featured in a magazine, Devin." Carol had stepped into the warmly-lit kitchen. A small basket of brightly-colored fruit held center stage in the middle of a large round pine table. To the left, a long granite counter ended at a large pantry. Off to the right, they could see a large dining room with a gleaming cherry wood table.

"I've been asked, but I prefer to keep this place private. A number of my restoration projects have been featured in various magazines over the years." Devin brought in the last of the grocery bags.

"Is this a wood-burning cook oven?" Ashley stroked the gleaming iron and metal appliance that was almost as tall as her. "I've only seen pictures of them."

"That was made in the early 1900s. I had it restored and converted to propane but it is an original." Devin went over and showed Ashley how the burners worked. "I'll give you the grand tour tomorrow after everyone has arrived. Basically, though, we're close to going off the electrical grid. I have a geothermal heating system that supplies the house and stable, plus we have solar and wind generation and propane for the fireplaces. Your brother would probably be very interested in all this."

"I'm going to text him. He'll be so jealous." Ashley went over to help put away their groceries.

"Can I offer you ladies a glass of wine?" Devin had put a cold beer on the counter. "Flynn will have decided by now which bedroom you will get, right Flynn?"

"I think these gorgeous ladies should share the Rosewood. I think you'll like the décor. How about we get you set up with your wine; you can have a sip, and I'll show you up?"

"I'll pass on the wine, Flynn. Do you mind taking me up now?" Ashley picked up her backpack. "I'm going to get ready for bed and do some course reading. G'night guys."

"Good night, Ash. I won't be long." Carol gratefully accepted the glass of wine Devin poured.

"Let's take it to the solarium." Devin picked up his beer and the bottle of wine and led the way.

"Oh, Devin. This is absolutely gorgeous. It's an add-on right?" Carol sank into a large wicker chair and set her glass on a gleaming glass-topped table. The soft green and brown tones in the room and ambient lighting gave the room an aura that said mellow and relaxed.

"Yes. I love sitting here watching the sun set over the meadow. In good weather, the horses stay out. I can see them grazing from here."

"What are their names?" Carol sipped the smooth Amarone appreciatively. "This wine is incredible."

"The stallion is Aerosmith, and the filly is Sabrina."

"Sabrina is a lovely name. But… Aerosmith? Is Steven Tyler your neighbor?" Carol crooked up an eyebrow.

"Well, he spent a lot of time in Boston. But it's actually a common name for stallions and geldings. We call him Aero for short." Devin took a pull on his beer. "Bring your wine and come with me. There's something I want to show you."

Carol picked up her glass and followed him towards the front of the house. They reached a heavy oak door. Devin opened it and waved Carol in. Her gaze was immediately drawn to a large antique fireplace centered against one wall. Above it was an oil painting of a large, chestnut horse with a long creamy white tail.

"He's magnificent. What kind? How old is he?" Carol looked around the room, noting the heavy oak desk that was the size of a dining room table.

"He's an American Quarter Horse and he's seven now. I've had him since he was a foal. He's been hand raised by Gregory and I."

Carol heard the love and pride in his voice. "He's a beautiful animal. I take it Allison didn't like animals?"

"No, and she didn't like the country at all. I'm glad now that she never came here."

"I'm with you. It feels safe here." Carol sipped her wine. "My condo won't feel like that until Allison is stopped. Even then, I don't think it will ever have the character this place has."

"I don't think any condo can really acquire the kind of character you feel in a house like this. It's part of the reason I'm so interested in Clara Wendover's house. There's a special feel you can only get from old hardwoods, whether in floors or furniture. How about we go back to the solarium for a few minutes? Maybe you'd like a little more wine."

"It's very good. A little more and I'm sure I'll be able to sleep." Carol could feel the cozy ambiance all around her. It's like the house had folded her to its bosom and was cradling her close.

Chapter Seven

Carol went over to the window and opened the curtains. Early morning sunlight peeked over the hills, bathing the dull green pasture in a soft light. "Look at this day. The weather is perfect. C'mon Ash, let's …" Carol smiled as she looked at the empty bed a few feet from hers. Right, she's up early to get ahead of her roommate in the bathroom.

But when Carol went to the hall bathroom, it was empty. No sign of shower activity. She brushed her teeth and hair, pulled on jeans and a sweater, and decided to follow the aroma of coffee that was wafting up the stairs.

"Am I the last one up? Where is everyone?"

Flynn was putting out a large bowl of fruit salad, a tray of bagels and muffins, and an assortment of cheeses. "Hello, gorgeous. Yes, you are last up. Devin is at the stable and Ashley has gone for a run. She said to tell you she'll catch up with you over breakfast around eight."

"Where do you live if you don't mind me asking?" Carol accepted a large mug of steaming coffee.

"Gregory and I have a lovely cottage on the property. You wouldn't have been able to see it from the laneway in the dark. It's a couple hundred yards west of the house. We love it."

"Do you take care of this house full-time?"

"Oh, no, darling girl." Flynn laughed. "A housekeeper comes in to clean. I have a gift shop and bookstore in town. You won't be seeing much of me today or tomorrow. This is one of my busiest weekends. I have a sacred mission to relieve as many Boston women of their money as I can in the next forty-eight hours."

66

"Sounds like you enjoy what you do." Carol chuckled. "I must see if my friend Jennifer would like to swing by your shop. Her partner is Ben Powell, the journalist. They have a few shekels between them."

"Ben Powell? She must bring him along. He is just the most handsome man and such a commanding presence. I would love to meet him."

"If you don't meet him at the store, they'll be here until Tuesday. Will you be joining us for Thanksgiving dinner?" Carol wasn't sure if it was her place to ask, but everything she knew about Devin made her feel it wouldn't be otherwise.

"Oh, absolutely. I've already picked out the china and glasses we'll use. You'll just love them, I know it. I found the set at an estate sale a couple of years ago and told Devin he had to have it. These dishes belong in a house like this, the glasses, too." Flynn rinsed his hands and headed for the mud room. "I have to dash now. Have a lovely day."

Carol topped up her coffee and went into the solarium. In the growing morning light, the casual warmth of the room contrasted with the bare trees and bushes outside the windows. Walking to one of the large windows, she was rewarded with the sight of two tall horses and the shorter pony, grazing at a feeding trough with fresh hay. She watched as Devin and Gregory strolled out of the stable, deep in discussion about something. When Devin looked up and saw her, he waved and pointed her out to Gregory, who also waved.

She knew she was blushing and felt a curious warmth seeing Devin's smiling face. He made for the house when he saw Ashley running up the lane. They met at the door and came in laughing. "He wouldn't leave me alone. At first, he just yapped and tried to stop me so I'd pet him. When I kept going, he ran along with me. He went home as we came by his lane on the way back."

Devin chuckled. "That would be marvelous Marvin. He belongs to my neighbors. As you saw, he's everybody's friend."

"I'm going to go up and shower. I'll be down in a few minutes."

"We'll wait for you."

"Great!"

"And how is one of Boston's top real estate agents this fine morning?" Devin went over and poured himself a coffee.

"Feeling much more human than I did last night. I slept like a baby. Didn't even hear Ash get up and get dressed."

"That often happens when people sleep here after being in the city. It's why I spend as much time here as I can. It's good for the soul."

"I would definitely have to agree with you on that. I feel like I'm on vacation at a New England Victorian bed and breakfast with a kick-ass kitchen. With a kitchen like this, I think even I could learn to cook."

"I'm glad you like it. I thought you might. And yeah, the kitchen really does kick ass. I have Flynn mostly to thank for that. He helped me get the right balance between tradition and convenience. Cost me a fortune though."

"It's worth every penny. Flynn told me about talking you into the estate sale dishes and glasses."

"He's so proud of that find. He swears the house wouldn't be the same without them."

They heard Ashley bounding down the stairs. She went straight for the bagels before she even sat down. "Let's eat. I'm starving."

"Can't have that in my house. Carol?" Devin held out a chair. "What's the plan for today?"

"Flynn wants me to bring Jennifer to his shop." Carol spread some cream cheese on half a bagel. "Ashley, you want to come too?"

"Sure. I'll shop, you pay." Ashley grinned across the table. "Sound good?"

"What happened to that extra fun money you were talking about?"

"It's more fun when it's yours." Ashley peeled a banana and bit off a large chunk.

Carol chuckled. "Devin, you said earlier you thought I'd like your house. I'm curious what made you say that. You've seen my condo. It's not exactly an advertisement for cozy."

"Wait until you see mine. To me it's just a place to sleep. This is the place I really live."

"I'm starting to understand why you feel that way." At the moment, she couldn't see the horses, but just knowing they were there made this place seem more real than almost anything she'd seen in many years. And being in real estate, she'd seen a lot.

"Do you ladies know how to ride?"

"Actually, Ashley had lessons not too far from here. So did I. Not in the same decade though."

"Would you like to do a bit of riding while we're waiting for the others to get here?"

Carol and Ashley looked at each other and smiled broadly. "Bet you never thought you'd have a Thanksgiving like this, did you Ash?"

"Definitely not. Ready when you are." Ashley picked up her dishes and loaded them in the dishwasher. Carol put the food away as Devin wiped the table and counters.

"Let's go, ladies."

"GREGORY, I'D LIKE YOU TO MEET CAROL AND ASHLEY BROCK." The stable was much cooler than the house but still comfortable. Gregory shook both their hands. "Pleased to meet you."

He looked down at their shoes. "Glad to see you both have sensible shoes. Boots would be better but the paddock and trails are dry this time of year, so you'll be fine. I'll just go saddle up Sabrina and Aero. Which one of you is going to ride Pablo?"

"Ashley, if you agree, I'd suggest you ride Pablo. He's actually right at the height limit to be called a horse but he's so much shorter than the other two that I've always called him a pony." Devin winked at her. "He thinks he's a horse though, so don't say anything."

Ashley laughed and went back to look at her steed. "Well, hello, you big beautiful horse." Pablo's ear pricked forward at the sound of her voice. He clopped forward to put his head over the gate. "You're a beautiful boy. I think we're going to be friends."

"He's a lover that one." Gregory pulled Pablo's halter off its hook.

The horse obediently put his head forward as it was slipped on. "Why don't you lead him out to the paddock, and I'll bring his saddle out?"

Within minutes, all three horses were saddled up and their riders seated. Aero was prancing, almost showing off to the visitors. Carol watched Devin sitting tall in the saddle of the sprightly horse and felt her heart beat a bit faster. *Oh my, he looks so handsome and virile. Good thing Ash is here to chaperone.* Then she chided herself. *This weekend is about friends and family. Just because he looks so damn virile on his horse doesn't mean I'm going to fall for him. And just because he's been a complete gentleman, doesn't mean that I'm ready to let my guard down—yet.*

"Lead on d'Artagnan. One for all and all for one." Ashley raised an arm with an imaginary sword and gave Pablo a nudge with her knees. The horse took three steps and stopped. Devin, Gregory and Carol tried in vain to hide their chuckles.

"C'mon Pablo. Don't make me look bad. I won't get you that carrot I promised." Ashley pressed her knees into the horse's broad flank. He took one more step and shook his head.

"As hilarious as this looks, it isn't fair." Devin's eyes danced with laughter. "You need to click with your tongue as you press your knees in. Like this." Devin demonstrated deftly. At one click plus knee pressure, Aero began a sedate walk. At two clicks he broke into a trot around the paddock.

Ashley imitated his actions and was rewarded with Pablo moving in behind Aero. Carol joined them on Sabrina. After three more turns around the paddock, Devin led them onto a trail that wound to the east of the stable.

Carol relished the cold air on her face. *If I were in Boston now, I'd probably be at the gym or showing a house. This feels like real exercise.* She watched Devin and Ash trotting side by side as they chatted and let her thoughts wander. *I might as well enjoy this weekend because, once I'm back in Boston dealing with Allison, Myra and possibly the media, this will be a memory I can cherish. This time, Myra's going to force me to take a leave of absence if Allison talks to the media. It could ruin my career.*

"Carol. Where are you?" Devin was suddenly beside her. "You're missing the ride." Carol shook her head slightly. She hadn't even seen Devin fall back to ride beside her.

"Oh, Devin, I'm sorry. I should be enjoying this, but I'm worried about work and what Allison may be up to now that she can't get at either of us. She's friends with the regional vice-president, who isn't my friend at the best of times. She's a queen bee and sees me as competition, which I'm not. She thinks I'm trying to hijack the hive."

"I can't tell you to stop worrying. I'm concerned too. But I can suggest you do your best to set it all aside, for now. Why don't you get up there with Ashley and spend time with her? Let me worry for both of us for awhile." Devin reached over and patted her thigh.

She smiled her thanks to him and caught up with Ash, her skin still tingling where he'd touched her.

"What do you think of him, Mom? Isn't he the greatest? And such a fine specimen."

"It was so kind of him to invite us here for the weekend to get away from that sick lady."

Ashley guffawed. "Mom! I was talking about Pablo."

Carol blushed to her roots. "Busted by my own daughter. I can't win." She smiled ruefully. "But what a great bust." She smiled over at Ash. "You got me there, kiddo. Don't you dare say a word, or I'll pull your tuition money."

"Mum's the word." Ashley feigned concern and grinned wickedly. "But yes, Devin is a fine specimen for a man his age. You should go for it, Mom. You deserve a good guy like him. The farm and horses are a major bonus."

"Just promise you won't say anything. I don't know what I'm feeling, and with the Allison situation, I'm not sure what's real and what isn't."

Ashley looked straight at her mother. "You'd have to be blind not to see that Devin cares about you. And I can see you're coming to care about him."

"It's only been a week. You're the one who flayed me for jumping all over a guy after one date. Devin and I have had dinner together once. And now we're here for the weekend. Don't you think that's rushing it according to your rules?"

"I believe this is different, Mom. I have strong instincts. My instincts tell me you can trust Devin with your feelings. And I'm betting your instincts are telling you the same thing."

"Ash, I'm confused. I'm not sure what I'm thinking. All I know is that this place feels special. I feel like I'm home, and I'm afraid of that feeling. There's a big part of me that doesn't want to trust again. I couldn't live again with a man who would cheat on me." Carol looked out over the meadow, resting as it waited for the winter snow to blanket it.

"Mom, if you want my opinion, this time, your feelings about Devin and this place are taking you in the right direction. I'm sure of it."

"I want to believe you so much, baby. I really do." Carol and Ashley reined in the horses as they saw a van coming up the lane.

"Party time." Ashley urged Pablo forward to trot down the lane and escort Lana and Mark's van up the laneway.

"Danny, get the leash and hold tight onto Charlie. We don't want to spook the horses and cause an accident." Mark looked a little nervous as the three horses sidled up beside their van. "Don't let him loose until Mr. Elliott says you can. Got it, big guy?"

"Sure, Dad. I got it. I've never been this close to a horse. They're huge!"

"You got that right. I've never been this close to one myself." Mark opened the window. "Hi Ashley. Where do we go?"

"Follow me." Ashley guided Pablo to the side of the house where they had unloaded the night before. Devin and Carol headed to the paddock to tie up their horses and join the new arrivals.

By the time the van rolled up to the side entrance, Carol and Devin had reached the house. Carol made the introductions. "Devin, this is Jennifer Barrett, my absolute best friend in the universe. This is her soon-to-be husband Ben Powell. This is Mark Powell, Ben's son and soon-to-be-husband of Lana Fitzpatrick. And this is Danny."

"When can I let Charlie out? When can I ride the pony?" Danny got out of the van holding Mark's hand.

Carol chuckled. "Danny is also known as the boy of a thousand questions. Be warned."

Devin squatted down. "Have you ever ridden a horse or pony before?"

"No."

"Well, then, we'd better get you up on one now. If you want to stay at this farm you have to be able to ride. That's a rule."

"I want to stay, and I want to ride a horse or the pony." Danny's six-year-old face was serious.

"Well, here's the thing, Danny." Devin stood up. "Pablo thinks he's a horse even though he's just on the line to be a real one. But if you say otherwise, he won't let you ride him. So just pretend he's a horse and he'll be fine. You ready?"

"You mean right now?" Danny's eyes went wide.

"Was there something else you wanted to do first?" Devin smiled over at Carol and Jennifer.

"Wow. I'm ready for sure. Does he bite?"

"He's never bitten anyone that I can remember." As Ashley got off Pablo, Devin picked up Danny and set him on the animal. "How about if Ashley walks you around a bit until you get used to him? She can tell you how to get him to do some of his moves." Devin winked at Ashley.

Carol felt a new warmth bathe her heart. Devin had captivated all of them in mere minutes. Danny was in the palm of his hands already. It had been the same with Ashley. *This man has a magical touch. He's completely sincere. Where have you been all my life?* The sudden thoughts came unbidden.

Devin looked over at her and smiled. It lit up his face, especially his eyes. "I'm so glad we're doing this Carol. There hasn't been a big Thanksgiving dinner held here in many years. It feels great."

Carol didn't know what to say. *He said we.* She pulled a hand through her hair to fluff it out. "You sure got Danny in the palm of your hand in record time. I don't remember Jim ever warming up to a stranger that fast at that age."

"Did any of those strangers have a pony?"

Carol chuckled. "No, I can't say that any of them did. I'm going to help Jennifer and Lana get settled in. Flynn told me what bedrooms to give everyone."

"I'll see you later then. Ashley, Ben, and I will stay with Danny and let you women take over my house and kitchen."

"You may never find things after we leave." Carol smiled at him.

"Then you'll just have to come back and tell me where everything is." Devin was rewarded with a definite blush as Carol turned to walk into the house. He was smiling as he walked towards the paddock.

DEVIN AND BEN WERE LEANING UP AGAINST THE PADDOCK FENCE, watching Ashley lead Pablo, with Danny asking question after question from his broad back.

"I don't have a saddle small enough for a child. But he can ride with me when we go out on the trails. That'll probably be plenty exciting enough for this weekend."

"So what's the story on this Wendover woman?"

Devin shook his head. He and Ben were head to head in height. He looked over at him. "I'm only beginning to see the patterns. But Jennifer is pretty convinced Allison is a psychopath. Detective Guzzo agrees. I'm becoming more convinced by the day."

"You know anything about psychopathic personalities?"

"Not really, at least not until the last couple of days. I haven't told Carol, but I've done some online research, and Allison really does fit the profile. Particularly, her long-time obsession over our break-up and now her obsession over me not getting her mother's home. She sees that as yet another public humiliation."

"From what Jennifer's told me, she won't stop until she ends the story her way. And if that means doing one or both of you physical harm, she won't hesitate."

"A week ago I wouldn't have agreed with you. Now, I do. And I'm just so sorry Carol's been caught up in her web."

"What's your plan?" Ben rubbed his hands together to warm them before shoving them in his jacket pockets. "Left my gloves in the van."

"I have spares in the stable. C'mon, I'll give you a tour." They headed towards the open doors. "Allison has been so unpredictable, I haven't really thought of a plan. My first priority was to get Carol and Ashley out of Boston for the weekend. Even at that, Allison called Carol on her mobile while we were driving here last night. A perfectly good fajita wrap became fox food in a ditch."

Ben looked puzzled and then laughed. "Carol upchucked?"

"Big time hurl."

"She always comes across as being one tough cookie, but Carol is very sensitive. Jennifer thinks the tough cookie routine is a cover for a broken heart over her ex."

"Makes sense. That, and the Demercado case, which I'm told you broke."

"I did, indeed. He's now rusting away in prison for the next ten years. Did she tell you he stole thousands of dollars worth of her jewelry on top of conning his way into her client's properties?"

"I did online research on the media coverage. She didn't have to tell me."

"Sounds like you're very interested in Carol's story." Ben let the statement stand between them.

Devin grinned. "I know a big brother when I see one. Yes, I'm interested in Carol. But I can assure you, hauling you all up here wasn't part of any grand seduction scheme. I just want her safe while Guzzo gets the troops lined up."

Ben grinned back. "Never said you're trying to seduce her. But if you get to that stage, you'll be one lucky fellow I'm sure. She's a fine looking lady with a sharp mind, too."

"Who knows how to take charge and get things done. You should've seen her ordering us all around once we decided to come up here."

"That's Carol at her finest. Speaking of which, if I know those ladies, we should be heading over for lunch. Jennifer was up 'til midnight putting things together."

"Let's get Ashley and Danny and get going then. I don't know about you, but I'm hungry." Devin called, "Ashley, Danny, time to wash up for lunch."

Gregory came out to tie up the horses.

"Let's just take off the saddles and let them feed. We'll be going out on the trail this afternoon while the ladies are off helping Flynn meet his monthly sales objective." Devin looked over at Ben, who nodded in agreement.

"They won't need any help from us, I'm sure," Ben said with a laugh.

"ANY FOOD IN THIS HOUSE?" Devin, Ben, Ashley, Danny and Gregory stomped in from the mud room. Their noses told them right away there was definitely something. The kitchen was filled with a tantalizing aroma.

"Hope you like Chinese hot and sour soup." Jennifer looked up from a large pot on the antique stove. "This stove is amazing. I feel like I should be wearing a floor-length dress and apron and maybe a matronly bonnet on my head. But then the rest of the kitchen says twenty-first century plus."

"Until Flynn gives you the grand tour, you won't know just how twenty-first century it is. It has bells and whistles I still haven't mastered." Devin went over to the pot, bent his head over it and inhaled reverently. "Anything we can do?"

"If you've washed your hands, you can go and sit down." Jennifer had taken over the kitchen. "No hands that have touched horses will touch this table or its food."

Devin heard a scratching noise as he washed his hands. Opening the mud room door, Charlie bounded in, wriggling with happiness.

"Like it here, fella?" Devin bent down to scratch his ear. Jennifer had only specified horses. "C'mon in. I'm sure we'll find some good leftovers for you."

Within minutes, they were all chowing down on hot bowls of soup with a large platter of homemade spring rolls.

"These spring rolls are delicious." Carol looked over at Devin who nodded in full agreement. "Ben, did you make these?"

"I made them awhile back. We just brought up a bag from the freezer. No big deal."

Ashley took a bite of hers. "Omigod. These are perfection. Can I get the recipe?"

"Only if you have a deep fryer."

"I'll just have to put in a mail order then. What do you charge for shipping?" Ashley grinned.

"Maybe I could come visit my alma mater and bring a bag along for a guest lecture to one of your classes. Once they're made we can heat them up in an oven."

"You'd come to Syracuse to visit me and do a guest lecture?" Ashley was wide-eyed.

"It's probably about time I visit." Ben smiled as he spooned up some of the fragrant soup. "They've been asking me for years. Now I have more time. Why don't you put one of your profs in touch with me?"

"I don't know any undergrad who has managed to land a Pulitzer prize-winning journalist to speak. Oh, Ben, thank you so much." Ashley shoved the rest of her spring roll in her mouth as Carol looked on smiling.

"From what I understand, the afternoon plan is this: Women are going to Flynn's shop; men are going riding. Drinks and hors d'oeuvres at six, compliments of Jennifer and Ben. Dinner around seven, compliments of Ashley and I, with able assists from whoever wants to make the salad." Carol beamed at everyone. "I haven't marshaled a family gathering in about fifteen years or a major dinner party in over a year. Looks like I haven't lost my touch."

Carol watched Devin as they cleared up the lunch and cleaned the kitchen. *He really likes this and feels comfortable,* she thought. *He and Ben have hit it off beautifully. Everyone loves this place. Danny is in heaven. Even Charlie has found his place.* The dog was sprawled in front of the living room fireplace, which had been turned on to ensure there was no chill as they were eating.

"Take the rental, ladies. There's unlimited mileage and well over half a tank of gas. It's all yours." Devin took the keys out of his pocket and handed them to Carol. "Just be careful when you're parking. Those pesky side mirrors get in the way sometimes."

"I think that's only a problem for large, black pickups." She grinned up at him. "We should be pretty safe."

"What will not be safe are your wallets. Flynn has immaculate taste and does a yearly buying trip in Europe and another here at home. Prepare to be impressed."

"There's safety in numbers. Between the three of us, we can take turns talking each other out of impulse purchases, right Jennifer? Ash?" Carol grabbed her tote off a side table and brought it into the mud room.

Devin looked on. "Good luck."

He looked at Ben. "How about we head over to the stable and organize for a trail ride? I see Gregory is putting the saddles back on. Let's go give him a hand." The two tall men walked out the door together.

"Great spread you have here, Devin. And thanks for the invite." Ben walked over to Sabrina, who stood almost head to head with him. "Jennifer was worried when Carol called to say she had to get out of town for the weekend. You actually made her day when you invited the whole clan here."

"I figured it was the least I could do after embroiling Carol in Allison's nastiness. She and Ashley seem to be enjoying the rural environment." Devin watched as Gregory adjusted Aero's saddle and rubbed the horse's nose. Aero whinnied and pawed the ground at their approach.

Mark and Danny emerged from the stable sporting bits of straw on their clothes. "Grandpa, come see. They have kittens." Danny grabbed Ben's hand and dragged him off.

"We'll be back shortly." Ben grinned and let himself be led into the dimly lit stable.

"You done any riding, Mark?" Devin realized all three men were well over six feet.

"No, I haven't. I may have gone on a pony when I was little but that is about it."

"Let's get you started then. You'll want to be one step ahead of your son, and he's already been in the saddle."

Chapter Eight

"HERE WE ARE GIRLS." With the van's GPS, Carol had no trouble locating Flynn's shop. "Isn't it lovely? Must be worth a small fortune in this location."

The narrow red brick Victorian dominated the main corner across from the town square. Tall windows were framed in crisp white sills, with intricate gingerbread trim surrounding the roof lines. One window held a display of colorful books while the other showcased a variety of collectibles and knick-knacks.

"I think we should all chip in and buy something for Devin as a thank you for this weekend. What do you think?" Carol led the way into the store as a silver bell tinkled lightly.

"That sounds like a fine idea." Jennifer stepped in behind Carol.

Flynn looked up from where he was wrapping a gift for a customer, who was still wandering about looking at the offerings. "Oh, it's my Boston beauties. Come right in, ladies. Let's see, you must be Jennifer. Carol promised me I could relieve you of some of your coin."

Jennifer smiled as they shook hands.

"And you must be the lovely Lana. And who are these little darlings?" Flynn looked down at the two baby carriers whose occupants were sound asleep.

"This is Angela, and this is Christopher. Their big brother Danny is with his dad and grandpa back at the farm."

"Well, put the little ones right up here on the counter so you can do some serious shopping. Did you have anything specific in mind?"

"We'd like to get a group gift for Devin as a thank you for his hospitality. I'm sure you'd know of something that would fit the bill."

Carol's practiced shopper's eye had already found several items that appealed to her inner decorator.

"You have come to the right person and the right place." Flynn beamed at them and walked over to a table of large coffee table books. "I happen to know that Devin would like to learn more about Thai cuisine. And we have a few imported from Thailand. They're the real deal."

Carol took the book Flynn offered her and flipped through the pages. "Devin is a cook?"

"Chef is more like it. Why do you think I helped him design that kitchen, love? He's very talented in the kitchen department. He's probably talented in other departments but I wouldn't know about that." Flynn winked wickedly and handed her another book. "This one is just for Thai seafood. I know he's done a couple of the recipes, but I'm sure most of these would be new for him."

Carol was chuckling as Flynn worked his magic. He knew how to sell a book the way she knew how to sell a house. "We'll take them both Flynn. We'll just have to get invited back to taste test a few recipes, right Ash?"

Ashley was holding a brilliant turquoise blue vase. "Sounds good to me, Mom. Not like we're conspiring to come back or anything, but it wouldn't hurt to start working up a plan."

"I like the way you girls think." Flynn took the two books and put them on the scuffed antique wood counter next to the sleeping babies. "You give Devin these books and he won't have a choice, will he? Nice strategy."

Within half an hour, the counter held a number of carefully chosen treasures. Ashley paid for the turquoise vase and handed it to her mom as a gift from her fun money. "It'll complement the afghan."

Carol turned the package over and then hugged it to her chest. "That is so thoughtful, Ash. And it's not even Christmas."

"It's more fun giving a surprise gift don't you think?" Ashley grinned.

"It is, for sure." Carol put the package into her tote next to the two books. "What have you come up with, Jennifer?"

"I thought this little lamp would go well in the twin's bedroom. What do you think Lana?"

"It's so cute!" Lana looked at the Winnie-the-Pooh lamp. "I would never buy it for myself."

"That's the idea. Grandmothers are supposed to spoil their grandchildren." Jennifer smiled at the pleased look on Lana's face.

"Is there somewhere we can go for some tea or coffee, Flynn?" Carol looked at her watch. "We still have some free time on our hands."

"There's a bakery and tea shop a block down on this side. It's called the Sweet Repose. Tell them I sent you. How much longer will the little ones sleep?"

Lana checked her watch. "Probably another hour at least."

"Then leave them with me and go enjoy some free mommy time. If one of you gives me a cell number, I can call you if they wake up hungry."

"Thank you so much, Flynn." Lana walked around the counter and gave him a big hug. "We'll be back in less than an hour. I can guarantee you they'll both be hungry when they wake up. You'll have maybe five to ten minutes of cooing before they announce it, loudly."

Flynn laughed. "See you in a bit then."

The four women strolled down the street together. Even before they reached it, the aroma of fresh tea biscuits wafted up the street. All memories of their lunch faded quickly. It was time for a good old-fashioned afternoon tea.

"I DON'T KNOW ABOUT YOU, but I wouldn't mind a little nap before dinner." Carol said, as she and Jennifer finished unloading the van into Devin's mud room. Lana and Ashley had gone ahead with the two infant carriers. "This past week has been beyond interesting, shall we say. Normally, I never nap, but here, I think I've been lulled. I feel like Dorothy in the poppy field. I'm ready to just lie down and sleep."

"You've been through an emotional wringer. No surprise your

system is telling you to take a break." Jennifer put on her slippers and took a bag into the kitchen. "Head up for a little lie-down. We want you fresh for dinner, and I need you bright and early tomorrow to work on the turkey."

"How long for the bird?"

"This one will be at least six hours. I figure if we have the full-scale dinner tomorrow we can work on leftovers on Monday. Less to deal with Tuesday morning, going back into town. You working Tuesday?"

"Yes, but we're taking Ash to the airport first for a mid-morning flight and to return the van. I won't really get to the office until noon. But with showings, I could easily put in eight hours anyway."

"You ever think of slowing down some? Maybe taking more weekends off?"

Carol smiled ruefully. "This is my first real weekend off since May. I didn't even take summer holidays. I somehow even managed to work the Fourth of July weekend. So yes, I'm planning to take more weekends off for sure. It means more evening showings during the week, but I've earned more down time."

"Now you sound sane. I was getting a bit worried, especially after last weekend. You were exhausted."

Carol sighed. "It was too much. I admit that now. I have to face the fact that I'm not thirty any more and not forty either. And to be honest, coming here has given me another reality check. I need some serenity in my life and you just can't buy that. Who needs to make two million a year in commissions and be too stressed to enjoy it?"

"Now you're thinking. Let's go have a nap." They walked up the stairs together and went their separate ways.

"Ben, can you open one of the Pinot's we brought, please?" Jennifer pointed to the corkscrew stand at one end of the long counter.

"I have quite a cellar. Let me bring up something. Flynn won't forgive me if I don't. He chose most of them and graciously let me pay." Devin stood back as his guests made themselves right at home in his kitchen yet again.

"Would you have a Pinot Noir?" Carol and Ashley were collaborating on the main course, which consisted of oven-roasted asparagus and potatoes and planked salmon with a coriander pesto. Devin saluted the women and disappeared down the basement stairs.

"Where are Mark, Lana, and the kids?"

"I think they all crashed from the fresh air and the riding." Ashley pared the ends of the asparagus and sprayed olive oil over them with a dash of Himalayan salt. "I can go wake them up if you want."

"Let's give them fifteen minutes or so. No rush." Jennifer arranged her hors d'oeuvres on a pretty platter and laid out cocktail napkins. "When you're finished there Ashley, can you go around and light some candles? Devin, where's a lighter or some matches?"

Devin set down the wine he had just brought up, found a lighter and handed it to Ashley. He looked around in wonder at the beehive of activity. *There haven't been this many guests here since mom and dad were here.* He realized the place hadn't seen this many guests in more years than he could remember. He felt the kitchen was finally being properly christened, even though he and Flynn had created a few special meals in the past months for local friends.

This is what this house needs, he realized, with a warm feeling spreading into his bones. *These people are helping me make this house a home the way no amount of decorating or renovating could do. This is a house that needs people in it. People who love the country, my animals and this house.*

He picked up the wine bottle and walked over to the counter to uncork it. As he did, he looked over at Carol. Their eyes locked. Devin could see her color heighten slightly as she smiled and looked away.

"Well, this house smells amazing." Flynn breezed in from the mud room and set his offering on the counter. "I called the bakery this morning and special-ordered fresh dinner rolls for us. I just couldn't resist. Gregory is washing up and changing out of his grubbies. He'll be over shortly. What's this, precious?" He tried to steal a little tart from the plate Jennifer was arranging and was playfully swatted away.

"Wait like everyone else. We'll be ready in a minute or two." Jennifer grinned at Flynn.

"Yes, girlfriend. If I must, but it smells so heavenly. You can't blame me."

"I don't." Jennifer laughed and shook her head. "You're such a character."

"And that's why you love me, right?"

Jennifer hooted. "How could I not? Lana, Mark, Danny… so glad you could join us. We were afraid you'd sleep through dinner."

"Must be the country air. We just conked out." Mark greeted everyone. Lana still looked half asleep. Danny had followed the enticing smells and was rewarded with his own plate of quiches to snack on. "I think the twins might be out for the night. We can hope." Mark put the radio monitor on the counter.

"Appetizers are out. Main course is on track. Choose your wine. Here's to Saturday night live at Devin's farm." Carol lifted her glass of Pinot as the others selected theirs.

"The ladies did some serious shopping at the store today, Devin." Flynn lifted his glass. "Did you have anything you want to share my Boston beauties?"

Carol and Jennifer smiled at each other. "Well, we did find a couple of special books we thought you might like. Of course, Flynn was advising, so we're not sure if they're really for you or more for him. You be the judge." Carol went to her tote, drew out the book package and handed it to Devin. "It's just a little thank you for inviting us here for the weekend."

"This isn't necessary." Devin took the gift-wrapped package and turned it over. Finding the tape, he opened it quickly and drew out the two books. "Flynn, you rogue." He grinned as he turned the books over and then opened them to flip through the pages. "You don't miss a thing, my friend. I have been lusting after these books since they came out last month. I was just waiting for them to be discounted on

Amazon before buying them. Nice work!"

Carol was pleased by his reaction. "You opened your house to a bunch of strangers for Thanksgiving weekend. And we've been able to sample this phenomenal kitchen. We owe you, big time. These books are our way of saying thanks, Devin, that's all."

"I wonder if I have the ingredients to make something for us tomorrow for lunch?" He winked at Carol, sipped his wine, and flipped through the pages.

"I have a feeling we'll want to keep lunch quite light tomorrow." Jennifer looked over to where Ashley was putting together a salad of mixed greens with strawberries and walnuts. "Plus, the oven won't be available as of mid-morning. I did the calculations on the weight and time and we'll need to get it in pretty early if we want to be eating by six."

Carol passed around the plate of mini quiches as Jennifer put the salmon in the oven alongside the half-cooked potatoes and asparagus. "Seems like all we'll be doing for the rest of the weekend is eat."

Ben popped a little tart in his mouth and licked his fingers. "Works for me."

As the adults settled into the business of fine food and drink, Danny played with his Game Boy and munched from his plate of quiches. Charlie lay quietly at his feet.

"Ah, Gregory is here at last." Devin opened the door to the mud room as his manager took off his boots and pulled on a pair of loafers. "Now we can get down to some serious eating."

"Sorry it took so long. Made a quick stop at the stable on my way over and caught my shirt on the latch. Put a real tear in it and had to go back and change." With Gregory in the kitchen, the large room seemed to shrink yet again. There were now four men over six feet, with Flynn and Carol almost that.

"Here's a glass of your favorite, my sweet man." Flynn handed Gregory a glass of Pinot Noir and guided him to the hors d'oeuvres. "Do you believe this party? We've never had this many people over. Isn't it fun?"

Gregory smiled and toasted his glass in the air to everyone. "Flynn has been dying to see Devin bring home a house load of guests. This is his wish come true."

CAROL LOOKED AROUND THE TABLE as they tucked into the main course. She couldn't think of a dinner gathering as warm and friendly as the mood in this room. The dinner parties she had hosted were calculated for business development. Only the right people with the right credentials got an invite to one of her catered affairs. As she chewed thoughtfully on a morsel of the succulent salmon, her reverie was broken.

"A penny for your thoughts, sweetie?" Flynn was smiling across at her.

"I was just thinking how wonderfully warm and friendly this all is. My dinner parties in Boston never have this kind of vibe."

"You're in real estate right?"

"Yes." Carol forked up a tender spear of asparagus.

"I imagine some of your dinners are like the ones I get invited to. They want free home decorating advice, and I happen to be the local expert. I don't turn them down because I know they'll lead to sales or referrals to the shop."

"Exactly. We're only as good as the buzz we create. But don't you find it a bit shallow, if you don't mind my saying so?"

"Not at all. It is a bit shallow, of course. But if you know the rules and understand it's just part of the game, then you won't invest your feelings in any of it."

"I think the difference between you and I is that you have somewhere and someone else to invest your true feelings in."

Flynn looked lovingly at Gregory, who was in a three-way discussion with Ben and Mark. "And you don't?"

"Of course I have Ashley and my son Jim, but they are in the exhilarating stage of being young adults who have left the nest. When they left, it became very clear to me that my nest felt quite sterile."

"Ouch. Aren't you being a bit hard on yourself?"

"You didn't know me a year ago. I'm quite a changed person, let me tell you." Carol broke off a piece of warm roll and put it in her mouth. "This is delicious."

"They refuse to give me the recipe, but I'm working on it." Flynn sipped at his wine. "I didn't know you until yesterday, but I would say whoever you are now is someone worth knowing and having as a friend. And knowing Devin, he feels the same way or you wouldn't be here."

Carol smiled. "Thanks, Flynn. It's good of you to say it."

"I've known Devin since we were children playing around the stable. He's a very sincere and honest person. The fact that he invited you here, with your friends, tells me he cares about you more than this altercation with Allison would suggest. He hasn't brought any woman here in the past eight years. Not since his fiancée was murdered." Flynn spoke quietly and directly to Carol.

"I vaguely remember the story. It was right around the time of my divorce. As I recall, they had been together for years." Carol blushed slightly and hoped her comment hadn't carried to other ears. She looked around. Jennifer had leaned in to whisper something in Ben's ear. He promptly broke into a broad grin. Mark was splitting a dinner roll in two to share with Danny. Ashley and Lana were chatting away to each other.

Devin said something to Gregory and then stood up with a broad smile. Picking up his wine glass, he said, "I'd like to make a toast. Here's to new friends and friendships. May this be the first of many meals we share together." When his eyes found Carol's, she smiled warmly at him and raised her glass.

Chapter Nine

"OKAY, GIRLFRIENDS, I expect this house to be absolutely swimming with delicious aromas by the time I get back tonight." Flynn stood at the kitchen entrance, watching the activities. "If you can't find something, just call me at the store."

"Thanks, Flynn. This kitchen is so well organized I'm sure we'll be fine." Jennifer and Carol were just getting their breakfast plates together. "See you later."

"How about we go eat in the solarium and watch our men at work?"

"Well, your men Jennifer. I don't have one." Carol took her coffee and plate of bagel and cheese with fresh strawberries to a small table near the window overlooking the paddock.

"Yet." Jennifer joined her. "I've been watching you and Devin make eyes at each other. It's pretty clear there's a strong mutual attraction happening."

Carol grinned and rolled her eyes. "I know, and I'm not sure what to do about it. I'm not even sure how I feel about dating right now. I don't want to do anything to jinx this amazing weekend."

"I think if you don't do something you'll jinx it. Devin looks like a man who wants to corral you in for a big, warm hug and some major kissing."

"I suspect he's a very fine kissing type, too." Carol sipped at her coffee and watched appreciatively as Devin led Aero into the paddock. "That man sure wears his jeans well."

"You talking about my Ben?" Jennifer teased. "Or maybe Mark? He works outdoors a lot so he's in great shape."

Carol laughed. "I'm talking about Devin. Ben and Mark are both great eye candy, but they're taken. And I no longer rob the cradle when it comes to younger men. I wonder how old Devin is?"

"I'd say mid-forties give or take. Is his age important?"

"Of course not, as long as his mother isn't my age." Carol chuckled. "I think Lance the leech's mother was only about two years older than me. What was I thinking?"

"Other than his seriously sexy body? You have to admit, you needed someone you could control."

"You're right. That whole control thing really controlled me for several years. Did I tell you I actually asked Ashley and Jim to plan what we'll do for Christmas this year?" She popped a juicy strawberry in her mouth.

"Wow. That's a change for sure."

"I had to remind myself to let go, but it was really worth it. They're both enthusiastically planning to take me somewhere and try snowshoeing." Another strawberry did a disappearing act. "I'm so happy. I haven't seen Jim since last spring. He stayed up at Thayer over the summer to do extra course work."

"Sounds like he's a bit of a workaholic, like someone else we both know."

Carol smiled. "I think we're all the same that way. When we find something we really enjoy, we stick with it. I have to say, though, the shine is really coming off my career at this point."

"How so? You always seem so involved with it."

Carol sighed. Devin, Mark, Danny, and Ben had ridden off on the horses. "That business with Michel has really made me see how shallow my relationships have been. You're a huge exception of course."

She smiled over at Jennifer. "My associates stayed away from me like I was contagious. The regional vice-president wouldn't see me alone. She always made sure someone was in the room when we spoke, like she wanted a witness." Carol chewed thoughtfully on her last bite of bagel and cheese. "Even when I closed the year only ten percent down despite the media and trial, people avoided me at meetings. Some still don't talk to me or even acknowledge my presence in a room. And these were people I thought were professional friends."

Carol stood up with her coffee and sipped it as she watched Ashley run to the paddock fence and lean against it to do some cool-down stretches.

"Are you thinking of quitting?" Jennifer stood and went over to put an arm around her friend.

"It's crossed my mind more than once, I have to say. Isn't she beautiful?" They both looked on as Ashley turned towards the house.

"She is beautiful. No matter what else happens, Carol, you have a wonderful daughter and son." Jennifer gave Carol a quick hug. The two women picked up their plates and mugs and headed for the kitchen.

"Hi Mom. Hi Jennifer." Ashley kicked off her runners and bounced lightly into the kitchen. "If you leave the food out, I'll just have a quick shower and come back to eat. It's so gorgeous out there today." She was up the stairs before they could say a word.

Lana came down the stairs rubbing the sleep out of her eyes. "Four a.m. feeding. I am so sleep deprived. Any decaf coffee?"

"You poor thing. Come and sit. I'll make you some fresh. You sure you don't want the real thing?"

"Can't. It could upset their tummies and they're already out of their home routine." Lana sat at the table with her head in her hands. "I didn't even feel Mark leave. Where have they gone off to?"

"They're all out on the trail with Devin. It's girl time here, apart from that big turkey." Jennifer had lifted the bird out of the large cooler she'd left plugged in overnight.

Lana reached out for a strawberry, then took a plate and started filling it. "This looks so refreshing. Cantaloupe, kiwi, strawberries, bagels. Who do I thank for this?"

"Flynn. I don't know when he sleeps. I guess Gregory is down at the stable pretty early, and Flynn just comes here and gets the food organized. The man is amazing."

Lana smiled as Jennifer brought over a steaming mug of coffee. "What's the plan for today? I want to be of some help."

"Once we get the bird in the oven, we'll all be off for a few hours. I suggest we get out for some fresh air and exercise and earn our dinner."

Ashley breezed into the kitchen and made straight for the food. "I'm starving. I did at least five miles. Marvin came with me again."

"Marvin?" Lana spread cream cheese on her bagel and took a large bite.

"Marvellous Marvin, the dog. He lives on the next farm."

"Speaking of dogs, where's Charlie?" Lana licked cream cheese off her fingers and picked up a slice of cantaloupe.

"Shadowing Danny last I saw. Those two are inseparable." Jennifer rinsed out the turkey and set it to drain. "They're going to have so much fun together after Ben and I head south."

"Where are you going this trip?" Carol had set herself up on the kitchen's island and was organizing a very large platter of sandwiches for their lunch.

"Ben thinks we should drive down to Charleston to rent a sailboat. He doesn't want to sail out of Boston in January. He plans to sail us to the British Virgin Islands. Maybe spend some time in Puerto Rico. It all sounds quite exotic," Jennifer sighed happily.

"Sounds wonderful." Ashley and Lana said it at the same time and giggled. They finished off the last of the fruit and started clearing the table and putting things away.

"I brought all the ingredients for the stuffing: pine nuts, cooked sausage, mushrooms and onions. I'm sure Flynn will approve." Jennifer pulled the ingredients out of her cooler.

"Isn't he a wonderful fellow?" Carol assembled half a dozen havarti and ham sandwiches with mustard and tomato. "He and Devin have known each other since they were little."

"He certainly knows how to design a kitchen. I'm starting to think I need to renovate mine. It hasn't changed since I was a kid. It's the original, other than adding the dishwasher." Jennifer expertly assembled all the ingredients for her dressing in a large stainless steel bowl.

Lana heard snuffling sounds from the baby monitor and headed back upstairs.

"Anything I can do, Mom?" Ashley surveyed her mother's efforts. "Maybe cut up a bunch of vegetables to go with those yummy looking sandwiches?"

"That would be great."

The three women chatted companionably as the lunch and dinner preparations slowly shifted into gear. By the time Lana came back down with the babies, the counter was clear to tuck them into their snowsuits for a walk along the trail.

"That three-wheel stroller you brought looks pretty high tech, Lana." Ashley smiled down at Angela and made cooing sounds as she helped the wriggling baby into her gaily-colored snowsuit.

"Mark decided we needed an all-terrain type to deal with snow and slush. I think it's going to come in very handy here." Lana finished suiting up Christopher. "You coming with us, Ash?"

"Of course. I'll push." The two young women put on their outdoor gear as Jennifer and Carol held the squirming babies.

"Lunch is any time you feel hungry. Nothing formal today." Jennifer handed Christopher to Ashley. "Dinner's at six, so don't eat too late."

"I can eat all the time. Just ask my mom." Ashley closed the mud room door and headed outside.

"Looks like the boys are back." Carol looked out the kitchen window and saw the horses walking into the paddock just as Ashley and Lana came along with the stroller. She watched them chat as she washed potatoes. "Looks like Mark's going with the girls and the twins."

Ben and Danny came into the mud room stomping to warm up their feet. "Carol, Devin is waiting for you to go out for a ride with him while the horses are warm. Any chance for hot chocolate for Danny and me?"

"Here's your chance, Carol. Don't you dare jinx it." Jennifer winked at Carol, who dried her hands on a towel and ran up the stairs.

"I'll be right down. Just want to get a turtleneck." Her voice trailed down to them.

"Two hot chocolates, coming up." Jennifer opened the fridge and pulled out the jug of milk. "C'mon over by the stove and warm up your feet."

Ben strode over to Jennifer and gave her his best Powell bear hug. "Hmm. This kitchen smells wonderful. What's for dinner?"

Jennifer laughed. "As if you didn't know. Did you have fun, Danny?"

"Devin showed us where a bald eagle is living for the winter in an old shed," Danny said, his eyes bright. "There were bones from mice and stuff on the floor."

"Did you see the eagle?" Jennifer asked.

"No. He wasn't home." Danny climbed onto a chair at the table as she poured milk into a pan and set it on the stove to warm.

"Okay, I'm off." Carol winked at Jennifer as she walked through the kitchen on her way to the mud room. "Hope I'll be warm enough."

"I'll keep a pot of hot chocolate going for when you come back. Have fun."

Devin watched as Carol walked towards him. Her turquoise blue turtleneck contrasted with a chocolate brown wooly scarf she'd artfully looped around her neck. *She'll have to get some better footwear and a warmer jacket if she's going to be riding regularly.* The thought popped unbidden into his head. *I want this woman in my life,* he thought with only mild surprise, *especially my life here on the farm.*

"Need a lift lady?"

Carol laughed. "Thanks for the offer. I think I can make it up. Where are we heading?"

"Want to check an old shed where a bald eagle is wintering over?"

"Will the eagle be home?"

"Not if we make enough noise coming up the trail."

"Okay then, let's go." Carol settled on Sabrina and brought the horse up next to Aero. Together, they walked the horses onto a trail that would take them around and behind Flynn and Gregory's little house and close to the property line.

94

"Everybody seems to be enjoying themselves." Devin was in no hurry. "I'm sorry about the circumstances, but I'm really glad you're all here. I really like Ben. I thought I had travelled a lot."

"He's been everywhere." The two horses seemed determined to walk as close together as possible. Devin's leg brushed up against Carol's. Her body betrayed her as she felt an involuntary tingle race through her. "He and Jennifer are just perfect for each other. He's bringing out a playfulness in her that I've never seen."

"He told me about her husband and daughter. It must have been so traumatic."

"I met her about a year after they died. She was just starting to redefine herself and her life without them. We met at yoga."

"And what about you, Carol? You seem to be redefining yourself too. How's that going?" Devin smiled over at her.

"I think I've made a lot of progress over the past year. Although you might not believe it, I'm coming to terms with my control issues. Well, as much as I can most days." She winked at him. "Bad mirror days being an exception."

"I'm glad we can laugh about that now." Devin grinned.

"When I saw your truck and that mirror, I saw my whole schedule going down the drain. I'm just so used to being in control."

"Do you feel in control here?"

"I don't feel the need to control anyone or any thing here. I can't really explain it except to say it feels great. My daughter is here, my best friends are here, I'm not thinking about work—well, maybe a bit—I feel very relaxed and at peace."

"I'm glad you feel that way here, Carol." Devin looked over to watch her face. "Would you like to come back, just you and I sometime?"

Carol cocked her head slightly. "What about Flynn and Gregory?"

"If I give Gregory the weekend off, we won't see either of them unless we invite them over." Devin gave his best roguish smile. "Is that a yes then?"

"It's a definite yes. Now where's this eagle you promised me?"

Devin grinned as he urged Aero into a brisk canter. "Follow me."

Carol easily kept pace, with the cool air lightly brushing her face.

A few minutes later, they pulled up the horses at a dilapidated wood shed. Dismounting, Devin tied Aero to an old tree trunk and then helped Carol down. When Sabrina was safely tied, they both looked around.

"Why is there a shed way out here I wonder?"

"I'm not sure, and I've never asked." Devin admired Carol's sleek physique. *She's like the horses, full of energy, gorgeous to look at and very proud and regal. She's a thoroughbred through and through.*

Carol stood quietly. "Is this for real Devin? I think you need to pinch me. I can't believe I'm in this amazing place."

Devin walked over to her and put his hands on her shoulders. They looked at each other deeply this time. No blushing. No shyness. "You know you belong here, don't you, Carol? Tell me you feel it. Because I sure do."

Carol's breath hitched slightly. "I do feel it. I can't explain it."

"Don't try. This is one moment you cannot control. Just feel, Carol."

Devin leaned down slightly. They were about to kiss when they both heard it—the keening cries of not one, but two bald eagles.

"Oh look, Devin." Carol whispered as she spotted the pair cavorting in the air above them. "They're so beautiful."

"They're a mated pair. I didn't realize there were two here."

They watched in awe as the two magnificent birds flew up and up and then nosedived down towards each other, only to twist and turn and fly away. Over and over again, the two majestic birds teased and played with each other not thirty feet over their heads. Finally, the female landed on a sturdy branch as her mate put on a show for them all. When it was over, both birds disappeared in a loud flapping of wings.

"I've never seen anything like that before." Devin had his arm around Carol's shoulder. She had leaned in to him as he cuddled her.

"Our own private show. Amazing. I've never seen an eagle in the wild, let alone a pair. They were definitely having fun." Carol hugged the warm feeling she felt with Devin's arm around her shoulder. She looked up at him.

"Weren't you about to kiss me?" She smiled invitingly.

"I was, and I will." Devin turned her fully into his arms. He pulled her chin up with a finger and slowly and gently covered her mouth. Carol felt herself melt into his body. She tasted him slowly and drank in his scents.

He broke away the kiss. "I've never met a woman like you, Carol. You're so strong, and yet I want to protect you." He ran a hand through her gleaming auburn waves. "We can never go back to just being friends. You know that, don't you?"

"Were we ever just friends, Devin?" Carol arched her head back as Devin pushed down the turtleneck to cover her neck in light kisses.

"I need you. Now. Here. Please don't say no." Devin looked up and saw Carol's glazed eyes. "I think you need me, too."

Carol nodded and watched in dazed wonder as Devin took the saddles off both horses and put them carefully on the ground. Then, he took the two saddle blankets and, walking over to her, took her hand and led her into the ancient shed.

"Maybe this is what the shed was for." She looked at him almost dreamily.

"My great grandparents did have a large family. Maybe this is why." Devin grinned as he spread one of the blankets on the cold earth floor and then opened his arms. "Care to join me?"

There was no hesitation as they cuddled in the cool semi-dark of the old shed. Devin reached into Carol's hair to pull his fingers through her thick locks. Tightening his embrace, he looked into her luminous eyes.

"I know it sounds trite, but I've been waiting for someone like you for so long." His voice was low as he let her go and stepped back slightly to unwrap her scarf and lay it across her shoulders.

Carol shivered slightly as he reached a hand under her sweater and gently rubbed her back. Even as her body responded to his cool touch, she felt her heart warming to his words.

"When I met you and saw the fire in your eyes, you reminded me of Aero and Sabrina." He traced a finger along the line of her shoulder. "So high-spirited and beautiful." Carol half closed her eyes as his hand slowly explored under her sweater. "I want us to take this slowly, Carol, but I don't think I can. You've touched my heart in a way no other woman has in many years."

Carol looked up into his eyes and nodded. "This is all so fast, yet it feels right."

"We're not kids, but right now I feel like one." He spoke quietly as he gazed into her eyes. "I'm in the candy store, and I want to taste it all, if you'll let me."

"We're in the same store." Carol stood on her toes and nibbled his ear. "You can only taste me if I can taste you."

Outside, Aero and Sabrina nuzzled heads as the eagles flew high in the soft November light.

Carol watched lovingly as Devin saddled up the horses. *Gord never made me feel this cherished,* she mused. *Or as fulfilled.* Her body still tingled with a sexual quivering she hadn't felt in years. *I am one well and truly loved woman.* His lingering scent caressed her like a warm embrace.

"Wonder if they missed us." Devin gave Carol a hand up onto Sabrina's broad back.

"You may blush to hear this, but both Jennifer and Ashley encouraged me to seduce you."

"I'd say it was mutual." Devin smiled, as he mounted Aero. "Ben played big brother and gave me the green light. Said you have a good mind, too."

Carol laughed. "That's my Ben. He's the brother I never had."

As they rode back slowly towards the house, Devin looked across at her. "I want you to know that I have never brought a lady friend to this farm. "You're the first and, I hope, the last."

Riding into the paddock, Carol looked up at the stately old house. *This man and this house. This could be my life if I let it.* As Carol got off Sabrina, she knew that, for the first time in a very long time, her need to control was not an issue.

JENNIFER WATCHED CAROL CLOSELY as she and Devin made their way to the house after stabling the horses. *Oh my*, she thought, *she sure didn't jinx anything. I'd say those two had a good roll in the hay somewhere.* She watched as Carol's hand glided up to smooth Devin's hair.

"Care for some hot chocolate you two?" she asked as they spilled into the mud room laughing.

"Yes, please." Carol pulled off her boots and then her scarf, wrapping it around Devin's neck. "We saw a pair of eagles playing in the air over an old shed." Carol was smiling brightly as she came into the kitchen and accepted a mug of silky hot chocolate.

"Do you know what it means when a pair of eagles play near you?" Ben looked up from a magazine he was reading.

"No, but I bet we're about to find out." Carol looked over at Devin, who now had a mug of chocolate and was warming his hands with it.

"In native culture, the eagle is believed to be the link between our world and the spirit world. When a pair of eagles play over a human couple, it's believed that the universe is giving you the opportunity to fly above your life's worldly levels, or above the shadow of past realities. Eagles teach us to give ourselves permission to be free to reach for the joy that our heart desires."

Carol and Devin looked at Ben in quiet astonishment and then looked at each other.

"Ben, what are you saying?" Carol felt her chest constrict. His words had neatly captured what only her heart had understood. As her mind absorbed his words, she felt all control slipping away and wondered only mildly if she would ever get it back. She smiled at Devin.

He appeared puzzled for a long moment and then smiled. "Damn, gotta hand it to those eagles. They know the real thing when they see it.

Carol Brock, I think that what the natives and the eagles meant is that you are now officially my woman. You ready for that?"

Carol grinned and tossed her head haughtily. "You ready to be my man, Devin Elliott?"

"Yes." Devin plopped down on a chair. "I need a beer, woman."

"And I'm sure you know where to find one."

"I'm home, dears." Flynn glided into the house. "I closed a bit early. There were only a few people the last hour, but they were all spending. I definitely met my sales objective. This house smells delicious."

"You put us to work Flynn, we deliver." Jennifer poured him a glass of Barolo. "I think there have been some developments since you left this morning." Jennifer could see Carol and Devin standing together in the solarium, their arms around each other.

"Dish, girl. What could I have possibly missed?"

"Look in the solarium and you tell me." Jennifer pointed Flynn's gaze towards the cozy scene.

"Oh my. He's never brought a woman here before, let alone put his arm around one. This is serious." Flynn took a sip of the wine and approved. "Anything else I should know before dinner?"

"They went for a very long ride on the trail. Seems there's an old shed near your cottage. Know the one?"

"Sure do." Flynn smiled as Devin put his arm near Carol's shoulder and drew her into a close hug. "How long were they gone?"

"At least two hours."

"I'd say they must have stopped for a good long time. Isn't that wonderful?" Flynn grinned and put his glass down to help Jennifer. "Devin is such a sexy man, and Carol is one hot mama. What a great pair they make,"

Jennifer laughed. "They told me a pair of eagles cavorted over their heads."

"You don't say. I hear that's pretty special in native circles."

"You and Ben must go to the same internet sites. He said the same thing and then quoted us chapter and verse on what it means."

"I knew Ben was special. Oh, not that way dearest." Flynn grinned and patted her hand. "He's safe with you. I would never go after any man who is already taken. But don't you just love his tight little butt?"

Jennifer let out a hoot. "Flynn, you're incorrigible."

"I know. I can't help it."

"Whatever do we do with you?" Jennifer grinned.

"Whatever you want, dearest. Just make sure it includes Gregory." He called out, "Carol, how about you and I finish setting the table for dinner. I want to tell you some of the history of the china and glassware I found that we'll be using tonight."

Carol found herself being led into the softly-lit dining room. "Flynn, we're only ten people. Why are there eleven settings?"

"I've always had this thing about having an extra setting in case someone arrives at the last minute. My mother did that. That way, she could always tell them that there was a spare place set and they were welcome to stay."

"What a thoughtful thing to do. I remember more than once scrambling to add a setting or two when my ex brought someone home completely unannounced. They always knew they were a last-minute addition."

Carol smoothed her hand along the gleaming cherry wood double pedestal table. A crystal chandelier centered above it cast a sparkling glow over the room that reached to its farthest corners. Flynn had set the table at the crack of dawn, before anyone was up. Now it glittered in the warm light as creamy placemats edged in gold thread reflected the light.

"Tell me about the dinnerware. The pattern is lovely." Carol picked up a side plate. In its center, a colorful bird with long elegant tail feathers was perched on a branch covered in delicate pink blooms. The smooth rim of the plate was edged in pale blue and gold.

"Look at the name of the pattern on the bottom."

Carol turned the plate over. "Paradise."

"When I saw that, I knew that set belonged here. It was made in the 1930s in Limoges, France. Two American brothers founded the original china import company in New York. Their sons bought the factory. " Flynn picked up a plate and gazed at it lovingly. "During World War II, the factories in Limoges were bombed and the patterns destroyed. It took me over a year to re-build the set up to twelve place settings. I still don't have all the cups and saucers."

"I hope these will be safe with Danny." Carol put the plate down reverently.

"Most of these have survived three generations of children." Flynn looked over the table like an inspector general. "And I don't think it was children who made the cups and saucers so hard to find. Do we have cranberry sauce?"

"Jennifer brought a big jar of her homemade sauce." Carol took the dish Flynn handed her.

"I'll get some more serving dishes, and we'll be all set. I think I hear Gregory."

At first, Carol didn't notice anything different. Jennifer was still getting things organized in the kitchen, with Ashley as her able assistant. Devin, Ben, Mark and Lana were in the solarium with the kids. But, there was another voice.

She looked at Flynn who was now grinning. Carol dashed into the solarium.

"Jim! Oh my God. Jim, it's you. What a wonderful surprise." Carol ran into her tall, strapping son's arms.

"Hi, Mom. It's all Ashley's fault." He grinned as he wrapped strong arms around his mother for a long moment.

Carol stepped back. She could feel tears of happiness coming on and looked in vain for a box of tissues.

Ashley stepped forward and handed her two. "Figure'd you'd need these."

Carol looked around at all the smiling faces. "This is a total surprise. You all knew and managed to keep the secret?"

Devin came and put his arm around her as Ashley explained. "I told Jim he'd never forgive himself if he missed Thanksgiving dinner with us. Dartmouth is less than an hour from here, so here he is."

"He arrived while we were out eagle watching and hid his car behind the stable. Jim stayed up in Danny's room with his gear until it was time to come down." Devin planted a light kiss on Carol's cheek, which was still damp from her tears of joy.

"All right, people. It's time to get this bird cut up and onto the plates." Jennifer motioned to Ben and Flynn and trooped them back to the kitchen to manage the final preparations.

"You said you had a term project you needed to work on." Carol, Jim, and Ashley stood by the window overlooking the now dark paddock.

"Turns out the workshop will be closed tomorrow for the holiday."

Carol hooked her arms with Ashley and Jim. "Let's go help Jennifer and Ben deal with their turkey dinner then." Together, they marched arm in arm into the dining room as Flynn and Devin came in with tureens of steaming hot vegetables.

Chapter Ten

"THAT WAS GOOD." Carol picked up her glass for a sip of wine. "Everything always tastes so much better when someone else cooks it. I'm so happy to be sharing this dinner with the favorite people in my life in this lovely home."

Devin held up his glass. "A toast to all the cooks. May they all return to cook another meal."

"To the cooks." Flynn raised his. "I can honestly say I had nothing to do with cooking this meal. It was just divine."

"Where's our pumpkin cheesecake?" Danny looked a bit bewildered as everyone chuckled and laughed.

Lana smiled and reached out a hand to tousle his head. "I think we're going to take a little break. How about you go and play for awhile and we'll call you when it's time for dessert?"

"I saw the desserts you ladies made. I left some room." Ben stood. "I'll go hang out with Danny for a bit. Devin, want to join me?"

"Sure." Devin topped up his wine and headed with Ben for the solarium. Mark, Jim, and Gregory came in next and soon all were deep in discussion about how best to shore up the Patriots' defense.

Carol listened to the male chatter and laughter as she carried dishes to the kitchen. *This is like an instant family,* she mused. *I could never have coaxed this kind of feeling at the condo. I've never seen Jim so comfortable and at ease.*

"Where do you want these?" Carol crossed to the kitchen sink area, where Flynn and Ashley held command.

"Over there, dearest." Up to his elbows in soapy water, he nodded with his head, his nose pointing the way. "There's a compost pail in the mud room for vegetable scraps, and then you can rinse them in this sink beside me. I don't put these lovelies through the dishwasher, although I'm sure the glaze is better than anything made these days."

Jennifer and Lana worked on the desserts, as the clean-up operation continued. "Notice how the men all disappeared when it came time to clear the table and wash up?"

Lana laughed. "Mark promised he's going to take over the dessert clean-up later. I'm sure he'll bring recruits."

As Carol made another trip for dishes, she felt the comfort of the old house all around her. *I don't want to leave here,* she realized. Her happiness dampened somewhat as she realized she would have to face Myra and the Allison situation. *I'll deal with them when the time comes. In the meantime, I'm going to enjoy this.* She was brought out of her reverie by Devin's low voice.

"Have you told Ashley there's been a change in the sleeping arrangements?"

"No, but I'm sure she's figured it out." Both hands full, she walked over to him and planted a kiss on his cheek, now sprouting some five o'clock shadow. "I'll make sure she knows though."

Devin picked up a load of dishes and followed her to the kitchen, where fresh coffee was being brewed. "Am I in the right house? This looks like dessert central."

Lana grinned happily. "I'm known for being a bit of a dessert queen. I love to bake."

"Is that warm blueberry pie?" Devin put the dishes on the counter and went back to stand guard over it. "This pie is mine. The rest of you are on your own."

Jennifer laughed. "You'll be fighting with Ben and Mark then. It's their favorite."

"Who's fighting?" Mark asked, as he and Jim walked into the kitchen, drawn by the smell of warm pumpkin and blueberries.

"As lord of this manor, I claim this blueberry pie as my own. I will fight any man who dares to challenge my claim." Devin tried to look stern but a smirk was playing at the corner of his lips and his eyes were dancing with mirth.

"Stand down men. I brought two. The other one is in the warming oven, along with a couple of pumpkin pies." Lana looked up at the three tall men who were now eyeing the other desserts.

"Whew. That was close. Great save, Lana." Devin put an arm around her petite shoulder and gave her a little hug. "Me and blueberry pies have a long and tasty history. I haven't had a piece outside a restaurant in ages, let alone in my own home."

"Well, you could have said something, silly man. I do know how to bake a decent pie." Flynn had emptied the sinks and was organizing coffee. "How about we each get a plate, load up desserts here at the counter and take them back to the dining room? I'll bring in the coffee. I made a pot of decaf too, and there's hot water for anyone who wants tea."

"If it's possible, Flynn, you're better organized than me. I'm impressed." Carol picked up a plate and chose a sampling of the treats. "I would have needed a catering crew to put this all together, I'm sure."

"It's easy once you get into practice." Jennifer stood next to Carol, savoring the sweet smells wafting in the air. "Ben and I started entertaining together last year when he moved in. With a little planning and two people, it's fun."

The conversation shifted back to the dining room as they again gathered at the table. Flynn turned the lights down slightly and took orders for coffee and tea.

Danny drooped first.

"Say goodnight to everyone, big guy." Mark took his sleepy son up to get ready for bed after he hugged his mother.

"You'd think those two were biological father and son the way they love each other." Jennifer smiled as her almost son-in-law and grandson disappeared up the stairs.

"You mean they're not?" Devin looked in surprise at Lana. "I just assumed you and Mark are his parents."

"Danny's father was killed in a military training accident when he was a toddler. Mark is officially adopting him when we get married next May."

"Let me get this straight then. If Mark is not Danny's father, then how come he calls you two grandma and grandpa?"

Jennifer and Ben chuckled at Devin's confusion. Jim, Flynn ,and Gregory waited with Devin for an explanation.

"Lana and Mark work at Brentwood Residence. They first met there after I steered Mark to his job as head groundskeeper. One day, Ben came to see Mark, and he introduced us. I was there visiting my father, who has since passed away." Jennifer took a bite of the pumpkin cheesecake and let it melt in her mouth before continuing. "I started going out with Ben, and one thing led to another, and I invited him to move in with me."

"Danny was so excited about having a for-real dad and a new pair of grandparents that he just started calling Mark dad and us grandpa and grandma." Ben picked up a warm date square.

"Well, I'm glad we got that all straightened out. Anyone for more coffee?" Flynn walked over to the gleaming sideboard, where an antique silver coffee pot was resting on a warming burner. "We can take it in the solarium if you're finished dessert or there's more in the kitchen."

Carol smiled as Flynn played the perfect hostess and thought, *I could take lessons from him.* As she held out her cup for a refill, she glanced over at Devin,her heart brimming with loving feelings she hadn't felt for any man in years.

"Anybody need anything before Gregory and I head home?" The kitchen was spotless, with no sign of the feast. "There are plenty of breakfast fixings in the fridge. There's fresh organic eggs and locally cured ham."

"Go home, Flynn. We can manage without you. You two have a day off, but drop by for lunch if you like. We'll take care of ourselves." With Carol at his side, Devin shepherded the two men towards the mud room. "The Powells will be leaving mid-afternoon. I know they'll want to say goodbye."

"See you for lunch then." Gregory helped Flynn on with his jacket, and the two walked away into the night; the bobbing lights from their flashlights soon disappeared down the trail.

Carol leaned into Devin as she watched them leave. "How long have they been together?"

"Must be fifteen years at least I would think." Devin hugged her. "They were among the couples legally married on May 17, 2004 when same-sex marriages became legal in Massachusetts. The governor ordered the usual three-day waiting period to be waived."

"I remember now." We were the first state in the entire country to legalize same-sex marriages. Flynn and Gregory made history that day."

Devin went to turn off some lights and dim others. "Shall we go up? Sounds like everyone else has settled for the night."

"Lead the way." Carol smiled and took his hand. Together they went up the stairs to the welcoming master bedroom.

Chapter Eleven

"WE'RE GOING TO HEAD BACK TO TOWN RIGHT AFTER LUNCH. Give you two, Ashley, and Jim time alone together." Jennifer joined Carol and Devin in the solarium. The sun had yet to peek over the hills. An early frost had dusted the tree branches and paddock fence with ice crystals that would soon sparkle before melting away.

"That was an amazing dinner. Thank you so much, Jennifer." Devin raised his mug in a silent toast. "Hard to believe we're going to be eating leftovers in a few hours."

"There aren't that many left. You men really tucked into that food with gusto."

"I feel I should go out and split wood for a couple of hours. But we don't heat anything with wood now." Devin chuckled. "But I could muck out the stable and give Gregory a break tomorrow."

"How about I organize breakfast? Fortify you for your labors?" Carol reached over and slipped her hand behind his neck and rubbed it.

"How about you stay right where you are and keep doing what you're doing?" Devin rubbed his head against her hand.

"Should we leave?" Jennifer grinned over at Ben. "I think they're trying to give us ideas, don't you?"

"I don't need anyone to give me ideas, my dear. I have plenty of my own when it comes to you. Breakfast sounds great. Stay put. I'll pull a few things out."

"I'll join you." Jennifer padded out to the kitchen with her mug.

"I think you chased them away." Devin stretched his neck forward as Carol rubbed it. "And you also got them to make breakfast. Nice work."

"They got the idea themselves. I just let them run with it. It's the mark of a good manager y'know." Carol took a long sip from her mug with her other hand. "It was so wonderful to wake up beside you this morning and know we have another glorious day here."

"One more sleep before we go back to reality."

"I feel better prepared to meet it though. We make a really good team."

"We do." Devin turned his head to look into her eyes. "All this trouble will have been worth it, if it brought us together."

"All it's cost me so far is a mirror and a fajita wrap and you paid for both." Carol chuckled at Devin.

"You throw up so prettily." Devin put his mug down and leaned over to kiss her forehead. "Maybe we should pick up another one at the airport tomorrow on the way in."

"No, thanks. I think I'll pass on them for awhile. More coffee?" Carol stood up.

"Sure. Thanks." He watched as Carol took their mugs over to the coffee pot in the dining room. *I can keep her safe here, but back in Boston will be a whole different game,* he realized. *We both have jobs and work to do. I can't watch over her and she wouldn't want me to anyway.* He looked out to the paddock to where the sun had turned the frost into sparkling diamonds.

"Here you go. Hot and fresh." Carol set down the mug. "Look at the paddock. That is so magical." She walked over to the window to admire the shimmering scene as the sun rose higher. Devin went over to stand beside her with his mug.

The smell of eggs, ham, and toast wafted into the now sun-filled solarium. "I think breakfast is ready. Would you care to join me in the kitchen, madam?" Devin hooked his arm through Carol's free one.

"I didn't think I could eat again for a week, but fresh country eggs and ham wins. Let's eat and then go for a very long brisk walk." Carol smiled up at him.

"Sounds like a plan. We should get Jennifer and Ben to come along. Jennifer's been doing all the cooking. She deserves a break."

"I don't think you'll get any arguments there. We do a lot of walking together in town. And she hasn't seen your lovely trail."

"Jennifer, you can't leave until you walk the trail out on the back forty." Carol and Devin strolled into the kitchen together to find Ben setting plates in the warming oven next to a mound of sliced ham.

"That's right. I haven't been for a walk or a ride. It's still early yet."

"What's for breakfast, grandma?" Danny zoomed into the kitchen, still in his pajamas. Charlie was right behind him.

"How about you let Charlie out and wash your hands. Your grandpa will fry you up an egg. Where's your mum and dad?"

"They said to tell you to go ahead without them. Dad said something about feeding time at the zoo."

They all laughed as Danny opened the door for Charlie, ran to the sink, rinsed his hands and ran to the table. "Can I have a banana?"

"Help yourself, Danny. They're for everyone." Devin reached into the bowl and took one. "Want to split it with me? It's pretty big."

"Sure."

"We're all going for a long walk after breakfast. Want to come along or stay here with your parents?"

"I'll stay with them. Morning is the best time to play with the babies."

"Was Jim awake when you got up, Danny?" Carol was in charge of buttering toast.

"No. He's snoring."

"Unlike Ashley, he's never been an early riser. He may sleep 'til noon unless the food smells wake him up."

"I'm taking orders for eggs. How many and how do you want them done?" Ben handed Danny his plate with an egg and some ham. "Help yourself to the toast son, and there's jam too if you want."

"That was a splendid breakfast, you two. But that's it. No more cooking for either of you." Devin led the way onto the path that would take them along the border of the property. It was still early morning cool, and a small wind was picking up. They were all wearing gloves, hats, and scarves against the chill damp air.

"This is what I needed." Jennifer and Carol walked ahead of the men and set a brisk pace. "You and Devin have become quite an item this weekend."

"I know. I never thought I'd end up in a man's bed within a week again in this lifetime. But this time, it feels like I've been waiting for him for years."

"How does Ashley feel about it?"

"She's the one who told me to make him a happy man. She liked him the minute she met him. Told me she knew he liked me the minute he walked into the condo."

"I've always known Ashley has good instincts."

"Yeah, well she distrusted Allison the minute she laid eyes on her outside my building."

"That's our girl."

"You've got that right. I don't know what Allison would have done if she'd actually gotten into the building. I'm trying not to let my mind go there."

"Probably just as well." Jennifer kept her elbows crooked and moved with purpose. "It's cold out here."

"We'll be in the trees up ahead. It should be less breezy. Glad I wore my turtleneck."

"When's Jim heading back?"

"Ashley's trying to talk him into staying overnight and leaving when we do in the morning. His first class isn't until late morning. Lana said she's leaving the dessert leftovers. Between Ashley's begging and the desserts, I'm betting he'll stay." Carol smiled. "Jim still doesn't know that women never argue fair."

"Poor him. He still has a lot to learn."

Behind them, Devin and Ben were in a deep discussion they had no desire for the women to hear.

"Guzzo knows me." Ben kept his distance from the women. "I know the case has nothing to do with me personally, but I can't help feeling there's more to Allison than meets the eye. You say her ex-husband died in a car accident just before the divorce papers were finalized?"

"You must have been out of the country. It was all over the media. He was a senior partner in one of the city's biggest firms and a big player on the Boston social scene." Devin pointed out a large hare lazily hopping away from them as if it knew it was safe. "His passenger that night was the wife of one of the firm's partners. They were not separated. She died in hospital."

"Did Allison inherit his estate?"

"She did. He hadn't changed his will to cut her out of it. His family, especially his ex, was devastated. He left Allison very well off. Let's say she didn't need to marry me for my money, although that was still a big factor in her decision, I'm sure. With Allison, there's no such thing as enough." Devin took off his cap, ran his hand through his hair and tugged the cap back down. "If you want to check into her, please do. It would help me feel we're doing something concrete."

"She doesn't know me, except perhaps from seeing me on TV. She doesn't know we're buddies. I think I should be able to work in the background without arousing any suspicions."

Devin suddenly looked at Ben and reached out an arm to stop him. "Okay Ben. We've only known each other a few days, but you know I'm the real deal. This may sound crazy but hear me out."

Ben looked puzzled. "Go on."

Devin stood for a few seconds collecting his thoughts. "Allison is adamant that I will never buy her mother's house. You heard what she did to my offer. If I gave you the money, would you be willing to buy the house? You could hold on to it for six months or a year and quietly sell it to me. She need never know, and life would go on."

Ben walked over and leaned up against a tree. "Is the house really that important to you?"

"I have a very sentimental attachment to the woman who used to live in it. She loved it like her child. And it's a very important piece of Victorian architecture. I promised her I would buy it and preserve it. This may be the only way."

"I think we should talk to Jennifer and Carol and get their take. I would support it in principle, but I want their input."

"Then let's go talk to them."

Carol reacted vehemently. "No way. This is not on. If Allison gets even a whiff of the fact that we all know each other, it will only drag Jennifer and Ben onto her hate list. Being second from the top of that list, I can tell you I wish I had never gotten on it. Devin, please, don't either of you take this any further. Promise me."

Devin looked somewhat embarrassed as the implications of Carol's reasoning struck home. "It could have worked, but I think you're right. I had no right to ask you folks to risk it. But it has given me an idea. I have a holding company I could probably use that she knows nothing about. I'll check into that."

"And I'll start checking into Allison's background when we get back."

"Checking into what about Allison's background?" Carol pinned them both with The Look.

Devin cleared his throat uncomfortably. "Ben and I think Allison may have murdered her ex-husband."

"But his death was ruled an accident." Carol felt the chill air right through her jacket.

"Wasn't she getting a generous settlement? I'm sure I read that somewhere." Jennifer put her arm around Carol who was now shivering beside her.

"Allison told me, some time after we met, that he'd been punished for his sins. It creeped me out, so I didn't ask her what she meant. I've never forgotten what she said though, or the look on her face. I put it down to one too many glasses of wine." Devin held out his arms to Carol.

"I think we'd better go back to the house. I'm feeling very chilled, and it isn't just the weather." She walked into his arms. He held her tightly for a moment before they all turned back towards the house.

FLYNN AND GREGORY CALLED TO BEG OFF LUNCH even as Jennifer and the family were loading the van. "They'll be over in a few minutes to say goodbye." Devin put his phone back in its clip, picked up the portable crib and brought it to Mark.

"You guys have a portable house happening here. Did you bring a bathtub too?" He smiled and handed in the collapsed frame.

"No, but it won't be this easy once they're walking. We have a few more months to get to plan B. I don't think travel will ever be this easy again for many years."

"Wait until Angela is a teenager. You'll probably need a trailer for her stuff." Devin peered into the cargo bay. "How did you all get here in one van? I'm impressed."

"Lana's the packer. I just drive." Mark hopped down. "That's it except the stroller."

"And here it is." Ben handed him the folded buggy. "It looks light, but it weighs a good forty pounds. I don't know how Lana manages it."

"Just don't try arm wrestling with her. She power lifts those babies about twenty times a day and can bench press the stroller." Mark tucked the stroller in and snapped the protective netting down. With the back door closed, they were ready to load people.

"I brought you a little snack for the road." Flynn arrived with his usual flourish, with Gregory following in his wake. "It's just a few things to keep Danny happy: raisins, some peanuts and dried apricots."

"Thanks, Flynn." Danny danced over to take the bag and get a big hug from Flynn. "My mother makes the same snack. Devin, can we come back some time and ride the horses?"

"You bet Danny. Maybe you could all come up over the Christmas holidays. If there's enough snow I can see about borrowing my neighbor's sleigh and take us for a hay ride. What do you think?"

"That would be so cool. Can I have a hug?"

Devin smiled and picked Danny up for a manly hug before handing him off to Mark. "Where's Charlie?"

"He's already in the van waiting. He's been there since I opened the doors. He's not taking any chances on being left behind." Mark watched Danny buckle up his seatbelt and then helped Lana attach the baby carriers on each side of him.

"Time to get on the road. Devin, it's been wonderful. Carol, I'm so glad we spent the weekend with you." Lana reached up to give both a hug. "You are all so tall compared to me. I feel like I'm in the land of giants."

"Carol. Devin. You take care of each other and you keep us posted. Remember, we're all on your team. And Carol, see you Thursday at yoga." Jennifer gave each a warm hug.

The men shook hands all around. Mark climbed into the driver's side with Ben beside him.

"Safe drive."

"Happy Thanksgiving!"

"THE HOUSE SEEMS SO EMPTY, and there's still four of us here." Carol walked into the solarium and plopped down on the larger of the two wicker couches. Come sit with me, Ash."

"This has been the best Thanksgiving ever, Mom. I can't even remember the last time I saw you so happy. I'm really happy for you and Devin." She picked up a pillow and afghan, stretched out beside her mom and put her head on her lap. "Are you going to move in with him?"

"I hadn't even thought of it. He's seen our condo, but I haven't seen his. Besides, I don't think we're at that stage. These are still early days."

"Well, whatever you decide, I'm good with it this time. I think you're good for each other."

Carol stroked Ash's long silky hair. "I have to agree on that. I just hope once we're back in the city this won't become a resort romance."

"C'mon, you don't believe that for a minute." Ashley looked up at her mother.

"No, I don't. Silly of me to even say it. Want to see if there's a

Backgammon board somewhere around?"

"Sure. Or Scrabble."

"Oooh, Scrabble. Maybe we could all play. Let's go find Devin. I think I saw him go in his den. You have to see it and the paintings of the horses."

"Devin." The door was open. Carol and Ashley walked in and saw him talking on his cell by the large bay window. He turned and motioned them in.

"I understand. I appreciate you calling. Please don't mention your call to her daughter. In fact, it would be best if you removed my name and number from your records. I'm really not the next-of-kin. You have her number? Good. Thanks."

Carol's eyes widened as she walked over to put a hand on Devin's shoulder. He looked at her and nodded as he closed the phone.

"Carla Wendover passed away this morning. Another stroke. They still had my name and number from when I brought her in so they called me first. If Allison ever finds out there'll be hell to pay for it, I'm sure."

"Oh, Devin. I'm so sorry. I never knew Mrs. Wendover, but I know she meant a great deal to you. I'm glad you weren't here alone to get this news."

Devin pulled her into his arms. "I'm glad you're here. Thank you."

Carol looked over and saw that Ashley had left them alone and closed the door behind her.

"Devin, is there anything I can do? Do you want me to call Flynn to come back?"

"No, I'll be fine. The nurse told me no-one except me has come to visit her in the past week. When they tried to contact Allison the other day about moving Clara into a long-term care bed, she told them to do whatever they wanted. She was too busy to get involved."

"Too busy stalking us, no doubt. That woman is so mentally ill. If it weren't for that, I would hate her. But she can't control her life or her feelings it seems."

"No, but she is sane enough to know that her mother needed her to step up to the plate and oversee her affairs. That nurse was not mincing words. Allison was rude and abrupt. She wanted nothing more to do with her mother."

"That is so sad."

"Let's find Jim and Ashley and go for a ride. You can ride double with me."

"Let's do it. And then come back for some hot chocolate." Carol could see Devin was mourning the loss of his friend. "You and Clara were great friends weren't you?"

"We were. I kind of adopted her. I really missed our weekly visits after she went in the hospital. She was a fine woman. She would have really liked you." Devin put his arm around her shoulder.

"Sounds like I would have liked her, too." Carol put her arm around his waist. Together they went to find the young people.

Chapter Twelve

"I REALLY HATE TO LEAVE. It's been such a great weekend." Ashley tossed her knapsack and boots into the back of the van.

"It was really great to meet you, Devin. Thanks for letting Ash invite me down." Jim stowed his bag in the back seat of his Corolla.

"Would you guys be interested in coming here for Christmas?" Devin looked over at Carol who beamed at them. "I talked to your mom, and if we still like each other by then, it would be great to have you spend it here."

"Are you serious?" Ash ran and hugged her mother and then hugged Devin. "You two better like each other come Christmas. That would be fantastic."

Devin and Jim shook hands. Devin reached out to pat the side of his arm. "Getting into Dartmouth is beyond special. It's number one in the country for undergrad. Keep up the good work."

Jim blushed with pride as Carol looked on. His own father had never, to her knowledge, ever complimented Jim on his academic accomplishments. As Jim drove away, Carol went over and hugged Devin.

"Thank you for that. Only someone like you would realize what an achievement it was for him to be accepted."

"I looked it up. Dartmouth only accepts one in ten applicants. Jim is in very good academic company." He looked at his watch. "Time to get on the road. I'll just say goodbye to Gregory, and we're off."

"When we get to the airport, I'll check for messages. I know I have nothing booked until this afternoon. I don't want to turn on my phone yet, in case you know who is still using up her minutes calling me."

The drive to the airport was over before they knew it. Soon they were saying goodbye to Ashley at the departure gate.

"Mom, Devin, you take care of each other. Let me know if anything happens with this Allison bitch."

As mother and daughter both wiped tears from their eyes and hugged, Devin's phone rang. Leaving the two leaky women, he walked over to the nearest window and watched a large jet taxiing in. "Elliott here. Who did you say you are?"

Devin eyes widened as he listened to the caller. "Can you text me your address and phone number please? I need to check with my office before I set an appointment. Yes, thanks. I'll get back to you as soon as I can."

Carol was dabbing her eyes and sniffling a bit as she rejoined Devin. "She's gone again. Sorry, it's like this every time now."

"It's fine, Carol. You're a loving mother. It's hard to say goodbye." Devin guided them towards the taxi stand. "That was a call from Clara Wendover's lawyer."

"What'd he want?" As they emerged into the cold air, Carol breathed deeply and steadied herself.

"He wants to meet me as soon as possible. Said he had instructions to call me when Clara passed away. Let's get a cab, and I'll call my office to check my schedule for today. Might as well get that out of the way."

"I need to check my messages, too." Once they were in the taxi, Carol turned on her phone for the first time since Allison's last call. She waited a bit nervously for it to load and then looked down in stunned surprise at the screen.

"This is impossible. The voicemail is full. That's never happened before." She scrolled through the list. With maybe a dozen exceptions, the number was the same. She scrolled to Allison's late evening call the previous Thursday.

Devin finished his office call and looked at her. "I need to call the lawyer back. Carol, what's wrong?"

"It's her. She's called dozens of times since Friday evening. Look at this. It's the same number she called from last Thursday night. I'm not even going to listen to them."

"Just don't delete them. You need to let the police look into this. It's part of her MO, as Guzzo calls it. Thank goodness we had the weekend to ourselves. Looks like it's going to be a hell of a week ahead."

"At least it's a short week." Carol listened to her other messages and made a few call-backs before the taxi arrived in front of her building. "Let me call Guzzo and see if I can pop in to see him. I want to authorize them to pull up my phone records and access my messages. I want this stopped."

"So do I. I'm meeting Clara's lawyer this afternoon." As they climbed out of the taxi, Devin looked down the street. Then he looked up the street. "Where the hell is my truck?"

With a scowl on his face, Devin pulled out his phone and called the police. "I need to report a stolen vehicle." He waited impatiently and was about to hang up when he was connected to what sounded like a teenage officer.

"Make, model and license number, sir."

"It's a Ford F-150 pickup." He gave the plate number and was put on hold.

"Sir, I ran your plate. Your truck is at impound. It was reported abandoned."

"It was parked in front of my girlfriend's condo for the weekend. Who reported it stolen?"

"I wouldn't know, sir. The City penalty is two hundred and fifty dollars plus one hundred and thirty in towing and storage fees."

"Where is it?" Devin's voice lost most of its fight.

"It's at Robert's on Goodenough Street."

After closing his phone, Devin paced in exasperation. "It's her. I know it's her. It had to be her."

"Let's find a bank machine and get you your truck back. I'll bring my stuff up later." Carol led the way into her building and down to her car.

Minutes later, they pulled up in front of the towing service. "Let me confirm I can have the truck before you leave?"

"I'll wait here and make a couple of calls." Carol watched him walk into the shop. Time to call Myra. I've put it off long enough. She went into her contacts, pulled up the number and pressed call.

"Myra. Carol here. You asked me to call." Carol didn't make any attempt at chitchat. With Myra it was strictly business.

"I think we need to consider this latest scandal you've drawn the agency into."

"I hardly think we're dealing with a scandal, Myra. Allison Wendover has made a completely baseless charge. She is facing criminal harassment charges and a slander suit. When the courts are finished with her, she'll probably be in prison." Carol felt no compunction about laying it out.

"Everyone is innocent until proven guilty."

"Everyone except me, that is."

"First, the Demercado case and now this, I want you to take an indefinite leave of absence."

"I assume you've consulted a lawyer."

"You assume correctly."

"I also assume you realize that you're leaving the company open to a suit over loss of livelihood?"

"I can live with it. I want you out of that office today. Colin has my signed letter. You'll need to call to be let in. We've already changed the lock passwords."

Carol closed her phone. Myra had hung up on her. She looked up and saw Devin walking towards her, waving a sheet of paper at her and smiling. She tried to muster a return smile and failed miserably.

"What's happened? Why the long look?" Devin got in the car and closed the door. "What the hell happened in the five minutes since I got out of this car?"

Carol shook her head and sniffled loudly. "Well, basically, I've been fired. I just spoke to Myra Stewart, the regional vice-president. I've been put on mandatory indefinite leave and they've changed the lock codes at the office."

"What are you talking about? You haven't done anything wrong. You're the one being stalked and harassed."

"Myra doesn't care. She's still pissed off at me for raining down the media during the Demercado case. There was a downward blip in new listings when that story hit the news. For an ambitious junior vice-president, it was a major blow. She's had it in for me ever since. I'm not surprised. But I am disappointed Colin didn't stand up to her."

"Probably can't blame him. He has his career to consider as well." Devin put his arm out and massaged her neck. "Now what?"

"Want to come with me to clear out my office? I don't know if I can face them alone." When she looked over at him, her eyes were swimming in tears.

"Y'know what? Come around here. I'll drive. We'll come back for the truck later. This is more important."

"Thank you," she whispered. "I'm not feeling very strong at the moment."

"Let's get you outta there, and then we'll go get some coffee and get ourselves organized. Allison has gone way too far. There is a thing called justice. We just have to find it."

FOR THE FIRST TIME IN HER TWENTY-TWO YEARS WITH THE COMPANY, Carol pressed the Visitor buzzer. When she identified herself, there was a definite hesitation from the receptionist.

"Come in, Ms. Brock." As the buzzer sounded, Carol and Devin entered the reception area.

"Alyssa. It's me. I'm still Carol. I haven't done anything wrong. This is all about office politics."

"I'm sorry, Ms. Brock. We have strict instructions. Colin will be out in a moment to escort you." The receptionist wouldn't make eye contact. "Please sign in here."

"What do you mean sign in? I'm not a visitor. I work here."

"If you want to go into the office area, you must sign in and out. I have my instructions."

"This is so insulting." Carol looked at Devin.

"Let's just get 'er done and get out of here. You don't deserve this, but she's been given marching orders from the powers that be. She'll lose her job if she does otherwise."

"You're right. Leave it to Myra to make everyone else do the dirty work." Carol saw Colin coming their way through the window in the door to the office area. "It's okay, Alyssa, I know you're just doing what you were told."

The young receptionist looked up gratefully but said nothing.

"Colin. I see Myra has roped you in to do the deed. Don't worry. I signed in."

"I'm so sorry about this, Carol. She wouldn't listen to reason. Insisted I enforce her letter and cut you off from all access immediately."

"Right now, I have larger problems to deal with, Colin. Allison Wendover has personally threatened me, left harassing phone calls and had Devin's truck impounded over the weekend. We know we're dealing with someone mentally ill, but I find it hard to believe Myra would fall for her story so quickly and easily."

"I think we both know Myra was just waiting for anything to happen to give her an excuse to push you out. She's very ambitious and you threatened her." They walked down the corridor towards her cubicle.

"She may be ambitious, but she's not very smart. If she was, she'd realize I have no ambitions to become anything more than an associate. I couldn't live the life of a desk-bound executive. I'd go crazy."

Devin piped up. "We need to use that word very advisedly."

"True." They reached Carol's cubicle. As she looked at it, she realized there was very little to show that it was hers. No pictures of the kids, no plants or fake flowers. None of her many awards were up. It was more a work station for transient agents than the station for a top agent.

"Guess I haven't left much of a mark here, eh, Colin?"

"You have, Carol. I'm just so sorry it has to end this way."

"You realize I won't come back. I have my pride."

"I know, and I'm truly sorry. I hope you sue the pants off the company and Myra. If you want me to be a witness for you, I'll be there in a heart beat."

"We both know you can't do that, Colin. Your career here would be over and you have your family to consider. You'd be seen as a snitch. No, thanks for the offer, but you still have a long career ahead of you and a very good one I'm sure. The day you knock Myra off her pedestal, I'll be cheering from the sidelines and buying drinks all around."

"I'll remember that." Colin hugged Carol. "C'mon. I'm sure you have much better things to do than stand around here with me. I won't forget you, Carol. And I am serious. If you think there is anything I can do to help. Please call me. You have my home number."

"Thanks. Well, Devin. I think we're done here. How about we go get your truck?"

Devin smiled and nodded. "Why do I get the feeling this is just the beginning of something much better for you?"

"I'm thinking the same thing. Those eagles were right. I feel I'm being set free and it actually feels pretty good. Goodbye, Colin. Thanks for sticking by me."

Carol and Devin took her two meager bags of office memorabilia back to her car. "Imagine. This is all I have to show for over twenty years in that office. Not even a send-off."

"Do you really want one?"

"No."

"You're walking away from a major and successful career. How do you feel about that?" Devin slipped into the driver's seat of her BMW.

Carol looked out the window thoughtfully as Devin pulled out of the parking lot. "I think I got from it everything I need to move on. And then some." She smiled thinly.

"You still need to put your talents to work. Thought about that?"

"Not yet, really. But I think I'll take a few weeks and just laze about until new inspiration strikes me. Do you mind if we spend a few days here and there at the farm?"

"How would you feel about going to the farm and living there with me? I only need to be in town a couple of days a week to keep on top of my projects. I can easily do most of it from the farm."

"Are you serious?"

Devin grinned. "You sound like Ashley. Yes, I'm serious. Pack up what you need and move up there. Let's see where it takes us."

"There is nothing tying me to Boston now. Nothing." Carol looked over at him with warm appreciation. "When can we go back?"

"Let's see Clara's lawyer after lunch and go from there. Maybe we could even go back tonight."

"Are you serious?"

"Carol. You're getting repetitive." Devin smiled and put his hand on her thigh and rubbed it. "You do love it there, don't you?"

"And just maybe I love you too." Carol put her hand over his and swallowed hard. It had just come out without thinking. She watched him closely for his reaction.

"If that's the way you feel, I'd be the happiest man alive."

Carol let out her breath with a whoosh. "I don't know what made me say that. It just felt so right."

"Trust me. It's right. Let's get some lunch and see that lawyer. I want to get out of Dodge, with you."

"MR. ELLIOT. GOOD TO MEET YOU, SIR. And you are?" Scott Haldimand shook hands with them as they stood in the reception area.

"This is my partner, Carol Brock. She's accompanying me as a witness. I'm not sure what this is about, but I would prefer she be in the room during our meeting."

"Understood. Please come in and sit down. Would you like a coffee or tea?" He ushered them into his brightly-lit office.

"Thanks, we just had lunch. Carol, you want something?"

"No, I'm fine."

"What's this about?" Devin asked as the lawyer sat behind his desk.

"I represent the estate of Clara Wendover. Mrs. Wendover's body has been released to the funeral home for cremation now that we have a death certificate. After learning of Mrs. Wendover's passing, I pulled out her last will and testament to begin the probate process. As the sole beneficiary of her estate, there are a number of matters you and I will need to deal with." He stopped speaking. "Is there something wrong? Were you not aware of her provisions?"

Devin sat in shocked silence before asking quietly, "Does her daughter know about this?"

"She is aware that she and her two brothers are excluded from the will, yes."

"What was her reaction?"

"I would say she was very upset. She hung up on me." He pushed forward a copy of the will. "I'd like to go through it with you now if we could."

Devin picked it up and looked at the date. It was about a year old. Near to the time Clara had made him promise to buy her house. "Is there anything in particular we need to do today? I want to take this with me and study it. Also, I need your advice on getting the locks changed on her house. Her daughter has full access and that needs to stop as soon as possible."

"As executor, I will order the locks changed today. I can have the keys delivered to you, if you wish."

Devin pulled out a business card. "Please have them delivered to my office. Could someone call me when it's done? There are some issues with Ms. Wendover that are currently under investigation by the police. Changing the locks needs to get high priority."

"Understood. I'll call the minute we're finished."

Devin stood. "I think that's it for now. I'm going to see if we can get the real estate agent for the house to let me in. Could I have a copy of the death certificate please?"

"By all means. I have spares right here. Here's three." He reached into a folder and pulled them out. "I can call the real estate company if you like. Who should I ask for?"

Carol spoke up. "That would be the manager, Colin Carmichael." She dictated the phone number to him as he dialed. They both sat down again.

"Colin. This is Scott Haldimand, lawyer for Clara Wendover's estate." He listened. "You've had a call from her then? Oh, good. Your advice to her was absolutely correct. Under no circumstances does she have any authority now to enter the house or remove any contents. Any inquiries should come directly to me as executor." He was shaking his head. "Devin Elliott is in my office. He'd like to come by and pick up a key if it's convenient. The locks will be changed later today. As you can appreciate, there will be no more showings during probate."

As he hung up, Scott looked at them, his eyes wide. "I think ballistic would be a polite term for what Mr. Carmichael just described. Apparently burn in hell came up several times. You say the police are involved?"

"Yes. There've been some incidents."

"What kind?"

"Threats, stalking, and vandalism. We're pretty sure she's a psychopath."

"May I offer some legal advice?"

Devin ran his hand through his hair in a gesture Carol was coming to realize meant that he was trying to collect his thoughts. "I'll take all the advice I can get."

"Most people doing the things you're describing are bullies. There may be mental health issues, but out of self-preservation they're usually still enough in control of themselves to stop short of breaking the law as they understand it. If you hit her with a restraining order she'll realize she will face criminal charges if she continues. In my opinion, it's worth a try."

"Are you offering to represent me on this?"

"I'd be happy to. It would give you a measure of legal protection I believe may help in this situation."

"Then let's do it."

"I can only do a civil restraining order. If she's charged with a crime, there could be a criminal one as well. That will be determined by the DA. I need her full legal name, date of birth if you know it, and address to get the file started."

Devin and Carol reached out and clasped each other's hands together tightly.

"Her name is Allison Clara Wendover. Her date of birth is February 13, 1976. I'm not sure where she lives now." He gave the last address he knew.

"Tell me about her activities against you." The lawyer typed as Devin talked, stopping to ask questions for clarification. After about five minutes he looked up. "She's a real piece of work. No wonder the police are interested."

"We actually think she may have killed her ex-husband. A former investigative journalist friend of ours is exploring that angle."

Carol joined the conversation. "If that's the case, it would mean even a restraining order may not stop her."

"I think you're probably right, but in the absence of a chargeable crime, the restraining order is our best bet. Right now, we can only deal with the facts at hand. I will craft a petition for a temporary Harassment Prevention Order. You more than meet the criteria for at least three incidents. I'm confident we can get an order for at least six months. That should give the police time to build their case against her." He printed off his notes.

"If you could review my notes and write in anything else, I'll be back in a minute. I need to re-schedule an appointment to open up some room in my calendar tomorrow to go to the court house." He left the office and closed the door behind him.

Devin looked at Carol. "I never thought it would ever come to this. I am so sorry to drag you into this."

"Let's not forget, this is what brought us together. I'm ready to take some punches to keep you in my life. As the Aussies say, *no worries, mate.*" Carol smiled brightly at him, doing her best to mask her worries.

"You have to wonder about the universe making you the listing agent for a house that I was about to inherit anyway. Does this mean I can take it off the market?"

"It's your house, and if you don't want to sell it, you don't have to. There have been no offers other than yours, which expired. Scott can just tell them no more showings until the listing itself expires. They'll pull the listing off the internet, any planned ads will be cancelled, and it will be as if it's no longer for sale."

"Okay, let's read this over, get Pasha, and go back to the farm for the night. You with me?"

"Where else would I be?" Carol reached up and smoothed her hand over his cheek. "You won't be rid of me anytime soon, Mr. Elliott."

As they were walking back to the truck, Devin grimaced and shook his head. "Things just got really complicated didn't they?"

"You think this will push Allison over the edge?" Carol shivered in the cold breeze.

"I'm so sure of it, I'm ready to call for backup."

"What backup?"

"That's the problem. I can't think of anything short of personal round-the-clock protection. I don't know about you, but I can't live that way." Devin pressed the remote to unlock the doors. "Let's get the key and the cat. I've had more than enough for today."

"We need a containment strategy." Carol climbed in the passenger side. "Right now, she's pushing all the buttons. We need to figure out how to push back and push back so hard she'll back off."

"You're absolutely right, Carol." Devin started the truck. "Bullies usually back down if you confront them."

"Let's work on that and hope it does the trick. I've had enough of her trying to ruin my life just because I was doing my job." Carol straightened the cuffs on her jacket. "We need a plan."

Chapter Thirteen

AFTER PICKING UP THE KEY AT CAROL'S FORMER OFFICE, they wound their way through the thick afternoon traffic. They were almost in front of the house when Devin spied Allison's car parked in the driveway.

He drove by without stopping. "Call 911. I'm not going in there without the police."

"I need to report a break-in. They're still in the house." Carol gave the address, answered a few questions and closed her phone. "They're on their way. I'll call Guzzo. He needs to know about this."

They watched from down the block as one, then another, and then a third blue and white entered the street with flashers on but no sirens. Devin went around the block and drove the pickup in behind the lead cruiser. He got out and quickly walked over to a slim officer in a bullet-proof vest who was climbing out of his squad car.

"My name is Devin Elliott. I have just inherited that house. The late owner's daughter is in there without any legal authority and she knows it. My lawyer is working on a restraining order as we speak. I have documents to prove she shouldn't be in there."

"Are you the one who called this in?"

"I am." Carol came over and stood beside Devin.

"We're going to enter the house now. If you would stay here, we'll bring the suspect out and determine what, if any, criminal activity has taken place."

He does not deserve this, Carol thought sadly as she watched two officers approach the house from the front. *He's never done anything to attract such negativity other than care about an older woman whose family*

131

was neglecting her. An officer rang the doorbell and waited.

Moments later, two tall police officers brought a squirming Allison out the front door hoisted by her armpits. Her legs were windmilling with agitation and her strident voice could be clearly heard.

"This is *my* house. You have no right to arrest me for trespassing in my own home." She twisted her head towards one officer and spit in his face. "I was born and raised in this house. I don't care what a damn will says. This is my house, and I can take whatever I want from it."

The officer came over to talk to Devin. "Sir. Could I borrow those documents you mentioned please? Maybe if we show them to her, she'll calm down a bit."

"Good luck, officer. She's had all day to work up to this. Are you going to take her in?"

"This kind of thing is a bit touchy, sir. It doesn't happen every day, but when it does, we try to avoid arrest and jail. If you insist, we will charge her and bring her in. We can charge her with resisting arrest and assaulting a police officer."

"Please call Detective Len Guzzo and do whatever he suggests."

"There are other problems?"

"Just call Guzzo."

"Roger that." The officer walked back to his cruiser while radioing back to his precinct. He stopped before even reaching the car and stood listening. He looked back at Devin and Carol and shook his head as his eyebrows crooked up. Putting the radio back on his belt clip, he walked over to where the two officers had Allison standing restrained by a squad car.

"Allison Wendover. You are under arrest for break and enter, attempted theft, resisting arrest and assaulting a police office …"

"Guess Guzzo told him something about Allison we'd rather not know." Devin took Carol's hand as they walked towards the house. "Let's find Pasha."

They walked into the house together and almost tripped over a small pile of boxes by the door.

"Seems there were more than a few things Allison wanted. She always told me she didn't give a whit about her mother's 'junk,' as she called it. Wonder what was so precious?" He opened one box and peered in.

"Blue Mountain pottery? What's so special about that? Clara said they used to rent a cottage in Canada for summer vacations. She liked the pottery and brought a few pieces home each summer. To her, it was just something pretty and a lovely memory of a place she really enjoyed."

They pushed the boxes back and split up to find the cat. With all the commotion and strangers, Pasha was probably well and truly hidden somewhere. Devin called to her softly over and over and finally went to sit in the living room. He sat on an old La-Z-Boy that had seen many better days. There was still a bright throw on it and a hand-crocheted pillow. He smoothed his hands over the arm rests. It had been Clara's chair for watching her favorite television programs.

Within a few quiet minutes, he was rewarded. Pasha crept out cautiously from somewhere in the back of the house.

"Come on, Pasha. Everyone is gone. It's just us." Devin spoke soothingly as Carol came slowly and quietly into the room and sat on the couch. "You remember Carol. She's my girlfriend now. What do you think of that?"

The cat ignored Carol, went straight to Devin and jumped into his lap, purring loudly. Carol watched with a smile as Devin scratched her ears and let his chest be used as a pin cushion by the kneading claws.

"I don't remember seeing a cat carrier. Do you know if there's one around?"

"Yes, it's in the closet under the stairs. You know the one I mean?" Devin stroked the cat lovingly.

"Good. I'll pick up the litter box and some supplies. I have a feeling Pasha is about to become a country girl." Carol stood up and stretched. "Wouldn't mind becoming one myself at the moment. Seems a whole lot saner."

"Let's get Pasha into the carrier, and I'll call Guzzo. Do you want to have your car out at the farm or here in town?"

"How about we figure that out another time? For tonight, let's all stay together."

"Sounds good."

Once Pasha was safely ensconced in the carrier, Devin put in the call to Guzzo.

"I was just about to call you. She's here being booked with breaking and entering and resisting arrest." Devin looked over to Carol and waited for Guzzo to continue. "She had a key because of the listing arrangement. But apparently her mother wouldn't let her have one for the past few years. Mrs. Wendover believed money and jewelry had gone missing. Allison insists she never stole anything. Says anything she took was hers and her mother had just forgotten."

Devin rolled his eyes wearily. "We're getting ready to go back to my farm for the night. Anything we should know?"

"She's claiming you duped her mother into making you her sole beneficiary. Says her mother loved her and her brothers and would never have written them out of her will."

"Clara's lawyer knew her quite well. He'll be able to set the record straight. And for the record, I didn't know until this afternoon that I was even a beneficiary, let alone the sole beneficiary. Ask the lawyer."

"I'm going to make sure Allison is kept here over night so you can get out of town and have a free evening. By the way, based on Carol's complaint, we were able to access her phone records. Allison called Carol about sixty times between Friday and yesterday; almost every hour with about a six hour break during the night. We've retrieved and saved well over a dozen text messages, most of them beginning with "bitch." Should make for some great evidence in court."

"Thanks for all your help, Len. I don't know what you said to the officer who called you, but he didn't hesitate to read Allison her rights on the spot."

"I just read him one of the more graphic text messages and told him I thought it best if Ms. Wendover could be taken off the street for a few hours. Apparently, he agreed."

"He sure didn't hesitate. I don't even want to know what was in the message, but I bet burn in hell was part of it."

"That was minor. Go. Get out to your farm and forget about this for the night. The case is building against her without any help from you. Trust me."

Devin closed his phone as Carol lugged a box of kitty litter to the door. "Here, let me take it from here."

"Good. I'll go back for the cat food. Do you want me to leave any here?"

"No. Pasha is going to be on full-time mousing duty for the rest of her life."

"Do you think you'll ever live in this house, Devin?"

"I'm thinking of selling my condo and keeping this as my city base. I'm only in town a couple of days a week but it would be great to have something like this as a second home. What do you think?"

"I think Clara Wendover would rest easy knowing her house is still being cared for."

"I do, too. Just sitting in her chair with Pasha felt really good and right. I'll give it a bit before changing things, but there will always be a little bit of Clara here. I'll be sure to do that. Speaking of which, how about we bring the bedspread from Clara's bedroom? It's Pasha's favorite spot for sleeping. It may help her settle in at the farm."

"Good idea. I'll get it." Carol walked away and up the stairs. The late afternoon sun had bathed the stairway in soft colors. Carol thought of the older woman she had never met. *Rest easy, Clara. You chose well. Devin is taking good care of things.*

Carol carefully folded back the brightly colored quilt. As she rearranged the pillows, she saw a notebook. Picking it up, she opened it. It was Clara's journal. She smiled as she flipped through the pages. Devin had clearly been a major part of her life. His name leaped off the page over and over again. *You need to come with me sister diary. Now I know how much Devin meant to you. He deserves to know that.* Looking in the bedside table, she found three more volumes. She tucked the diaries on top of the folded quilt and made her way back down the stairs.

"Got the bedspread. I found her diaries too. There may be something the police can use. Anything else you want to bring home with you? Maybe some Blue Mountain pottery?"

"Definitely some Blue Mountain." Devin grinned. "I don't know about you, but I'm partial to that large fish thing. It would make a dandy door stop."

"Whatever you say, Devin. Just promise me you won't start trolling garage sales to find more."

Devin look offended. "You mean you don't want to add to the collection? It would fit right in to the solarium."

"Don't you dare." Carol feigned horror. "Your choice. Me or the pottery."

"Okay. You win. No Blue Mountain pottery at the farm." Devin put on his jacket. "Let's get out of Dodge and catch the sunset on the road. How about we stop by your place and you can pick up whatever you need for the next few days?"

"I'm with you." Pasha started yowling before they reached the truck. "I have a feeling it's going to be a long ride."

It was dark by the time they drove up the lane at the farm. Devin had called ahead to let Gregory know they were coming. Soft yellow lights bathed the front and side of the house as they pulled up.

"We're home, Pasha." The cat had yowled piteously all the way from Boston. No amount of talking or sticking fingers through the grate had calmed her. Devin turned off the truck and the yowling stopped. "Welcome home, girls."

"How about I go and see about putting together a little supper? I'm sure there must be something we can muster." Carol got out of the truck, retrieved her weekender, and waited as Devin unlocked the door leading into the mud room.

Stepping into the kitchen a moment later, they both smiled and linked arms. The kitchen table had been set with two settings. Two tall pillar candles flanked a bright fuchsia pink flowering Christmas cactus. An ice bucket stood to the side with a bottle chilling in it. A salad bowl with tongs sticking out graced another side. And the smells in the room announced something was warming in the oven.

"This is signature Flynn." Devin brought the carrier into the room and set it on the floor near the oven. Pasha remained quiet. "You know what this means?"

"Other than he is very caring and adores you?" Carol set her weekender near the stairs, took the bedspread, and opened it on the floor beside the carrier.

"It means you have his official seal of approval. He has never ever done this before."

"Have you brought other lady friends here before?"

"Well no, but—"

"Then he's just being Flynn. He is a gracious host of this property, and he is welcoming us home the way he would anyone. Let's not read too much into this."

"Okay, but I still believe you have the Flynn seal of approval big time." Devin walked over to Carol, wrapped her in his arms, and noisily nuzzled her neck. "You have mine."

Pasha let out a mournful yowl. They both laughed. "Guess Pasha agrees."

"I think it means we need to let her out to find her litter box."

"Minor detail." Devin walked over and unclasped the door off one end of the carrier. Pasha emerged slowly. After carefully sniffing the air and exploring for several minutes she approached the litter box briefly but kept on walking. She circled back to the bedspread, sat down on it, and started cleaning herself vigorously.

"Would you like a glass of wine, madam?" Devin went to the ice bucket and drew out a Pinot Grigio.

"I would love one. This has been a day to remember and maybe someday to forget."

"You're right. I'm not sure I want to let you out of my sight until Allison is stopped. If you don't mind, I'm feeling a bit protective about you just now."

"Two months ago, I would have rejected anyone who wanted to be protective of me. But Allison is one very sick lady. I don't know how to deal with it alone, and I don't want to. Between you and Guzzo, I feel I can handle it just because I know I'm not alone. Does that make sense?"

"It does. How about we work on Flynn's dinner?"

"It's going to be an early night, isn't it?" Carol asked.

"Yes."

Pasha meowed loudly.

"I think that's a food meow," Devin said. "Let me get her organized and then we can eat in peace."

THE NEXT MORNING DAWNED COLD AND BRIGHT. Carol turned on her back and stretched languidly. She could already smell coffee. *I could get used to this,* she mused as she looked around Devin's bedroom and wiggled her toes. The large four-poster bed dominated one side of the room while a large dresser and mirror took up the far wall. Getting up, she walked over to the window and pulled back the heavy drapes.

She was rewarded with the sight of Devin and Gregory riding up the lane, the frosty breath of the horses sending up little puffs of steam. *Looks like they've been out for a good ride,* she thought, as she watched them get closer.

Pulling on her silk dressing gown and some warm slippers, she padded down the stairs. By the time Devin came in, she was in the bright solarium and just finishing her first cup of coffee.

"You should have woken me up. We could have all gone for a ride." She strolled back into the kitchen for a refill and a morning kiss.

"You looked so relaxed and warm, I almost didn't get up myself." Devin picked up his mug from the counter and held it out for a refill. "We'll take Pablo out this afternoon if you like. I need to pick up a few things in the village. Want to join me? We can drop by and see Flynn. Bring him up to date."

"And I might actually buy a book." Carol opened the fridge door and surveyed its meager contents. "I haven't read a book in months. Looks like we need to get in some more food if we're going to spend time here."

"LOOK WHO'S BACK ALREADY." Flynn came around the counter to give Carol a warm hug.

"Thanks so much for the lovely dinner last night. Your beef bourguignon was divine." Carol hugged him back. "Amazing flavor. I need your recipe."

"And you shall have it. The key is long, slow cooking and half a bottle of red wine. Gregory told me about that nasty woman, Allison. I'm glad I'm not on her radar."

"We wish neither of us were. Speaking of which, I should call Guzzo and get an update. Want to have lunch with us?" Devin pulled out his phone.

"I can close the shop for an hour or so. It's never that busy during the week." Flynn tapped Carol on the arm and motioned her to follow him. "Come and see something. I found it at a bankruptcy auction." Approaching an antique table, he gently opened a cotton towel that was protecting a framed oil painting and propped it against the wall.

"Oh, Flynn. I don't know a lot about art, but that is one fine Impressionist painting." Carol looked at the mottled browns and greens of a country meadow and the forest behind it. "It reminds me of some places I've seen in Connecticut in the spring. So lush even the air smells green."

"I'm taking it to New York or Boston to get it dated when I get a chance. I strongly suspect it's mid-1800s. The canvas stretching and framing are almost definitely from that period." He stood back to gaze at it. "Isn't it gorgeous? You almost feel you're in the picture."

"It's lovely. What do you think it's worth?" Carol could imagine the painting in Devin's den.

"A few thousand I imagine. I can't decipher the artist's name."

Devin walked over. "Allison put in a not guilty plea and got a sympathetic hearing from the judge in chambers. She must have been at her most charming. She's out on her own recognizance. No trial date set."

"I wonder if that judge knew about some of her other antics."

"Without proof, it couldn't even be brought up. It's still all conjecture at this stage." Devin looked at his watch. "Flynn, why don't you close up and come with us?"

"Already decided. We can go whenever you're ready. I'll just get the keys."

When they walked in to the Sweet Repose a few minutes later, they were welcomed by its portly owner. "Flynn, Devin. I can't even remember the last time the two of you came over for lunch. And who is your lovely friend?"

"Carol, meet Eric Lesage. His wife, Sheila, is slaving over the hot stove out back. Carol is visiting from Boston."

"We won't hold it against you, my dear. We've forgiven Devin. Just waiting for him to see the light and commute from here." He showed them to a window table. The bright dining room overlooked a small ravine with a stream running through it. Dozens of birds and squirrels flocked to the feeders dotting the yard.

"This is beautiful. You can't tell from the outside how big it is. I thought it would just be a few tables." Carol gazed around the spacious dining room with its exposed beams and large gas fireplace holding court at one end of the room. "This must be gorgeous in the winter with the snow."

"We can seat up to sixty people, more in the summer on the patio." He put menus in front of them. "We have Sheila's cream of squash soup on today. The noon specials are on the blackboard over there. Can I get you a glass of wine?"

"This is my first day of a well-earned vacation. A glass of Chardonnay, please. I already have my eye on that filet of sole."

"I'll have the same." Flynn closed his menu as Devin ordered a beer and chicken parmesan. "You're on vacation, sweetie? You weren't when you left here this morning. Dish girl."

Carol smiled ruefully. "Let's just say it wasn't my idea. The regional vice-president of my company decided the situation with Allison didn't have good optics, as she put it. I'm on indefinite leave of absence."

"I'm so sorry to hear that. Devin tells me you're one of the best."

"How the mighty fall. But to be honest Flynn, I have no intention of going back to it. I've been in it for over twenty years. I used to love it, but it almost cost me my kids. No career should be allowed to demand that kind of sacrifice."

"Have you thought about what you want to do next?" The conversation halted briefly as their drinks were served.

"I want to take a few weeks off to get my life back in balance. It's coming up to Christmas. In the new year I'll revisit it. For now, I need a total break."

"I hear you, girl. But here's an idea you might want to consider." Flynn sipped his wine thoughtfully. "I've been talking for at least a year about bringing in a partner. From what I know of you so far, I think we could work quite well together."

"Nice thought, Flynn, but I don't know the first thing about running a store like yours."

"You know about selling, right?"

"Yes, but—"

"And you know what Bostonians are buying these days, right?"

"Yes." Carol cautiously set aside her objections. "I do know about all the latest trends, and I can sell for sure. I never thought about it, but I have a lot of transferable skills."

"Of course you do. And with the right tutelage from me, I'm sure you'd be up to speed in a few weeks." Flynn smiled smugly. "Promise me you'll consider it after New Year's."

"What are the hours like? I want most of my weekends off."

"We're closed Monday and Tuesday. We can take turns on weekends. We can split the rest of the hours between us and still have lots of spare time to go to auctions, craft fairs, and whatnot. I do quite a bit of buying online. You interested?"

"How's the pay?"

"I'm looking for a partner, not an employee. We'll work out profit-sharing based on what you invest."

"Would you go for fifty-fifty?" Carol sat back as their soup arrived.

"For you, I just might." Flynn looked up. "This smells heavenly. What's the herb?"

"It's cardamom."

"I may not be much of a cook, but I sure know how to eat." Carol picked up her spoon and dipped in. "Oh my. This is the perfect day for this soup."

"Enjoy." Eric left them to greet a couple that had just arrived.

"This all assumes that I will be living in this area next year." Carol spooned up more of the fragrant soup and looked at Devin and Flynn.

Devin grinned. "Looks like Flynn just invited you to move in with me, Carol. Is that what you just did, Flynn? You could have checked with me first, Mr. Matchmaker."

"How am I doing so far?" Flynn beamed at them.

"How's he doing, Carol?"

"He's doing well." She tried not to laugh in her soup. "I accept your job offer. Only after the first week of January though."

"It's really slow then. Make it late January and you're on. Our lawyers can work out the details. But, just out of curiosity, what would you be planning to invest?"

"I need to know more about your sales and inventory. I could go well into the six figures if needed."

Flynn almost choked on a spoonful of soup. "You have that kind of money to invest?"

"I've been in Boston real estate for twenty years. I have a nice nest egg." Carol sipped her wine.

"I told you she's quality." Flynn looked at her with new appreciation.

"You did say that. You were clearly way ahead of me and my poor male brain." Devin grinned at them. "I was still stuck at beauty and brains."

"Here's to my new partner." Flynn raised his glass

The main course arrived. Carol savored a delicate piece of the sole. "I know quality when I see it, but I've never gone looking for it in the way you have, Flynn."

"Trust me, girl, a few weeks with me and you'll be hooked. If you thought selling real estate was fun, wait until you go out on a buying trip. I know you'll love it. Think of it this way, you'll be spending the store's money and not your own."

"But the store's money will be my own."

"Not after you sell at retail for about a hundred per cent more than we paid, dearest."

Carol popped some broccoli in her mouth. "I'm getting the picture now. Tell me more."

"Would anyone mind if we talked shop some other time?" Devin asked. "I'm feeling a bit excluded here. I know the restoration market for a house, but not what goes in it."

Carol and Flynn laughed in unison. "Sorry, Devin. I'm monopolizing Carol. She's your date."

"That's what I thought. Seems you had other plans." Devin reached out and rubbed his hand against Carol's cheek. "I'm just kidding. Glad to see you two are making these plans. It means Carol can't leave, and that was my plan."

"It almost sounds like you two were collaborating on enticing me out here. Dinner last night. Good coffee this morning. Now, this lunch. I smell a conspiracy." Carol finished the last of her meal and put her knife and fork down. "Wonder what's for dessert?"

Almost two hours passed before the threesome was back on the sidewalk and heading to the store. "That was delicious. Thank you so much, Devin, for suggesting it. And thank you so much for paying for it, Flynn."

"Business expense. We were talking business."

"I know all about write offs."

Carol's phone chirped. "It's Jim. Just a second." She listened. "Shit. I knew this would happen. Thanks dear, we'll check it out." She looked at Devin and Flynn with pained eyes.

"The media have the story. Allison must have called someone the minute they let her out of jail. I need to make a couple of calls and the numbers are on my laptop. Do you mind if we head back to the farm?"

Chapter Fourteen

BY THE TIME THEY REACHED THE FARM, Carol had put things in motion. "Nobody can reach me out here. I want to stay off the media radar until Scott gets the restraining order and we have our messaging straight. Allison is the criminal not us. I want the world to know it. Let's go online and see what they're saying."

Moments later, Carol had her laptop set up, had done a search and come up with four online stories and video clips. "She and Myra worked this together. Look at Myra talking about how fast she moved to ensure other clients wouldn't be affected by this latest scandal. What a bitch. She's ruining my reputation all over again."

"Do you care?"

"I care for my kids more than me. I'm changing careers, and I'm fine with that. I just don't want Jim and Ash to be tainted by this. For them, I need to clear my name."

"So what do you want to do?" Devin followed Carol into the kitchen.

"I'm going to see if Scott Haldimand will take this on. I'd ask Avery Hutchinson but she'd be in a conflict of interest situation with the agency. Much as I respect her competence, I need a different lawyer." Carol organized a pot of coffee and went back to her laptop. "We'll work on a prepared statement to give to the media the minute he gets the restraining order and go from there. Do you have his card handy?"

Carol left a voice message from her phone. "Could I borrow your phone? I want to keep mine free until he calls back."

Devin handed over his phone, poured them both a coffee, and went off to his study, leaving Carol to man her battle stations.

Fifteen minutes later, Carol sought out Devin in his study. "Scott's working on the statement. He expects to hear about the restraining order before the end of the day. Thanks for the use of your phone."

"You're one gutsy lady, Carol." Devin slipped the phone into his pocket. "I was impressed before, but I'm truly impressed now. I don't know where you draw your strength from, but if you could share your secret you'd have a bestseller on your hands."

"I work in a highly competitive field. To get where I was until this happened, I had to be stronger and faster and smarter. But this past year has taught me so many lessons. And one of them is that, when it comes to my family, no-one threatens us. I'm just doing what I have to do to protect my family."

"Ashley and Jim would be very proud of their mother if they could see you right now. Why don't you give them a call or text them and bring them up to date? Then we could go for a walk or a ride."

"Thanks, Devin. I will text them an update. I don't think this story will go much farther than Boston, but Jim had already heard through Facebook, so I should keep them in the loop. Excuse me, I'll be back."

As Carol walked back to her laptop and phone, she suddenly had an inspiration and called Jennifer. "Is Ben around? I need some media advice."

Ben's deep, measured voice came on. "Hi Carol. Looks like the media wolves are out for a feeding frenzy, and you're on the menu."

"Tell me about it. Any advice? I've decided not to go back into real estate, but my kids will be affected if my reputation is smeared. I can live with this, but I don't want to put them through it. The last thing I need is for this story to become a case study in one of Ashley's journalism courses."

"I hear you. You working on an official statement?"

"Yes. I should have it by the end of the afternoon."

"That's a good start. What else are you doing?"

"We have a lawyer working on a restraining order against Allison for harassment, threats, and vandalism."

"Can you prove all this?"

"Not entirely, but the police are investigating. That should provide reasonable doubt about her allegations."

"Reasonable doubt may work in a trial, but it will only feed the media machine. Doubt and drama is what a good story is all about. They'll have a field day with this, and you'll be lucky if the real truth sees the light of day."

"What can I do, Ben? I'm at my wits' end." Carol scrolled through her Facebook messages. "I need to do damage control here big time, and you're telling me the truth isn't enough?"

"With your permission, I could make a couple of phone calls to some heavy hitters I know. I can't stop the news machine, but I'm pretty sure I could make the doubt and drama turn in your favor. You game?"

"You know I am. Bring it on."

"Okay then. You keep working with your lawyer on that statement, and let me work my network. I'll get back to you as soon as I can. You willing to be interviewed one on one live?"

"Yes, definitely. This needs to be dealt with once and for all so I can get on with my life and my kids can hold their heads up wherever they are. I'm back at Devin's farm."

"All right then. Let's work this. Have you asked Jim and Ashley to work with you on Facebook and Twitter? I bet they can make this go viral in no time."

"Jim has a gazillion friends on Facebook, and so does Ashley. I've got a few hundred friends on my personal page and over a thousand on my real estate page. As soon as we nail down the statement, we'll start posting."

"Good girl. One thing to consider though: you may want to take down your real estate page. Anyone can join right?"

"Good point. Myra and Allison could send people to it to leave nasty posts. I'll ask Colin to double-check that it's been suspended right now."

"I still have my best camera equipment. How about we do an interview tomorrow and post it to YouTube? I can make sure it gets to some of my media buddies. They'll know what to do with it."

"Talk about hitting back hard and fast. Let's do it." Carol smiled as she closed her phone. *I have just launched my secret weapons,* she thought. *Allison and Myra won't know what hit them.*

CAROL CHANGED INTO HER FAVORITE SILK DRESSING GOWN, poured them both a generous glass of wine, and tucked herself into a wicker chair in the solarium with one of Clara's diaries. *Who needs to buy a book,* she mused, *when I have first hand stories about Devin and Clara to read?* Opening the latest book, she took a sip of wine and began to read.

… Devin visited again today. He is such a good man. Says he found Pasha's favorite food and treats on sale and couldn't resist. I have enough food for her for at least two months. He won't admit that he's the one who organized the food bank extras, but I know it's him.

She flipped to another page.

… Allison was here today. Now she claims she's allergic to Pasha, but we've always had cats. This sudden allergy makes no sense. She is so distant too. And she can't seem to sit still. I always knew she was different. I don't understand her, but I still love my only girl. I just wish I could reach her somehow.

Carol idly flipped through some pages as she sipped her wine. A quiche was warming in the oven. The fixings for a salad were waiting to be combined and tossed. Devin was in his study. Suddenly, she stared at the page as what she was reading began to seep into her consciousness.

…Allison came by tonight with a bottle of wine. I think she'd already had some before she came over. She was excited. Kept talking about winning and making the bastard pay for his sins. I asked her what she meant, and she just smiled. Said he crossed her one too many times, and now it was time for payback.

Carol's hand started to shake. She put the glass down and read on.

...I think she killed Charles. She said something about loosening his brake line so there would be a slow leak. He would have what would appear to be an accident, and she could get the house and his money before the divorce papers are signed.

Seems Allison has finally remembered what she told me and she's scared I'll tell someone. I promised her I wouldn't. I'm going to have the locks changed. I can't trust her. She's so threatening. And she's starting to take things. When I say something, she tells me I must have Alzheimer's and she's going to have me put away. If it weren't for Devin, I'd be afraid to live here. She knows he comes every week.

"Devin, there's something you need to read." Carol walked into his study with the journal in her hand. "I think your case against Allison and her murdering her ex is documented in this journal I found."

Devin took it out of her outstretched hand. "Where did you find this?"

"The first one was under a pillow on Clara's bed. I found more in her bedside table. At first, I was curious about how she described your visits. She loved you as a son. You must know that."

"I do."

"But she also described Allison's visits. It's all there. I think Guzzo will find more than enough to start checking back on the ex's death."

"Interesting. Clara couldn't control Allison while she was alive, but she may lead us to the truth after her death."

"Clara was afraid of her own daughter." Carol looked up at the painting of Aero. "How sad."

"Clara changed the locks so Allison couldn't get in the house without her there. She changed her will to exclude her. She deeded the house to me. I didn't know what she'd done, so I couldn't help. She never said anything to me directly."

"Maybe she hoped Allison would turn around."

"No. She knew about Allison's mental health issues. She told me more than once about her strange behavior and activities. But, it's almost impossible to get help for someone who denies there are any problems."

Carol's phone chirped. "It's Jim. Hold that thought."

"Hello, you. What's up?" Carol listened intently and began to smile. "You'd do that for me? Okay, I will never admit to knowing about this but go for it. And Ben is going to interview me and put it up on YouTube. I'm waiting for the statement from the lawyer so we can all post it on our Facebook pages. Stay tuned dear and thanks. Love you."

She turned to Devin with a huge grin on her face. "I've always known my son is extremely adept at programming and computers. What I didn't know is that he is an amateur hacker in his spare time."

"How about you share his plan over dinner? That quiche smells wonderful, and I'm hungry." Devin took her by the hand and led her to the kitchen. "I'll toss the salad if you serve."

When they were settled with their food and their glasses topped up, Carol explained. "Jim located Myra's Twitter account. It's a public address she promotes openly. He's started tweeting messages to all his followers about Myra's smear campaign and asked them to re-tweet to their followers."

"What's the purpose of that? I have no idea how it works."

"He's basically sending out headlines: my mother's boss fired her for doing her job because a rich friend doesn't like her. The old David and Goliath theme. He's using tags to attract lawyers, human rights activists and the media to tweet Myra. What he hopes is it will start trending and catch the eye of the media."

Devin's phone rang in his pocket. "It's Scott. Devin here. How's it going? Yes, she's right here." He handed the phone across.

"Hi, Scott. What's up?" Carol ate some quiche as she listened. "I'll read it over right now if you want to stay on the line." She walked over to her laptop and opened the attachment he'd just sent.

"This looks very good. You've hit all the key points. I have a retired journalist friend who's going to help me get this on YouTube and to the media. My son and daughter and I will be posting it on Facebook as well." Carol walked back to her supper. "What's the status on the restraining order?"

She beamed. "Excellent. Nice work, Scott. I'll look forward to getting a copy of it. Oh, it's there? I didn't notice it. I'll open it after I finish my dinner. No, it's fine. This was important. Do you want to talk to Devin again? Okay, we'll chat tomorrow. Thanks again."

She closed the phone. "Scott got a six-month restraining order against Allison. She is not to come within one hundred feet of either of us. He had a police statement about the ongoing investigation that convinced the judge."

"I don't know about you, but I feel a lot better already."

"Me too. There's been a constant underlying stress since she started all this. Now we have to hope she can control herself and leave us alone." Carol finished up her plate and set it aside. "I need to get on my laptop and get this statement to Jim and Ash and onto the internet. I also want to call Ben back and set things up with him. Do you mind handling the dishes?"

"You go do what you need to do. I'll clean up here and get a pot of coffee organized for the morning." Devin picked up the salad bowl and carried it to the sink.

"What are your plans for tomorrow?" Carol shifted to where her laptop stood ready.

"How about we both go to town, you pick up your car, and see Ben; and we'll meet back here for dinner?"

"That sounds like a good plan. How about a morning ride before we leave?" Carol looked up from the keyboard.

Devin cocked his eyebrows up and smirked. "Exactly what kind of ride did you have in mind?"

Carol dissolved into laughter. "I meant on horseback. But let's see what happens when we wake up. Or maybe later."

Chapter Fifteen

"TIME TO RISE AND SHINE, GORGEOUS." Devin playfully tickled Carol's ear, where a small diamond stud earring was half-hidden by her hair. "I think I hear Sabrina calling you."

"Tell Sabrina to have a nap." Carol snuggled down into the covers. "It's too early. And it's probably cold."

"C'mon, city girl. You need to practice being a country girl." Devin turned over on his side and carefully got out of the bed. Standing beside it, he reached down and grabbed the bedspread and sheet in his hands and flung them back in one smooth movement.

"You beast! You are so mean!" Carol clutched her pillow tight to her chest. "That is cruel and unusual punishment."

"C'mon. Get dressed, and I'll show you a sunrise that will make up for it."

"Only if there's coffee in advance."

"Can't you smell it?" Devin pulled on his bathrobe and slippers.

"Hmm. I can. Okay, you win. Let's go get that coffee."

"Right this way, ma'am." Devin held out her dressing gown to her and then led her towards the stairs. Minutes later they each had a steaming mug in their hands.

"I swear the coffee here tastes better than in town. And I buy a premium brand." Carol sipped the hot brew appreciatively as she looked out over the paddock and the pasture beyond. "We even beat Gregory this morning."

"He'll be surprised, but I think he can handle it." Devin walked up behind her and rubbed the small of her back. "Flynn left some croissants from the bakery for breakfast."

"He's so thoughtful. We should have them over for a dinner we make this weekend."

"You can be my sous chef, and we'll try out some of those Thai recipes." Devin finished off his coffee and put the mug on the counter. "I'm good for now. How about we get dressed and get going? I'm sure Sabrina is calling you."

"Let's go. This is going to be a long day. I want to have this ride to remember all day long."

"And don't forget the ride last night." Devin smiled impishly.

"You're so bad." Carol tapped his butt playfully as they went back up the stairs.

THEY WERE HALFWAY TO BOSTON when Carol finished studying the statement. "Scott has done a great job. I've almost got it memorized now." Carol had the printout on her lap. "Throw some practice questions at me. I need to figure out how to use only our key messages without straying into libel land."

Devin did his best imitation of Ben. "Tell me, Ms. Brock, why would the regional vice-president of your agency launch a personal vendetta against you? What happened to innocent until proven guilty?"

"I honestly don't know. I was just doing my job. I showed the house to four potential buyers that day. One came forward to put in an unconditional offer. I wrote it up and gave it to Ms. Wendover. She refused to sign it. It happens. She had twenty-four hours to consider the offer."

"She claims you colluded with Mr. Elliott, a friend of the family, to fix the price. What do you say to that?"

"I say, it simply isn't true. There are very strict ethics governing real estate transactions. I've been in this business many years and have always abided by the ethics of my former profession."

"Former profession, Ms. Brock?" Devin grinned.

"I don't plan to return. Ms. Stewart has created an atmosphere that is intolerable to me at this stage in my career. She has made sure any enjoyment I could have in my work has been tarnished. I refuse to live under that kind of shadow."

"You're going to do great, Carol. I'm not a journalist, but I know you're speaking from the heart. That's what counts."

Carol smiled and put the statement in her tote. "I'm counting on it, too. I'm ready."

As the sun rose slowly over the Boston skyline, they cranked up "Dream On" and rocked their way to town.

"I'll see you later, sweetheart. Call or text—I want to know how your day is going." Devin planted a light kiss on Carol's head. "I'm going to take the diaries over to Guzzo and drop over to Scott's for an official copy of the restraining order."

"I hope you realize there are very few people on the planet who can kiss the top of my head without standing on their tiptoes." Carol turned up her face. "Kiss me where it counts. Right here on the lips."

Devin laughed. "You are some piece of woman." He gave her a good lip lock. "That will have to keep you going all day."

Carol fluttered her eyelids. "Oh my, sir. I believe I may swoon."

"Just don't swoon when Ben is interviewing you. It might beg his journalistic integrity." Devin combed one hand through her thick wavy tresses.

Carol laughed. "I've never swooned around Ben. He's my buddy."

"A Pulitzer prize-winning buddy. You can't do better than that. I'll be interested to see what he does with your story."

"Me too. So I'd better get going. I'm supposed to meet him in half an hour on the Common. He's doing the interview himself with a tech guy he knows behind the camera. Speaking of owing someone dinner."

"Be safe, Carol. You know I love you." Devin tilted her chin up with his hand. "I'm becoming attached to your face, your lovely eyes, and your beautiful smile."

"And I love you, Devin Elliott. You're not going to be the one that got away again. You're stuck with me for better or for worse."

"Well, I'd say we're already at worse, so I can only look forward to better." Devin smiled at her and wrapped her in a warm hug.

"HI CAROL. WE PICKED A PERFECT SPOT, and the weather is great."
Ben introduced her to his camera man. "When I told Ed about my
equipment, he couldn't resist. The foreign correspondents get the best
equipment. You could only dream of it, right Ed?"

There was a mumbled response as they organized the set-up.

"Here are my thoughts." Ben handed a well-padded aluminum case
to Ed. "I want to set this up so we can get a 30-second, a 60-second,
and three-minute clip. The long one will be for YouTube. So just work
with me as I do the interview. I'm hoping we can get this in one take
but, if you aren't sure what to say just put your head down and we'll
turn the camera off. You got that?"

"You're the boss on this, Ben. Whatever you want. Let's do it."
Carol had applied extra make-up at Ben's suggestion. "Are you sure I'm
not wearing too much make-up?

"The light in late November is not the best at any time of day.
Trust me, a little extra color will work to make you look fresh, vital,
and above these nasty allegations." Ben held a light meter to her face.
"What do you think, Ed?"

"The camera will love her. I'm all set here."

Ben smiled at Carol. "He's one of the best camera men I know. All
right then, let's do it." Ben combed his fingers through his hair and
snapped his collar straight. "In three, two, one…

"I'm here with Carol Brock, one of Boston's top real estate agents.
Less than a year ago she faced a major scandal after her ex-boyfriend
conned her. Now in prison for ten years, Michel Demercado stole her
client lists and conned his way into their properties to steal art and
collectibles. Now Ms. Brock stands accused of an indiscretion that,
if proven, will cost her the real estate license she needs to earn her
livelihood. She is accused of colluding with a potential buyer to fix the
offer to purchase price for a property. That's a major ethics breach."
The cameraman changed his angle slightly to put the focus on Carol,
who stood tall next to Ben and looked directly at the camera.

"Ms. Brock. What do you say to these allegations?"

"They are completely untrue. For over twenty years, I have followed the ethics guidelines of my profession. My clients have rewarded me with their business, their trust, and many, many referrals."

"Then what happened this time? These are very serious allegations." Ben kept his face solemn.

"I really don't know. I showed a property during an open house last weekend to four potential buyers. One came forward with an unconditional offer. I worked up the offer with him that evening and presented it to the seller the next morning. She later cut it up in tiny pieces, put them in an envelope and tracked me down at my home. She had my daughter deliver it to me. Oh, and she phoned me the night before and threatened me if I, quote, aided and abetted the man who made the offer."

"Forgive me for saying this Ms. Brock, but this seems pretty melodramatic wouldn't you say?"

"What she said to me on the phone was not melodramatic. It was clearly very threatening."

"You've talked to the police I take it?"

"I have. A judge has granted a six-month restraining order against Allison Wendover. If she comes within one hundred feet of me or any member of my family, she could land in jail."

"Do you have any idea why Ms. Wendover has targeted you?"

"She was once the girlfriend of the man who put in the offer. They broke up six years ago."

"Did you know him before he viewed the property?" Ben looked her straight in the eyes.

"I had met him for the first time less than three days earlier. He backed in beside my car in a parking lot and ripped off my driver's side mirror."

"And that was your first meeting?"

"I'd never set eyes on him before."

"You're sure of that."

"Quite sure."

"Ms. Brock, you have been put on an indefinite leave of absence by your company. Why is that?"

"I was told by the regional vice-president that the optics of this current case are not good for the company's reputation."

"But you say you have done nothing wrong. Were you given any other reason?" Ben was getting ready to move in for the kill.

"I've always been led to believe that a person is innocent until proven guilty. I have been threatened and harassed, and that person is still considered innocent. Yet I have lost my job and income and livelihood and I am innocent. I'm being treated like a criminal and I have done nothing wrong." Carol's emotions flooded in as she spoke.

"Do you feel you've been treated fairly by your employer?"

"Not at all. After twenty solid years of loyal and ethical service, I feel I've been kicked to the curb for no good reason."

"Thank you, Ms. Brock." Ben turned back to look straight into the camera. "This is Ben Powell."

"Okay. What do you think, Ed?"

"It's good. With a bit of minor editing we'll have it out for tonight's newscasts."

"Carol, leave it with me now. We'll go into the editing room and pull the pieces together. I'll have it up on YouTube within a couple of hours. You, Jim, and Ashley can tweet it out and set up your Facebook links. We'll see where it goes from there."

"You're amazing, Ben. Thank you so much. I feel we're turning a corner here." Carol stood on her toes to plant a kiss on his cheek.

Carol was walking back to her car when her phone chirped. She recognized the caller and shook her head almost wearily. "What do you want Myra?"

"Your little campaign on Facebook and Twitter doesn't change the fact that you are never listing with this company again. But if you don't stop, I'll make sure you never work in real estate again in this state."

"Myra, get a life." Carol shut her phone and rolled her eyes. *I need to figure out how to block her damn calls. Between her and Allison, they make quite a pair.*

"How did it go?" Devin was waiting at the door to the mud room as she pulled up beside the house.

"Ben is such a pro. He had his questions ready. We were done in under fifteen minutes."

"Wow. I thought you'd be at it all morning."

"Nope. I actually had time to go back to my condo, clean up the fridge and get some fresh clothes. Do you mind helping me empty the trunk?" Carol stretched to loosen up after the drive.

"Are you moving in, madam?"

"I thought you invited me to."

"Good thing I have a spare closet or two." Devin reached into the trunk and heaved out two large suitcases. "You going on a long trip?"

"I hope not. What I'm really hoping is to not have to go to Boston for at least a week." Carol pulled a small box out of her back seat that held all that was left from her fridge in town. "I need to get on my laptop. Ben said he'd e-mail the short clips and send me the link to the YouTube interview. I can hardly wait."

"Me, too. You go get set up. I'll take care of this stuff."

"Thanks." Carol set the box on the verandah and retrieved her tote and laptop.

They had barely put anything away when Carol's phone rang. "Carol Brock here. Ben, I didn't recognize the number. What's up?" She nodded to Devin when he brought a bottle of wine out of the fridge.

"Already? Okay, sure. We'll put it on right now. Thanks a million, and give my love to Jen." She hung up and strode quickly into the solarium and turned on the television. "Ben said they're running his story after the commercial break. Come quick, Devin."

Devin grabbed two glasses and the bottle and followed Carol into the softly lit room. Outside, the lighting around the stable and paddock cast a warm glow. He set the glasses down and poured a glass for each of them as the anchor's face appeared. He handed a glass to Carol. They both sat down.

"All of Boston is buzzing with the latest scandal to hit real estate agent Carol Brock. As many will remember, Ms. Brock was conned a year ago by her boyfriend, who went on to steal over a million dollars worth of fine art and ceramics from her real estate clients. By the time Michael Demercado was arrested, most of the stolen property was retrieved but Ms. Brock's career was in shreds. Fast forward and now Ms. Brock is accused of colluding with a potential buyer to fix the price for a sale. But has she done anything wrong? Pulitzer prize-winning journalist Ben Powell interviewed Ms. Brock today."

Carol and Devin sat mesmerized as Ben's interview was played. Carol reached over to clasp Devin's hand as she watched herself on television. "He was right about the extra makeup."

"This is really good, Carol. You come across as honest and trustworthy and definitely the victim." Devin squeezed her hand.

"No wonder he won a Pulitzer. I had no idea it would come across so well." Carol squeezed back. "Whoa. What's this? They're interviewing Ben!"

They both sat in rapt attention as the anchor interviewed Ben remotely. "Why did you get involved in this, Ben?"

"As a journalist, I always ask myself about the motivations of people. I have explored this case closely and cannot figure out the motivations of Myra Stewart other than professional jealousy. As for Allison Wendover, that is a matter for the police and courts now."

"What attracted you to this story and Carol Brock's plight?"

"I have known Carol Brock for over a year. She lives by her values and ethics every day. There is absolutely no way she would compromise her career, her values or her ethics to do what she is accused of."

"How can you be so sure?"

"We've had many discussions about values and ethics. I'd bet my Pulitzer that she's the real deal." Ben sat back.

"That's a very tall claim."

"Which I don't take the least bit lightly." Ben looked every inch the senior journalist

"Thank you, Ben. There you have it, folks. Ben Powell is a

household name for millions of Americans. I've known him for almost thirty years. If Ben believes Carol Brock is innocent, the least we can do is give her the benefit of the doubt. That's all the news there is. Good night folks."

Carol's eyes were swimming with tears as the newscast ended. When her phone chirped, she had to blink several times before she could see the screen. "Jim, hi dear. What's up?"

She looked at Devin, crooked up her eyebrows and then walked to her laptop. "Just a second, let me call up my Facebook page. Oh, my God. Devin, come and see this!" She tilted the screen a bit so they could both see the messages. Jim had already posted the link to YouTube and the number of likes and comments already numbered in the hundreds.

"Now I know why Myra called me. I hadn't had time to check. I can only imagine what's happening on Twitter." She checked and started to laugh. "This is amazing. Talk about the power of social media. And it's all so positive. There are even job offers and a bunch of media interview requests. I'd better take care of this. Love you, Jim."

"Let's see the YouTube video. Whatever Ben did, it's getting a lot of reaction. He must have sent the link to every media outlet in Boston." Carol continued smiling as she clicked on the link.

"I'm going to pull out something for us to eat. There's some leftover quiche we can warm up." Devin felt relieved to see Carol feeling so upbeat. *She has gone through such a wringer the past few days and it's been because of me,* he thought as he set things in motion for their supper. "Let's see that video."

"Ben said it would be about three minutes. Here it is." They watched as the Boston skyline appeared. The title '*What happened to innocent until proven guilty? Carol Brock's story*' materialized onto the screen. And then Ben started his intro segment.

When it was finished, they looked at each other and grinned. Devin stood up first and then Carol. They hugged and danced around the kitchen table like a couple of children on Christmas morning.

"He did it. That was so amazing." Carol's eyes were sparkling. "No wonder Myra is so upset. And there is nothing she can do. There is no slander in anything either he or I said. Whatever Scott charges me, it's worth every penny."

Chapter Sixteen

THE NEXT MORNING they ate a leisurely breakfast before heading back to Boston.

"Guzzo called while you were in the shower. He read the diaries and he's convinced Allison was behind the so-called accident." Devin pulled out from the laneway onto the county road. "There was never a case file opened when Allison's husband died, so he's starting from scratch. He's going to talk to the officers who were at the scene."

Carol looked out at the rolling pastures as they passed a large tractor with a trailer of hay behind it. Being able to drive through such beautiful countryside helped her get a calm focus. "It's like Allison is a ticking time bomb. On one level she functions well, but when someone gets on her bad side, watch out."

"Her ex was the first, and I was the second. Wonder if there were others?" Devin said and then fell quiet.

The traffic was getting noticeably heavier when Carol's phone chirped.

"Hi Ben. Yes, we're just outside Boston now. I have three interviews lined up plus a live interview for an afternoon drive home show. Your story has really attracted attention." She smiled as she listened and then her eyes widened. "Are you serious? What time? I wish I could be there, but I'm doing an interview a half hour later. Darn."

Carol said goodbye and closed the phone. "There's been a new development. The senior vice-president of the company is holding a news conference at eleven this morning. I'll be very interested to hear what he has to say about all this."

"I was thinking..." Devin was in heavy traffic now. "How about we stay overnight at my condo? The media on this is going to be heavy for at least another day. It would save us the drive and you'd be more available."

"It's a good idea, but we'll have to swing by my place for a change of clothes."

"You mean you have some left? I thought you brought it all to the farm yesterday."

Carol laughed. "That was only part of one closet. I have outfits for every possible occasion. And shoes to go with them. I may need to take over one of your bedrooms at the farm and turn it into a ladies dressing room."

"Didn't you say something about simple and informal being good?" Devin glanced over at her.

"I did. And I am going to simplify my life. I'm sure I can cull about half my wardrobe and give a lot to the Goodwill. In fact, if we stay at my place instead of yours tonight, you can help me decide what to keep and what to give away. We could start with my lingerie collection if you like."

"Oh, you don't have to give any of that away." Devin put a pleading look on his face. "I rather enjoy helping you out of them."

"You sure?" Carol grinned wickedly. "Simple and informal. I'm sure I don't need a dozen bras in so many different styles and colors."

Devin groaned. "Let's sort some stuff to give away, but the lingerie is off limits."

"If you insist." Carol smiled smugly as Devin pulled up to where she was doing her first interview. "I'll meet you at my condo around four, and we can think of what to do for dinner then. We could always order in and watch the news."

"Sounds good. I'm sure there'll be lots to see online too."

"I especially don't want to miss any coverage of that news conference. Should be interesting." She leaned over to give him a warm, seductive kiss before getting out of the truck.

CAROL CABBED HER WAY FROM INTERVIEW TO INTERVIEW, finally

making it back to her condo late in the afternoon. Opening her door, she stepped in and sat down to take her boots off. She hadn't even taken her coat off when her phone chirped.

"Hi, Devin. Where are you?" She started undoing her coat and abruptly stopped. "Oh no. A fire? When did it happen?" She couldn't help it. Her eyes started to tear up. "Are the horses all right?"

They quickly agreed to head back to the farm. Carol knew Devin needed to see for himself that everyone was all right. "I'll be downstairs waiting for you in five minutes."

Watching Devin speed down the street minutes later Carol knew they were in for a tense drive. It didn't help that a mix of rain and snow was coming down and the temperature might dip below freezing before they reached the farm. Getting into the warm truck cab, she stowed her tote behind her seat and looked at Devin. She saw the worry etched in his face and leaned over to kiss him.

"Let's get you home and keep the family together. These are your babies." Carol watched tears fill Devin's eyes.

"They are my babies. You're the first person who's ever said that, but that's what they are to me."

"You think Allison is involved?"

"She's the only one I can think of, but how would she know where to find us?" Devin was grim as they drove. "If my horses have been harmed in any way she will pay."

"Devin. I'm so sorry." They rode on in silence.

DESPITE THE POOR DRIVING CONDITIONS, Devin navigated the roads back to the farm in record time. He pulled up by the paddock and jumped out of the truck, with Carol right behind him. The three horses were huddled as far away as they could get from the smoldering ruins of the stable.

"How did it start?" Devin questioned Gregory closely. "Where were the horses?"

Gregory was a man of few words. Carol could see he was uncomfortable.

"I had just gone back to the house for lunch. I left the horses out after mucking their stalls. I had just put fresh hay down. Figured it would be good to let the place air out before bringing them back in." He leaned against the fence with his head down. "I heard a muffled boom. At first, I figured a semi had blown a tire out on the road. But then I smelled smoke and came back running."

Devin put a hand on Gregory's shoulder. "Did you see anyone hanging around?"

"Matter of fact I did." Gregory straightened up. "When I left to pick up a load of hay from the McAllister farm this morning, I saw a car at the side of the road near the end of the laneway. A woman was taking pictures. I figured she was a tourist."

"How long were you gone?"

"About two hours. McAllister helped load the hay, and then I gave him a hand with a couple of things."

"No sign of the lady and the car when you got back?"

"Nope. The road was empty."

They all turned at the sound of a vehicle coming up the lane. Devin smiled. "You called the vet?"

"Figured we should get them checked over. Make sure they didn't inhale too much smoke."

"Thanks Gregory." Devin walked towards the truck. "Thanks for coming out Val. Appreciate it." A chunky blonde woman emerged from a truck that had seen better days.

"Carol, I'd like you to meet Val McCormick, the local large animal vet. Val, this is my friend Carol Brock."

Valerie stuck out her weathered hand to shake Carol's. "You his girlfriend?"

Carol smiled. "Yes, I am."

"Took you long enough, Devin. The vet looked Carol over like any other farm animal and grinned. "Definitely worth waiting for in the looks department. She got brains too?"

Carol burst out laughing. "Yes, she does. Enough brains to go into partnership with Flynn next year."

"That'll do. He's a bright fellow for sure. He's talked me into buying more things than I'll ever need." Val took Carol's arm and started them walking towards the paddock. "When Gregory called and told me what happened, all I could think of was Sabrina. Don't tell Aero, but she's my favorite."

"Mine, too. I think Pablo's figured it out though."

Devin and Gregory looked at each other. "Did you see what I just saw?"

Gregory gave a wondering smile. "Val isn't one to cozy up to someone that fast. She's usually much more reserved."

"Can you imagine what this is going to mean to Flynn's sales if she can rope in a down and dirty country woman that fast?" Devin grinned. "I'm impressed."

"Me, too." Gregory and Devin watched Val check over each horse and talk to them quietly. Carol took Pablo by the halter and petted his head soothingly. As Devin and Gregory joined them, the three horses remained calm despite the acrid smell of burned wood and leather.

"Do you have any idea who would do this?"

"I do. What I don't know is how she found my farm and how she set the fire. She's never been here and I've never told her where it is."

"Have you thought of a GPS tracking device? Check your truck. Tom and I put one on mine. It's come in handy a couple of times when I had engine trouble." She walked over to her truck, opened the door, reached in under the dash board and pulled out a palm-sized device with a short antenna. "This is the transmitter. A lot of trucking and rental companies are using them now to track their fleets."

"It's how the police caught Michel, too." Carol flinched at the memory. "He didn't realize the car he'd rented in Detroit was equipped with one. He led them straight to every fence he knew."

Val looked at Carol more closely. "Now I recognize your face. You're that real estate agent from Boston who got fleeced by a sleazy con artist."

"The one and the same." Carol waited for her reaction.

"You saved a lot of women a whole pack of trouble when you shut his operation down." Val smiled warmly at her. "Seems to me you did us all a favor."

"Never thought of it that way." Carol smiled. "Thanks, Val. That was such a nice thing to say."

"And I'm not known for being nice, am I, Devin?" She cackled a broken laugh, turned and headed back towards her truck.

"I can't win, no matter what I say, so I won't say a thing." Devin patted Aero's head as the horse whinnied.

"I think Aero is telling you you're a wise man." Val chuckled as Flynn drove up the lane.

Val got in her truck and looked at Carol and Devin. "There's a new ultra-thin model that can be hidden under carpets or in door panels. It has a two-month battery life. We thought about it getting but it was expensive for what we need." She started up the truck.

"I think you're on to something with the GPS. We'll check both vehicles after we get some of this mess cleaned up. Thanks, Val." Devin slapped the hood of the truck as she drove off.

"I closed up early when Gregory called." Flynn jumped out of his car and walked briskly over to Gregory. "You all right, my sweet man?"

They hugged without reservation. Flynn looked at all of them.

"Who did this? It was no accident from what Gregory said."

"We're pretty sure it was Allison. Gregory saw a woman hanging around near the end of the driveway taking photos this morning. She probably put a GPS tracking device in the truck somewhere." Carol walked with him towards Devin's truck.

"Now that you mention it, it's probably the only way she could figure out how to find us short of hiring someone." Flynn had already reached Devin's truck and was checking under the dashboard.

"Let's check under the hood, too." As Devin and Flynn continued searching the truck, Carol went into the solarium and powered up her laptop. After a few minutes of online research, she ran outside. "If you find one don't remove it. Some of them send a warning if you remove it."

"Just in time, Carol. There it is." Flynn had pulled up the cargo liner in the truck box. "I can get you the make and model without moving it."

Carol took down the information and went back to her computer, with Devin, Flynn and Gregory right behind her.

Devin peered over Carol's shoulder. "Very sophisticated. This is designed specifically for weak signal areas. If you move it, she'll know right away. It's transmitting to her smart phone. She knows exactly where we are right now."

"We'd better check my car, too, then. It may be the way she found out where I live." Carol looked up from the keyboard. "How about I make a pot of coffee while we figure out our next moves?"

Flynn waved to her as he moved towards the counter. "I'll make the coffee while you do your research. The more we can tell the police, the better. As soon as things cool off outside we should try to find out how she started the fire."

"One of the volunteer firefighters told me the most intense heat was near the main door to the paddock. Said that means there was an accelerant used. They were pretty certain it was gasoline." Gregory shared his new information grimly. "There must have been a timer too if she set it up while I was away and before I put the horses into the paddock. Wanted to give herself time to get away."

"She meant to kill the horses and possibly Gregory with them." Devin spoke the chilling words quietly. They looked at each other in horror as Devin and Carol's phone chirped almost in unison.

"Hi, Ben. What's up?" Carol massaged her forehead as she paced with her phone. She listened and nodded. "Thanks, we'll be sure to watch for it. Listen Ben, we've located a sophisticated GPS transmitter in Devin's truck. Allison's been here to the farm. She set fire to the stable.

"No, the horses were outside when the fire started, but that didn't appear to be part of the plan. She set the fire to start near the main doors to the paddock. If Gregory hadn't put the horses out so he could muck the stalls they all could have been trapped."

Devin had walked out of the solarium with his phone. "Thanks for calling, Scott. We can use a bit of good news right now."

"Scott got a call from Colin at the real estate office. That press conference was to announce that Myra has been put on a leave of absence without pay pending an internal investigation."

"That's what Ben was calling about too. Apparently the entire news conference is on YouTube and may be a top story at six. He also mentioned that after his story yesterday, the television station got three calls from people who have a history with Allison. They referred the callers to the police." Carol gratefully accepted a mug of fresh steaming coffee from Flynn.

Flynn put out some fresh cookies from the town bakery. "I'm going out to check over Carol's car. I bet there's one on hers, too. I'll wear gloves so I don't mess up any fingerprints."

"Thanks for everything, Flynn." Carol took a sip of the fragrant brew and put in the call. "Hi Len. It's Carol."

She brought him up to date about the fire and the GPS and gave him the make and model. She was just about to hang up when Flynn ran in brandishing a small transmitter. "Just a second. There was a GPS tracker on my car too." She looked up at Flynn. "Where did you find it?"

"It was in the pocket behind the passenger seat."

Carol relayed the product information. "I can send you photos of the one in Devin's truck. According to the web site, it's the same kind that the police use for surveillance."

Carol listened for another minute before ending the call.

Devin grinned. "You have a thing about taking pictures and sending them to the police, don't you?"

"Hey. Look where it got me with you." Carol smiled warmly and reached for a cookie. "Let's go take some pictures, Flynn."

"I'm with you, sweetie. The sooner we can get Ms. Wendover away from here, the better we'll all feel."

IT WAS ALMOST DINNER TIME WHEN GUZZO CALLED BACK. Carol spoke with him as Devin looked on questioningly. When she ended the call she looked thoughtful.

"Guzzo learned that there's only two distributors in Boston for the

GPS tracker we found in your truck. The person who sold it to Allison remembers the transaction very well. He was trying to sell her a simpler one, like the one Flynn found in my car. But, she insisted she needed the kind we found under the liner. It's twice the price plus the tracking package. He found it strange she insisted on that model. He had never sold one for other than professional surveillance."

"What's the plan now?"

"Guzzo wants you to bring the truck by tomorrow. A technician will dust the truck and GPS for prints. The serial number is already proof that Allison bought it. He also told me that the former principal of Allison's high school contacted the police after Ben's story. Apparently Allison had a history of bullying other girls." Carol went over and opened the fridge door. "What do we want for dinner?"

"How about I make us a frittata? Keep it simple and use up a few vegetables." Devin came up behind her as she started handing out things from the fridge.

"While you do that, I'm going to do some yoga for awhile. For some reason, I'm feeling a bit stressed."

"We need to set up a space to work out and maybe get an elliptical. I usually work out in town but, if we're going to spend most of our time here, we should organize." Devin put four eggs in a bowl next to a chopping block. "I foresee see a sunny addition to the end of the solarium."

"I'll see you in fifteen or twenty minutes or when it starts to smell really good." Carol went upstairs to change.

As she sorted through some clothes to find a workout suit, she realized, *I have two enemies. I doubt I'll ever cross paths with Myra again. Scott can handle the lawsuit. And it's going to cost the agency big time before I'm finished with them. But Alison isn't done yet. She's going over the edge, I can feel it.*

Chapter Seventeen

"I can stay here for the day. Gregory will be around." Carol toweled her wet hair briskly. "I have a feeling Allison is done with us here, unless she's planning to burn down the house next."

Devin looked at her sharply. "Don't even joke. I'm still trying to wrap my mind around that stable fire."

"I'm sorry. That was flippant." She hung the towel on a rack. "It's hard to believe any human would harm an animal in that way. I can't let myself imagine it, but I know it happens."

"Call me overly protective, but I would just feel a lot better if we stayed together or at least in close proximity."

"You're right. I wouldn't want you almost two hours away if anything happened to either of us. But I reserve the right to return to my former independence once the Allison situation is resolved."

"And it will always be your right. It's why I fell in love with you. Don't you dare change that." Devin smiled appreciatively as he watched her brush out her hair. "And promise me you'll never cut your hair short. It's so lovely just the way it is."

"I can promise you this. I will never cut it short like Allison's."

"Thank you for that. When I look back now, I can't understand what made me go out with her. Everything about her was sharp." Devin walked up behind Carol as she looked in the mirror on top of the antique dresser. He put his hands on her shoulder and leaned in to smell her damp hair. "You, on the other hand, are like Sabrina. Beautifully defined features, large expressive eyes, lovely long legs and a luxurious mane of hair."

"I never thought I would enjoy being compared to a horse." Carol

smiled and turned in his arms. "What time do we have to leave?"
"Later than originally planned."

"AFTER I DROP YOU OFF AT YOUR CONDO, I'll bring the truck to the
police station. What are your plans?"
"I left a message for Jennifer to see if she's free for lunch. And I
have a standing weekly Skype call with Jim between his classes this
afternoon. It's almost like we're at home together."
As they drew up in front of her condo, Devin looked at her
pensively. "Have you considered selling your condo and making our
arrangement more permanent? There will always be a place for Ashley
and Jim to call home—at the farm and here in town."
Carol looked into the hazel eyes that had glowed with passion only
hours before. "I'm thinking about it. I know my heart is with you."
"I'm ready whenever you are. I won't rush you. But, I truly want
my home to be your only real home."
"It already is." Carol leaned her head back on the headrest and then
turned her head to face him with an intimate smile on her face. "Guess
I'd better find me a real estate agent."

"THERE ARE SEVERAL CLEAR PRINTS ON THE GPS TRACKING DEVICE,
SIR." The police technician pointed with a gloved finger. "She may have
wiped off the top but she missed enough spots that I'm sure we'll get a
clear match. I found more on the truck box liner."
"She was fingerprinted here not two weeks ago. How long before
you can run them?" Detective Guzzo stood with Devin as the tech guy
carefully lowered the device back into place.
"I should have results in the next twenty to thirty minutes, sir. I
can call you."
"We'll go for a coffee and meet up with you later. I may have some
other questions for you."
Guzzo led Devin to his office after pouring them both mugs of hot
coffee. "I live on this stuff. Can't be good for me, but I'm hooked. That

and chocolate. I'm a caffeine addict."

"How many hours a week do you put in? You're never far from the end of a phone." Devin looked around the small overcrowded office.

"Enough hours that I've gone through three wives and two girlfriends in twenty years and each one faster than the one before. Guess I'm married to my work."

"I was engaged years ago. She was murdered. The case was never solved. " Devin shook his head sadly and sipped the strong coffee. "Since then, I always thought my work and my farm were enough. Now I know differently."

"You and Carol Brock are an item?"

"Yes."

Guzzo nodded. "She is one bright and independent lady. She impressed us all during the Demercado case. Other victims would have come undone on the witness stand the way the defense was badgering her. She didn't give an inch. How is she holding up over this Wendover woman?"

"All in all she's doing extremely well. Like you said, she doesn't give an inch."

"I heard that boss that caused her grief has been shunted aside. Nice piece by Ben Powell."

"Ben certainly put in a prize-winning performance. Carol's plight even got picked up by CNN." Devin finished his coffee. He sensed the guy talk phase was ending.

"We had a call from one of Allison's neighbors." Guzzo put his mug down to pull out his notebook. "She claims Allison called her at least six or seven times about her dog barking too early in the morning. She explained that it couldn't be her dog. The woman says she always took her dog out for a walk each morning around seven and then it stayed inside all morning. Numerous other people walk their dogs around the same time." He flipped the page over. "She said Allison refused to accept her word that it wasn't her dog that was the problem. She told her if she didn't get the dog to stop barking, she'd do something about it."

Guzzo looked at Devin. "Three days later the dog died after

eating meat laced with rat poison that someone had tossed in the neighbor's yard."

CAROL'S PHONE CHIRPED AS SHE WAS SORTING PILES OF CLOTHES. She looked at the display and smiled. "Jennifer! Hope you're free for lunch today. Excellent. Where shall we go? My treat."

They agreed to meet before noon at the bistro where Devin had first taken Carol. They were seated immediately. "I still haven't had their burger platter. It looks so good."

Looking over their menus, they speculated on what to order. Tall glasses of iced tea arrived as they placed their orders. Carol looked around. Although very trendy-looking, the restaurant had a warm and inviting air with its chocolate brown décor and the scattered tables with leather tube chairs grouped around them.

"I've decided to sell the condo and move in permanently with Devin."

"Oh my, that was fast. You sure about this?"

"I don't think I've ever been so sure of anything, Jennifer. I feel like I've known him for years, instead of weeks. I care for him deeply. There is a place in my heart that has finally opened again, and it's because of Devin and the kind of man he is.

"For one thing, he's such an animal lover. I've seen him with the horses and Pasha, Clara's cat. The animals seem to know they're safe around him. I feel the same way." Carol sipped at her ice tea.

"He told me about his fiancée. He still finds it hard to believe she was so brutally murdered. Said he had nightmares for months."

"He does come across as a very caring and thoughtful man." Jennifer smiled. "Seems to me you've finally found your soul mate."

"And he has horses, which I love." Carol grinned. "Bonus!"

They stopped talking briefly as their food arrived.

"He's certainly stood with you all the way on this Allison business." Jennifer plucked a French fry from Carol's plate. "Mmm. Those fries are excellent. But I'll be good and eat my salad."

"Help yourself. There's too many for me." Carol took a bite of her hamburger. "Memories of backyard barbeques at your place. I knew this would be good."

"If we get a good day over the winter, we can send Ben out. He loves barbequing, even when it's quite cool. Tell me more about your plans with Devin."

"He's talking about renovating the Wendover house and using that as his Boston base. He'd sell his condo after the renovations are completed."

"And what will you do now that you're leaving the Boston real estate scene?" Jennifer appropriated another fry.

"That's right. We haven't spoken for a couple of days!" Carol sipped her iced tea. "Devin and I had lunch with Flynn. Somehow the talk got around to what I plan to do with myself. Next thing I knew, Flynn was talking me into coming in as his partner in the store."

"What do you know about running a bookstore and gift shop?"

"That's what I said. But I know all the techniques of selling. I love to shop, as you well know. And I'd have a lot more time for myself. No night hours. Every other weekend off."

Jennifer looked at her friend. "This sounds like a very sane life you're describing."

"I think sane is the word. Flynn warned me it gets pretty wild over the summer with all the tourist buses coming through. But he said, all in all it's manageable and we set our own sales goals. I know all about that."

"So when do you start?" Jennifer smiled.

"Late January, in time for the Valentine's Day shoppers. You know, I just had a great idea. You and Ben are leaving after New Year's for your southern sailing adventure. Would you like to do some buying for the store?"

"You mean spend other people's money? It's very tempting."

"I'm sure I just saw a little shopping devil appear on your shoulder with a big smile on her face." Carol chuckled and signaled for the check. "This just became a business expense."

"Ben told me there are all kinds of rules about bringing goods back to the States for re-sale. I'd want to check this out further before committing."

"Oh yes. We definitely want to do everything by the rules. No question. But are you interested in theory?"

"You bet I am." Jennifer insisted on covering the tip. "I ate half your fries."

As they left the now bustling bistro, Jennifer offered to drive Carol back to her condo. The two chatted happily as they crossed town in the ever-present snarl of traffic. As they turned onto her street, Carol noticed the solitary figure standing across from her building and scrunched down in the seat.

"Jennifer, keep going to the back entrance. Allison Wendover is standing across from the front entrance. I can't get out here."

Jennifer looked straight ahead and drove around to the back of the building into a visitor's spot. "I'm coming in with you, and we're calling Guzzo."

"I'm already sending in the call." The two friends walked briskly to the back entrance where Carol keyed them in. "Len, it's Carol Brock. Allison Wendover is in front of my building right now. Is there anything you can do?"

"No, she hasn't come within the hundred foot radius. She didn't see me. We're going in through the back entrance." Carol had a death grip on her phone as they walked to the elevator. "Devin is with you? May I speak to him please?"

"Devin. We need to go to Plan B. Obviously, Allison knew you had come here this morning. That tracking device was still sending her your location. Can you disable the thing and pick me up at Jennifer's in half an hour? I know it will alert Allison, but we can't let her know about Jennifer and Ben and who knows what she'll do if you drive up in the truck. I don't want her to know about the back entrance although she's probably cased the entire property."

Carol listened as they rode up the elevator. "This has got to stop. Allison is not stupid. She's pushing the limits without actually breaking the law. I understand Guzzo's hands are tied until the arson investigation unequivocally points to her, but there has to be something we can do."

Carol took a deep breath. "I'll meet you at Jennifer's in half an hour. Just promise me you will disable that damn tracking device before you leave the police station. Thank you," she added, as she closed the phone.

DEVIN HANDED GUZZO BACK HIS PHONE. "Now, what?"

"Now, we find out whose fingerprints were on that tracking device. The tech guy emailed me to come down. Let's go."

"I have to pick Carol up in half an hour."

"This won't take long."

A couple of minutes later they were looking at three screens displaying a series of fingerprints. Devin stared at them without comprehension as the tech guy pointed to the first set.

"These are Allison Wendover's police prints from when she was picked up after the break-in at her late mother's home in Dorchester." He pointed to the next display. "These are the prints I lifted off the tracking device. We have a definite match. He then pointed to a third set of prints. "These are the prints we found at the unsolved murder scene of a woman who was killed about eight years ago. They are a match for Allison Wendover."

Devin recognized the case number and paled. He leaned heavily against a wall. "Guzzo, that was my fiancée. She murdered my fiancée and then put the moves on me. And now she's after Carol."

"Where's the washroom. I think I'm going to be sick." Devin staggered from the room as Guzzo guided him.

Guzzo came back to the technician's desk. "Why weren't her prints run against cold cases when she was arrested last week?"

"No one said anything about priors. We're swamped here."

"Okay, sorry. I understand. Make sure those files are on my desk as soon as possible. Guzzo made a couple of calls while he waited for Devin.

Devin walked back slowly. His face pale and drawn, a dazed look on his face. "My God. She had set her sights on me even though she knew I was deeply in love with Marilyn. They were best friends." He shook his head slowly.

"Devin, call Carol." Guzzo snapped him back. "Tell her to get the hell out of there as fast as she can and under no circumstances is she to go anywhere near Wendover."

Devin's hand shook as he put through the call. He pulled the other hand through his hair as the call went straight to message. "Oh God, Carol. I need to speak to you. Now!"

CAROL GATHERED A FEW THINGS TOGETHER that she really wanted to bring to the farm. "I'm not moving out just yet, but I do need to mark my territory a bit at the farm, so to speak."

"There's plenty of room for you to do that. It's a big place."

"Jennifer, when we leave, I'd like you to take the two bags to the car and go out through the back entrance. I'll meet you out front. I want Allison to see that I'm leaving."

"You sure you want to do that?"

"Trust me. I have a strategy. I'm just going to text Jim that our weekly chat won't be happening, and then I'll be ready to go." Carol decided not to tell Jennifer about her plans. Better she not know.

Minutes later, the two friends parted at the ground floor, with Jennifer walking out the back entrance. Carol watched until she was sure she was at the car, and then strode purposefully out the front door of her building with her phone in video mode. Holding the phone facing out, she marched straight toward the dark silhouette standing just back from the sidewalk.

"Hello Allison. We meet again." She stood tall and firm, exuding a confidence she hardly felt. "But this time, you are in violation of a court-ordered restraining order. What are you doing standing in front of my building? What business do you have here other than to harass and try to intimidate me? Answer me that." Carol stopped less than ten feet from Allison, whose eyes had gone black with anger.

"Who the hell do you think you are, bitch, and what the hell do you think you're doing? You have stolen my house. You have slept with the devil. I will see you burn in hell before you get that house or my man."

Carol held the phone in her hand as steadily as she could. From the corner of her eye she saw Jennifer pulling her car out onto the street and counted the seconds until she could run to it.

"He hasn't been your man for six years, dear. You really need to move on with your life. Hope it's a good one." Carol turned on her heel and sprinted to Jennifer's waiting car. "Let's get the hell out of here before she can follow us."

"What were you doing, Carol? Are you trying to inflame her? She's a psychopath. You can't expect her to react rationally on any level."

"I don't expect her to. But I now have proof that can be taken to a judge and used to get a warrant for her arrest. She's broken cover that she is willing to kill, and I have it all on video… live at five." Carol sat back as they left her neighborhood. Every part of her was shaking but she hadn't felt so alive since the day she kicked Gordon out.

Devin was waiting when they got back to Jennifer's. "What took you so long?"

"I gave Allison a chance to do a little public venting before we left. I have it on video."

Devin grabbed her by her shoulders. "What have you done? Guzzo and I just learned that Allison's prints match prints found at the scene of the murder of my fiancée eight years ago. Her throat was cut and her body left in a ditch."

Carol paled. "I just wanted to confront her and get proof that she's stalking me. Guzzo's hands have been tied. She never quite crosses the line. I thought I'd force her over it and get the evidence we need to get her arrested and held."

"If you have forced her over the line, and it sounds like you have, we need the police right now." Devin called Guzzo. "He's on his way. He's already called out the troops to pick her up. They're looking for her now."

Ben called them all into the house where they quickly gathered in the kitchen. "She doesn't know about this place right? The house and phone are in Jennifer's name. Even if she Googles me, she'll never track me here. You're safe here."

"I'm going to call Gregory. He needs to know what's happening. This is escalating." Devin strode towards the living room even as he called up Gregory's mobile.

"Carol, give me your phone. I'll transfer the video to my system and clean up the sound and video quality. No editing of course. I'll make a copy for Guzzo. Won't be long."

"Ben, you're the best." Carol gave him a grateful hug before he went to his office.

"I think we all need a pot of fortifying coffee while we're waiting for Detective Guzzo." Jennifer busied herself. "Any one want anything to eat?"

Carol shook her head. "You know what I ate for lunch, I'm fine."

"Devin? Did you have lunch?"

"No, but I'm really not hungry at the moment. Thanks anyway." Devin paced the kitchen a few times and then went to stand by the patio door overlooking Jennifer's back yard. He watched Charlie snuffling around the base of a large tree near the end of the yard. "Looks like Charlie's treed something."

"Probably the neighbor's cat." Jennifer took out several mugs. "He does it every day at least once a day."

Devin jerked around at the sound of the door bell. "Stay put, Jennifer. I'll get it. Must be Guzzo."

A moment later the burly detective had joined them in the kitchen. "We've got her mug shot on all the squad car displays. A couple of plain clothes are watching her townhouse."

"Coffee, detective?" Jennifer had the pot in her hands.

"Yes, please. Nice to see you again, Ms. Barrett."

"Call me Jennifer. What do you take again?"

"Just black. Thanks."

"What's this I hear about a video?" Guzzo sat down at the table as Jennifer put a mug in front of him and filled it.

Carol cleared her throat. "I confronted her outside my

building. Ben has my phone and is making a copy of the video for you right now."

"That was a very gutsy thing to do Carol. Ill-advised and dangerous but very gutsy. And I don't think any judge will censure you for what you did. You have stopped someone who will likely be considered a serial killer."

"Let's just underline dangerous." Jennifer took her mug of coffee and sat down at the table. "You and I both know it, detective."

"And we both know your friend here." Guzzo glanced over at Carol with a hint of a smile.

Ben came into the room with a laptop under his arm and a USB stick in his hand. "That was quite the scene, Carol. She is one very sick lady."

"Tell me about it. Did you get anything decent? I'm sure I was shaking like a leaf."

"Maybe afterwards but not during. I couldn't have shot it better." Ben held out the stick. "Here, Detective Guzzo. This is for you. We can all see it on my laptop if you like. You okay with that, Carol?"

"I think so. If it bothers me I'll just leave the room." Carol sat quietly at the table as Devin stood behind her. Ben called up the video and hit play.

Carol's strong clear voice suddenly filled the kitchen, now bathed in late afternoon sun. Devin rubbed one shoulder. She gratefully leaned her head against his arm as the vivid encounter was replayed. When Allison ground out her angry retort, she shuddered involuntarily. As Carol's final words rang out, there was a noticeable relaxing of the tension in the brightly-lit room.

Devin broke the silence first. "She's gone over the edge. She's lost all perspective and control."

"I would have to agree with you, Devin. She's not armed that we know of, but she is a definite danger. The APB is to consider her armed and dangerous."

"What now?" Carol had both hands clasped tightly around her mug to try and mask her nervousness. Whether it was the caffeine, seeing the video, or both, she felt a strong urge to run out the door and just keep on running until she dropped.

Devin heard the stressed pitch of her voice, put his mug down, and began massaging the tense muscles in her neck.

Rubbing the stubble on his chin thoughtfully, Guzzo spoke. "Until we have her in custody, neither of you can go to your condos or your farm. She knows where you live. If we're lucky, she'll go back to her townhouse and we'll pick her up tonight. If she goes underground, it will take longer. How much longer, I have no way of knowing."

"You two will stay here tonight, no arguments." Jennifer looked at them both with concern. "You know this is the safest place right now."

"Thanks, Jennifer." Carol looked up at Devin, who nodded.

"Good. That's settled. I'll be on my way then." Guzzo stood up. "Thanks for the great coffee Jennifer. As soon as I hear anything, I'll be in touch."

"Why do I get the feeling this will be a very long night?" Carol collected mugs and brought them to the sink, where Jennifer rinsed them and put them in the dishwasher.

"I just hope they arrest her tonight. I think we'd all sleep better."

"Ben and I are going up to his office for some guy talk. You ladies need us for anything?" Devin handed his mug to Carol and gave her a light kiss on the forehead.

"I think we'll just sit here and have some more girl talk. You go on. We'll figure out dinner later." Jennifer walked to the patio door and let a wriggling Charlie loose in the kitchen.

Carol smiled and sat down as Charlie flung himself at her in joyful welcome. She scratched his ears. "I think Devin and I will want to have a pooch of some kind. Something big and friendly but willing to be a guard dog when needed."

"You love it there, don't you?" Jennifer sat down at the table.

"I do. I think I'm a country girl in my heart of hearts. I've always lived in the city, but some of my fondest memories are from the year I took riding lessons. On those Saturday mornings I was up at five without an alarm just itching to get out to the stables. I begged my parents for a horse, but they didn't want to complicate things."

181

"What do you mean 'complicate?'"

"My father travelled a lot for work. My mother said she had enough on her hands with taking care of the house, teaching school, and raising me. She was right, of course."

"But it was your dream."

"Yes. And it looks like, after forty-three years, that dream is coming true."

"Have you told Ashley and Jim about what's happened since Thanksgiving?" Jennifer glanced up at the clock. It was only four o'clock but the sun had set, and the remaining light was weak. She went around turning on lights.

"I've avoided telling them some of the grittier details. They don't know about the stable fire yet. But it was Jim who helped take Ben's story viral through Facebook and Twitter. It gave him a role to play in all this that he seemed to need. I know Ashley is super busy just now, but she's as aware as I want to let her be."

"That little control thing again?" Jennifer smiled and put her hand over Carol's. "There are times when having control issues is a good thing. This is one of those times."

"I hadn't thought of that, but you're right. I just don't want her to waste time worrying about me." Carol's face relaxed. "When this is all over, I'm sure there will be things we'll laugh about."

She combed both hands through her hair and fluffed it out. "Did I tell you Myra phoned me before she got sacked? She said if I kept up my little campaign, as she called it, she'd make sure I never worked in real estate in Massachusetts again."

"What did you say?"

"I said, 'get a life' and hung up on her." Carol grinned smugly. "I would love to have seen the look on her face."

"That's priceless. Wonder what will happen to her?"

"I really don't care. She never cared anything about her people other than making sure they were holding the career ladder she was climbing."

"Enough about her then. What shall we have for supper? We have lots of fixings for salad—"

Ben marched into the kitchen with Devin right behind him. Suddenly, the room seemed smaller. "Devin and I have agreed to cook dinner for you ladies. We would invite you to get yourselves a glass of wine and go sit in the living room. First though, the chefs need a beer."

"Carol, how about you and I go set up the spare room? I have a spare bathrobe you can borrow, and I'll get out towels."

"Thanks, Jen. I actually wouldn't mind lying down with my laptop for awhile before dinner. A little downtime would be good."

"Let's get you set up then."

A few minutes later, Carol was wearing a fluffy bathroom and was stretched out on the roomy bed with her laptop beside her. She gazed around the room. Its soft yellow walls soothed her, while the thick cotton quilt promised to keep them warm during the coming night. She snuggled down and lay her head back on the pillow. *I'll just rest my eyes for a few minutes and then catch up on emails.*

She was running through dark streets, the sidewalks slick from a cold, driving rain. Whatever was after her was getting closer. She could almost feel its panting, hot breath and hear the rapid footfalls closing in on her. She dared not look behind her. She had to run as fast as possible. It was the only way to get away. It was the only way to save Devin. *I have to outrun this monster or we will both die.* But she couldn't keep running so fast. Her heart was pounding. The air was searing her hot lungs. She stumbled and felt the hot breath pulsing against her neck.

"Carol." Devin was beside her on the bed stroking her forehead. "Carol, you've had a nightmare. It's okay. I'm here. We're all safe."

Carol opened her eyes wide. She was still curled in a tight fetal ball. "It was so real. I couldn't run fast enough to get away. I thought if I could just get away, you'd be safe."

"It looks like you got away then because I'm here, and I'm safe." He lay back, cradled her closely in his arms, and kissed her forehead.

"That's some sexy bathrobe you're wearing, my dear."

"Did I shout?" She snuggled into his arms, appreciating the feel of his strong work-hardened muscles.

"Let's just say Charlie was cowering under the kitchen table when he heard you."

"I can't remember the last time I had a nightmare." She stretched out but still lay against him. "You smell good. What are you two cooking?"

"Cooked and eaten. You were out like a light when I came up to get you for dinner. But we saved you a plate if you're hungry."

"After the race I just ran in that dream I think I could eat something for sure. What time is it?"

"Almost nine o'clock."

"Oh my. Anybody mind if I eat in this bathrobe?"

"I doubt it. C'mon down."

"Any word from Guzzo?" Carol already knew the answer.

"No. Nothing."

Chapter Eighteen

"It's been three days now and still no sign of Allison, not even a sighting despite putting her picture out to the media." Carol sipped her coffee and looked at Devin reading the morning paper. "I don't know about you, but I'm getting cabin fever. I want my life back, and I'm sure Jennifer and Ben would like theirs back too."

Devin put the paper down. "How would you like to come with me to check on a project that's going into its final phase? We could get away from all this for a bit and pretend we're normal people living an ordinary life."

"Normal. Ordinary. Suddenly those seem like two very enticing concepts. I could go for that."

"Let me make some calls, get things set up. When could you be ready to leave?"

"This afternoon too soon?" Carol took her cup to the sink and rinsed it. "My turn in the shower."

"I'll get to work on it right now." Devin folded up the paper and set it back on the table.

"Hi Jennifer. We're on our way to the airport. We're going to Savannah for a few days to check on one of Devin's projects. Hopefully, the police will turn up Allison while we're gone. You know how to reach me. Thanks so much for taking care of us. I'll call you when we get back." Carol ended the message and closed the phone.

"It was good of Ben to offer to put the truck in their garage. There isn't any way for Allison to track it now but I feel better knowing it's off the street and out of sight." Devin looked out the taxi window at the early afternoon traffic congestion.

"What time do we get in?"

"We should be at our hotel in time for a late supper."

"Did you let Gregory and Flynn know?"

"Taken care of."

"It feels so much dryer and warmer than Boston. I haven't been here in years." Carol pulled her little carry-on behind her as they walked into a luxurious waterfront hotel lobby. "And I've never packed this light. I need to do some shopping."

"We both do. Ben and I are the same height and size, and he has excellent taste, but I still prefer my own clothes."

Carol laughed. "I tried on a pair of Jennifer's slacks. They were about four inches too short in the legs. I didn't realize how much taller I am than her."

Checking in at the front desk, Devin was handed a message. "Guzzo called. He needs to talk to us. Let's get up to the room and give him a call."

Their suite overlooked the Savannah River, which now sparkled with myriad lights under the twilight sky. Looking out, Carol saw a riverboat docked across from the hotel. Looking around inside, she appreciated the spaciousness of the suite after sharing one small bedroom with Devin for almost four days. *I'm really used to having my space, although I don't mind sharing space with Devin. But sharing Jennifer's house among the four of us with none of my belongings was starting to wear on me. Normal. I would love to feel normal again.* She looked over and smiled as Devin emerged from the bathroom.

"Detective Guzzo—Len. Devin here. We just got in. Any news?" Devin looked over at Carol and nodded slightly. "It's a start. At least you know she's still in Boston somewhere. We'll be here for two or three nights. Hopefully, you'll be able to arrest her before we get back." He closed the phone and set it for silent.

"She went to an ATM machine. She kept her face down but the security camera got a full body shot… same height and build. She appeared to leave on foot. Her bank called it in when the transaction cleared her account."

"But where could she possibly hide for this long and not be recognized?"

"Guzzo told me they're going to start canvassing the homeless shelters and drop-in shelters within walking distance of the ATM. I can't imagine Allison surviving on the streets, but then I couldn't imagine her killing someone, either."

"What would you like to do this evening?" Carol wanted to get away from all the Allison talk.

"How would you like to dine al fresco, madam?"

"It's the end of November."

"It's Savannah. There's a good restaurant down the street that has gas heaters and plastic curtains around their patio. On a nice night like this, it'll be open for sure."

"Sounds wonderful after being cooped up indoors for the past three days."

"Let me call down for reservations. Seven o'clock good?"

"Perfect."

"WHAT DO YOU THINK?" Devin held out a chair for her as they were ushered to a candlelit table.

"It's lovely and very warm. This is such a treat." The old Victorian building's interior featured tables with linen cloths and chandeliers hanging from the ceilings. She couldn't imagine it as a private residence back in its day. The outdoor patio was less formal but still elegant.

"I think we both deserve it. By the way, Gregory called while you were in the shower. The insurance adjuster came out today and wrote off the entire structure and contents. We're clear to go ahead and have a new stable built."

"What about all the tack and saddles?" Carol picked up her menu. "Aero's saddle must have cost a small fortune."

"Everything was inventoried with the date of purchase and amount. I'm very particular about keeping good records. Never thought I'd need them for this, though." Devin eyed his menu. "Mussels sound good. How about you?"

"Sounds great. Add a salad, and it's a perfect supper." Carol smiled and felt herself relax. "It was a good idea to get away."

"How about we make some plans for Christmas? Get our minds off our problems?" They held hands across the small table.

"That reminds me. I need to get in touch with Ashley and Jim to let them know about selling the condo."

"Do you think they'll mind about us moving in together so quickly?"

"No, I think they'll both be fine with it. Ashley was trying to match make the day she met you." Carol smiled as their waitress brought glasses and a bottle of Pinot Grigio.

"Jim and I have connected by email. He sends me the odd engineer joke. I send him architect jokes. He's a bright young man. They're both bright." Devin and Carol raised their glasses to each other in a silent toast. "I'm guessing they got their brains from their mother."

"Why, thank you. I'll give my ex some credit for brains, but not for common sense. They definitely got that from me."

Devin's phone vibrated in his pocket. "I'd better get this."

"Elliot here. Hi, Len, we're just having dinner." He listened quietly. "That's very encouraging for sure. Thanks for calling." He turned the phone off.

"Someone recognized Allison's mug shot at two of the shelters. It seems she's going to different shelters and not staying for more than one night at a time. She's keeping to herself. No one remembered her talking to anyone."

"She needs help and she won't ever get it on the street." Carol looked at the steaming bowl of mussels being put in front of her. "We'll all breathe easier when she's arrested. This smells wonderful."

"Okay, no more talk about Allison for the rest of the evening. This is our first night out in Savannah. Let's make a good memory." Devin popped a mussel into his mouth and closed his eyes with pleasure.

"I'm with you." The sounds of people, cars and boats mingled with the hum of conversation in the restaurant. "This is a great place to bring a date."

"Who says you're my date?" Devin chuckled as Carol's eyes sparkled with humor.

"You're paying for this. That makes it a date in my book." Devin shot back. "It's a business expense. I'm here purely on business."

"Then where's your client?"

"I expect he'll drop by when we're having coffee."

"You mean he's here?"

"This building is one of my projects." Devin smiled broadly. "Pretty special isn't it? I have three others I want to visit while we're here."

"It's so charming and Old World. I hadn't thought of you restoring a restaurant."

"It's much more than the restaurant. There are guest rooms on the upper floors. My company re-wired the building to conform to current codes and make it possible for people to use all their technology without blowing the circuits. Putting in Wi-Fi without being obvious is a science in these old buildings."

"I hadn't really thought of it that way. But owners don't have a choice. We all want to be plugged in all the time." Carol spooned up some of her broth.

"And have a coffeemaker in each room and a hairdryer in the bathroom." Devin ripped off a piece of roll and soaked up some of the broth. "This was a multi-million dollar restoration project. We only had six weeks to do the restaurant in the off season. We're doing the rooms and suites a couple at a time."

"Well, you're clearly doing a great job. It's beautiful and still completely authentic from what I can see."

"That was the idea." He smiled at her as he finished the last mussel. "There are three rooms left to do. You can come with me and see them tomorrow if you like."

"I'd like that. I'm still interested in real estate even if I'm not selling it. And besides, it will give me ideas for buying for the shop next year."

"Thinking ahead and planning. I have a feeling we'll have a lot of good years ahead of us, my dear." Devin reached out and covered one of Carol's hands. "We make a good team."

"Devin, good to see you again!" The Southern voice belonged to a very well-dressed man walking towards their table.

"Paul. Figured we'd see you before the evening was over." Devin stood up to shake hands. "I'd like you to meet my girlfriend, Carol Brock. Carol, this is Paul Rendquist, Paul meet Carol."

Carol smiled as he took her hand and raised it to his lips. "Very pleased to meet you, Carol. Do you by any chance have a twin sister who is single and available? It doesn't matter if she doesn't live here. I can change that."

"I'm so sorry, Paul." Carol's eyes sparkled with mirth. "I don't have a twin sister for you, I'm afraid, and I would think my daughter is at least a decade too young for you."

"I am devastated. Your beauty suggests that you could only have been born in the South. Tell me this is true."

"Apologies, again. I'm a Boston girl going back three generations."

"I am crushed and defeated." Paul pulled up a chair and signaled for a waitress. "May I offer you a cognac and coffee? It's on the house."

"Thank you, but I will pass on both and just finish my wine." Carol realized she hadn't been this relaxed since being at the farm.

Devin accepted and soon the two men were talking about the next room on the project list.

"There's a story that says that room is haunted. No-one has heard or seen anything in years but we keep the story going. It helps business. I'm hoping we'll get on the Ghost Tour one of these days." Paul swirled the cognac in his glass and lifted the bowl to his nose to savor the aroma of the golden liquid.

"Our guys won't be worrying about a ghost I'm sure, story or not. They're pretty excited about the plans we drew up."

"And so am I. I'm glad you're heading up the project. Can't think of a better person for it." Paul picked up his coffee. "Carol Brock. You're the real estate agent who was having a little trouble recently right? I saw

Ben Powell's report."

Carol realized with a little sigh she wasn't going to get past this story for awhile. "Surprised the story got this far south."

"I spend a lot of time on news web sites." He smiled kindly. "Everything back to normal now?"

"No. After this, I think I'll be looking at a whole new normal some day." Carol finished her wine, set the glass down and stood up. "If you'll excuse me, I'll just go to the ladies room and freshen up."

Both men watched as Carol walked away. Devin smiled ruefully. "We were hoping to get away from it all by coming here."

"Sorry Devin. I wasn't thinking."

"We'll be fine. There's still an issue of Allison, who is trying to hunt us down."

Paul's eyes widened. "I hadn't heard about that part of the story. You two broke up years ago."

"In my mind, yes. But not in hers. It turns out she's a psychopath who is still fixated on me and incensed that her mother willed me her Victorian." Devin sipped at the cognac. "She burned down my stable. Luckily, no-one was hurt and the horses were in the paddock. She's threatened Carol and she's been stalking both of us."

"We're hoping she'll be arrested before we get back. Her prints match those found where Marilyn was killed."

"Oh God, Devin. All this time and you didn't know."

"I went out with that crazy bitch for a year. She was the one always talking about how tragic Marilyn's death was. How she knew how much I loved Marilyn and how much I missed her."

"Wish there was something I could do to help."

"Keep me here for a couple more days and you will have helped a great deal more than you know."

"I can keep you busy for sure."

Their talk turned to technical issues when they saw Carol walking back onto the patio. They both stood as she reached the table.

"What gentlemen!" Carol smiled at Devin as she held her chair. "I could get used to this."

"A fine lady like you deserves only the best manners a Southern gentleman can offer." Paul remained standing. "I need to get going, but I look forward to seeing you both tomorrow. We should have lunch together."

"That sounds like a fine idea. It's been awhile since I sampled the lunch menu." Devin put his credit card over the bill their waitress had just delivered.

"We always have fresh Pecan pie. You won't want to miss that."

"We'll have to hit the gym for sure and that means some shopping first." Carol grinned. "Think I'd better get back and rest up."

"Oh no. Carol's getting organized and I'm included." Devin chuckled. "If you think I'm organized Paul, you haven't seen Carol in action. She's formidable."

Carol laughed and smiled at them both. "See you for lunch tomorrow."

Chapter Nineteen

"I'm way ahead on my Christmas shopping now, thanks to this trip." Carol looked out at the passing landscape, her bags neatly tucked in the trunk of the airport taxi. "I think Ashley will love the sweater I found."

"Judging by what we're bringing back with us, I'd say we've significantly enriched the merchants of Savannah." Devin grinned over at her.

"Just doing my best to keep the local economy afloat." Carol smiled back. "It'll be good to get back though. I want to list the condo before things go quiet over Christmas. I'll be staging it myself just by packing and moving a few things out."

"You can move a lot of things to the Dorchester house. It could use some better furnishings."

"I was thinking the same thing. I want to leave the main furniture in place until it sells. Then I'll get the movers in. Ashley and Jim's bedroom sets would fit in well. It would make it more like home for them, too." They were deep in discussion as the taxi pulled up at the departure level.

"Hi Jennifer. We're back safe and sound." Carol smiled at the sound of her friend's voice. "We should be at your place within half an hour or so.

"Nothing on Allison. She's keeping herself well hidden." She nodded her head. "See you in a bit then."

She smiled, closed her phone, and looked over at Devin. "Hope you brought an appetite for dinner tonight. Jennifer and Ben have been cooking again."

"I think we need to figure out some way to repay them for putting us up like this. We could have checked into a hotel until she's arrested."

"Too late now. Knowing Jennifer, she'd never hear of it anyway. It's just the way she is." Carol put a hand over Devin's. "I'm very lucky to have a friend like her. They're one in a million."

"I feel the same way about Gregory and Flynn. I never worry about the farm. They take care of it as if it were theirs." He paused. "Wait a minute. I have an idea. Didn't you say Jennifer and Ben are picking up their sailboat rental in Charleston?"

"That's the plan, why?"

"I have a client there with an amazing inn that my company renovated last year. We could rent them one of the suites and have everything billed to me. It's in the French Quarter and very close to the harbor. What do you think?"

"It's a very romantic idea. We could give it to them as a Christmas gift they can't refuse." Carol patted his leg. "You are so thoughtful."

"How about we put all your shopping bags in the truck cab?" Devin paid the taxi driver as they pulled up in front of Jennifer's home.

"Good idea. I'll just get someone to open the door. Be right back." Carol grabbed her new suitcase and walked up to the front door.

"SCOTT JUST CALLED." DEVIN WALKED INTO THE KITCHEN to the smell of fresh coffee. "I'll have a quick bite of breakfast with you folks and be on my way. He wants to meet me at the Dorchester house as soon as possible. Something about estate papers he needs me to help him find."

Carol poured coffee for them both. "Jennifer and I are going to take Charlie for a nice long walk after breakfast and then she'll drop me off to pick up my car. I'm going to call Colin today about listing the condo."

"Sounds like we both have places to go and people to see." Devin patted Carol's thigh as she sat down. "I'm going to check with Guzzo.

I think we should be able to go back to the farm. There's no evidence Allison has been anywhere near her car in over a week. She hasn't been seen near her townhouse. It's a safe bet she's on foot and couldn't get to the farm even if she wanted to. Every car rental agency is on alert and her credit cards are being monitored."

"I agree. I'd like nothing better than to fill up my car with some stuff and get moving." Carol spread strawberry jam on a piece of homemade apple muffin and popped it in her mouth. "Oh my, this is really good. You have to have one."

She broke off another piece and slathered jam on it. "Open up. Sin at seven."

Devin obediently opened his mouth for the morsel and rolled his eyes in appreciation. "We need the recipe for this for sure. Delicious."

They finished their breakfast and parted ways. "I'll see you later, sweetie. I'll call you after I speak with Guzzo. We can make our plans from there."

"You be good and we'll talk later." Carol rose up on her toes to plant a warm kiss on his lips. "Mmm. You taste like strawberry jam."

"You do too."

Devin parked in the driveway of the old Victorian. Looking at it, he admired its gracious angles yet again. *It's such a stately old place,* he thought, as he made a mental note that the whole verandah and stairs needed a fresh coat of paint. *After the repairs and renovations, not before*, he reasoned.

He strode up the stairs and walked to the door. He was mildly surprised to find it open a crack. Scott must not have shut it properly. Calling out Scott's name, he pushed it open and walked in and made his way toward the living room.

In the brief seconds it took for his brain to register what he was seeing and who was in the room, Devin felt a sharp sting in his neck. As he lost consciousness, his last coherent thought was *how did she bring down two grown men without a fight?*

195

CAROL AND JENNIFER WALKED BRISKLY along a path on the Common as Charlie pulled them eagerly forward, only to stop abruptly to sniff a bush or bench. "Devin and I will likely head back to the farm today or tomorrow. Allison's car hasn't moved in over a week and she hasn't used a credit card either."

"At least she's not stalking you anymore. That must be a huge relief."

"It is for sure. It's never happened to me before. That feeling that you're being watched is really eerie."

They'd been out for about half an hour when Carol's phone chirped. She looked at the number and then at Jennifer with a quizzical look on her face. "Wonder who it is? I don't recognize the number at all."

"Carol Brock." She suddenly stopped cold, her eyes wide and staring. "I'm listening."

Jennifer watched as Carol's face drained of color. "I don't have a car at the moment. It will take me at least an hour to get there."

Carol was shivering with more than the cold. "I understand, Allison. I will not call the police. I promise. I'll be there as soon as I possibly can."

"Oh God. She says she's drugged and tied up both Scott Haldimand, the estate lawyer, and Devin at the Wendover house. I'm to get there within one hour or she'll give them both lethal doses."

"C'mon then, let's get you to your car." They both looked at their watches as they broke into a run. Charlie raced to keep up with them. "How long from your condo to the Victorian?"

"At least half an hour, if the traffic isn't bad."

"Which it always is." Jennifer aimed the remote and had the doors unlocked before they reached her car. "I'll do my best to get you home as quickly as possible."

"Just don't speed. The last thing we need is to get stopped for a traffic ticket."

"I hear you loud and clear." Jennifer pulled out smoothly into the traffic. "You promised Allison you wouldn't call the police."

"I did. But you could call. This is a hostage taking by a wanted felon. I'm sure Guzzo would get a SWAT team out."

"Call him and then hand me the phone. Bring Charlie with you. He could create the distraction you need to get Allison off guard."

"It's worth a try. You know she's planning to kill Devin, Scott, and me?"

"I know. But you're not going to let that happen, right?"

"Damn right. She's messed with my life, my family, and my career more than enough already. She may be mentally ill, but she is a cold, calculating and ruthless bitch who is going to be stopped. Today." Carol no longer shivered. Adrenaline was pouring into her body, firing her up with grim determination that Allison's show was ending once and for all. "Her run is about to end if I have anything to do with it."

Jennifer smiled as her friend dialed up the detective's private mobile number and handed the phone back to her. "Detective Guzzo? It's Jennifer Barrett. Allison has taken Devin Elliot and Clara Wendover's lawyer hostage in the house in Dorchester. Carol is on her way there now. Allison insisted she not call the police and to come alone." She swallowed nervously and nodded. "Thank you. She's wearing a lime green car coat and has Charlie, my cocker spaniel with her."

"Good luck, Carol." Jennifer watched as Carol hurried to her car with Charlie in tow.

THE POLICE HAD SEALED BOTH ENDS OF THE STREET by the time Carol reached the Dorchester neighborhood. They were waiting for her as she drove up to the barricade.

"Ms. Brock, I'm officer Charlemagne. Detective Guzzo is on his way. How much time left in your hour?"

Carol looked at the car clock. "Ten minutes."

"He won't be here in time. You'd best get going. Stall her as long as you can while we get our team in place. Wear this." He took what appeared to be a woman's brooch out of a case and bent forward to attach it to her coat lapel.

"This will transmit everything to us. Try to let us know where in the house you are at all times in a way that won't alert her that we're listening in. Can you do that?"

"I'll do it. Thanks, officer."

Carol parked the car a few houses away from the Victorian. She could already see one black-uniformed officer with a rifle climbing a fence near the house. Another had come out onto the balcony of a townhouse unit across and down the street. He would have a direct line of fire at the front of the house, she realized, holding tightly to Charlie's leash and shifting her large tote on her shoulder. A small can of pepper spray was in her right pocket. She thanked Jennifer silently for having it in her glove compartment.

As she neared the house, she noticed the front curtains were closed. She spoke quietly towards the transmitter. "The living room drapes are closed. They were open the last I saw. They may be in there."

She took some deep breaths as she climbed the front stairs. The front door was open a crack. Stepping in, she unleashed Charlie and called out Devin's name. The dog's paws scrabbled on the hardwood as he surged forward towards the smells of his friend. Carol heard the muttered oath and waited for Allison to show herself.

"Damn dog. Get out of here you stupid animal." There was a muffled thump and Charlie yelped in pain.

Carol edged towards the sounds. "She's in the living room on the right," she whispered.

She spoke out. "Allison. I came as you asked. I got here in under an hour as you demanded. I have not called the police as you also demanded. What do you want?"

Carol heard Charlie whimpering but didn't dare go to him.

"Come into the living room, Carol. I want you to see your big man Devin helpless as a fish out of water." Allison's voice was flat and emotionless. "I want you to see what a woman can accomplish when she puts her mind to it."

Carol stepped to the entrance and saw Devin unconscious on the floor. Scott's wide eyes looked pleading. His hands were tied in front of him and his mouth was covered in duct tape.

Then she saw Allison with a syringe in her hand. She stood still, well out of range. "It's a bit hard to see in here. Can we open the curtains a bit?"

"I can see well enough."

"What do you want Allison?"

"I wanted this house. That was all I ever wanted."

"That's not exactly true. You also wanted Devin." Carol took a deep breath and let it out slowly.

"But he doesn't want me. He thinks I'm too needy. Well, I don't need him or this house now. They say you can't take it with you. But I'm going to. I'm going to take it all with me when I die."

"There's no need for anyone to die, Allison. You need help. You're sick."

Allison's words ground out caustically. "That's what my mother said. She pleaded with me to see a shrink. What do they know?"

Charlie had stopped whimpering but his breathing didn't seem right. More than anything, Carol wanted this to be over.

"What happened to your first husband, Allison? It wasn't an accident was it?"

Allison sneered. "He didn't deserve me. I was his trophy wife. His first wife bore his three brats and took care of his home. But she wasn't a party girl any more and he liked to party. When I came along, he was ripe for the picking."

"Why did you kill him?" Carol kept her voice even.

"He was still paying support to wife number one and his snotty kids. His lawyer had worked it so I would only get one-quarter in the settlement. It wasn't enough to support my lifestyle. I knew he had cut his ex and the kids out of his will. I got it all when he died."

"Why did you set the stable on fire at Devin's?" Carol wondered how much longer she needed to stall before the police were ready to make a move.

"He stole this house from me. I wanted him to feel the pain of loss the way I did."

"Well, the horses survived. They were put outside before your bomb went off." With her eyes adjusted to the filtered light, Carol saw Allison's eyes narrow. "Where did you learn about explosives?"

"Everything is on the internet. It was quite simple really. I bought the ingredients from different places and put it together with a fuse and a timer. "

Carol saw Devin twitch. "What's the plan, Allison? What's next?"

Allison sniggered. "You will die. We will all die. But, you can choose how to die."

"What do you mean I can choose?"

"I have enough sedative in this needle to kill one of you. You choose who gets the lethal injection."

"What will happen to the other two?" Carol realized grimly that she already knew but she couldn't help asking.

"The other two will die of smoke inhalation or burn to death. Choose Carol. There isn't much time left."

Devin groaned and tried to move.

"Choose now, Carol."

Carol saw the Blue Mountain pottery fish on the table only two feet away. This fish may be out of water but it isn't helpless, she thought as she lunged towards the table, grabbed the pottery and heaved it towards Allison. Years of yoga had given her strong arm muscles that were now fueled by a surge of adrenaline more powerful than anything she had known since giving birth.

The fish hit Allison full in the forehead and shattered on impact. A sharp shard gouged her right eye, leaving her howling in pain as she crumpled to the floor. The syringe rolled harmlessly away.

"That's for Charlie, bitch." Carol lunged towards Allison and emptied the can of pepper spray in her face. "This is for Devin and Scott."

"Come in, now!" Carol roared into the transmitter as she dove to the floor. "We're all on the floor."

Suddenly the front and back doors flew back on their hinges.

Heavy footfalls could be heard over Allison's anguished howls. Within seconds, the officers had Allison handcuffed and were carrying her towards the front door.

Carol slid over to Charlie. She felt cautiously around his ribs and was rewarded with one large wet lick on her hand. "You done good, Charlie."

Carol heard Devin groan and pulled herself over to him. "You okay, big guy?

He groaned, opened his eyes and closed them again. "What happened?"

"Allison happened. Tell you all about it later." Carol was on her feet looking at the SWAT team guys when she suddenly remembered what Allison had been talking about.

"There's a bomb somewhere. She's done it before. Trust me, she's planning to burn the place down. It's probably downstairs. We need to get out of here fast."

Even as she said it, the old house shuddered as a muffled boom reverberated through it. Within seconds, smoke billowed around the edges of the door to the basement.

"Call the fire department now!" Carol shouted into the transmitter. "We need to get out. Devin, can you stand?"

He groaned again groggily. Two officers hoisted him up by his armpits and dragged him towards the front door. Two others grabbed Scott and rushed him towards the door. They were almost there when another muffled blast shook the house.

"Everyone out now!" The team leader barked out the order.

Carol picked up Charlie as gently as possible and walked quickly through the front door and down the front stairs.

Within minutes, fire trucks rolled down the street as breaking glass signaled the basement windows breaking from heat. Soon they saw flames flickering behind a ground floor window.

Devin leaned heavily against a squad car taking in deep breaths. "Can they save the house?"

"We're not sure yet, sir. An ambulance is on the way to check you over. Want to sit in the car until they get here?"

"No, I think I need the fresh air." He looked around for Carol. "Do you know where Ms. Brock is?"

"I believe she went to put a dog in her car. Said she'd be right back for you."

Devin took in a deep breath. "Oh, good."

"Scott, you okay?" Carol, Devin, and Scott stood huddled together as they watched the firefighters bring the blaze under control.

"I've been better. She was good. She altered her voice just enough that I didn't realize it was her. Told me she was calling from the alarm company and that there had been a break-in. Said I needed to go over and re-set the alarm. So I went."

When I got there, she jabbed me with the needle before I could do a thing. Next thing I know I wake up and my hands are tied. She told me if I made you the least bit suspicious she'd kill me."

"You gave a great performance Scott, I'll give you that. I had no inkling there was any problem."

"I like my life as much as the next person. I didn't think today was a good day to die."

"I'm with you a hundred percent on that, buddy." Devin looked at Carol who nodded. "You okay to drive home, Scott?"

"I am. No problem. I guess the police are finished with me?" He massaged his neck.

"Here comes Guzzo. We can check right now. This guy never goes home, I tell you."

"Len. How are we doing? Can we leave?"

"You can. It's all up to the fire department now. There's one thing though. How did Allison know you were out of town or back in town?"

Devin looked sheepish. "I think that happened through my office. I called in this morning and learned that a female reporter had repeatedly called looking for an interview about one of my projects here in Boston. Our receptionist told her I was out of town and couldn't be reached. She kept calling back. The receptionist finally got fed up and gave her my return date. I'm betting it was Allison."

"You're probably right. She may be mentally ill, but she's very cunning. I'll give her that." Guzzo jotted down Devin's comment in his notebook. "I'll want to talk to that receptionist and let her hear Allison's voice to see if she recognizes it."

Devin looked at the smoking house as a squad of firefighters continued to rain water into it. He put his arm around Carol. "I hope we can salvage this."

"If anyone can salvage it, you can." Carol pulled herself reluctantly out of his embrace. "We need to get Charlie to the vet. I can't rest until we get him looked over."

"Of course! Scott, sorry you got dragged into this, but it's over. Thanks for everything. We'll be in touch." Devin checked to see if his truck was in the clear. "Let's get the number for the nearest animal hospital. I'll meet you there with Charlie."

"Already have it. There's one over on Morrisey."

"Let's go. Have you told Jennifer?"

"No. Let's see what's up. I don't want her to worry needlessly."

"Good point. I'll follow you."

"Hi Jennifer. Charlie is a hero. He may have saved four lives. Allison is in custody. She tried to burn down the house but failed." Carol looked over at the dog who lay quietly on the passenger seat. "As you know, Allison doesn't like animals. Charlie has three cracked ribs.

"I'm bringing him home as we speak. He's a bit drugged but he's not in pain. I took care of the bill."

"If Charlie saved even one life, the cracked ribs are worth it. I'm so glad I made you bring him along." Jennifer punched her arm in the air in a victory salute.. "Are you coming back here for the night?"

"Thanks, but no. We really need to re-connect with the farm and the horses."

"I hear you. I'll see you in a bit."

Chapter Twenty

"Where are you?" Carol was about an hour from the farm. Her BMW was fully loaded with boxes and clothes on hangars.

"I'm about half an hour outside of Boston. You?" Devin smiled over at a dozen bags of bootie from Carol's shopping excursions in Savannah. "I'm starting to wonder how we're going to fit you into the farm. Maybe I should build you a house for your collections."

"I promise it's not going to be like that." Carol grinned at the phone. "Most of it is for Christmas. Which reminds me, don't you dare poke around in those bags. Some of it is your Christmas gifts."

"I can't poke, I'm driving."

"Good, just keep it that way." Carol turned onto the road that would take her to the farm. "I hope you have no plans for this evening other than to feed me wine and some food and cuddle up near the fireplace."

"My plan exactly. Since you're going to get there first, you're in charge of food and wine."

"If Flynn hasn't beaten me to it."

"Ah yes, the Flynn factor. I did call ahead." Devin grinned. "We'll both be pleasantly surprised I'm sure."

Carol found the hidden key and opened the door to the mud room. The comforting smell of lasagna filled the air. Taking off her boots, she walked through the kitchen and into the solarium, basking in the warm feeling of being home. Oh how romantic, she broke into a warm smile as she looked around.

The lights were all dimmed. A number of candles stood ready. A small table had been set a few feet away from the glowing fireplace. A small bouquet of fresh flowers sat on a cheerful checkered yellow table cloth next to a silver ice bucket chilling a bottle of wine.

Flynn did it again, she thought as she let the room infuse her with its welcome ambiance. *But first, I need to unload the car and make room for the stuff coming in the truck.* She walked briskly back to the mud room and slipped her boots back on.

Walking towards the car, she looked over at the new stable that was beginning to take shape. Already, the roof trusses were up and she could see a sizable pile of lumber and roofing materials stacked under a tarp.

"Need some help?" Gregory walked into a pool of light near the paddock. "I'm just finishing up here."

"That would be great. I brought a full carload." Carol gave him a quick hug. "If you could bring the boxes into the mud room, I'll take them in from there. Devin should be here in ten to fifteen minutes with another load."

"Where are you going to put all this stuff?" Gregory winked at her. "Seems like you're going to need your own house."

Carol laughed outright. "That's exactly what Devin said. Women need a little more than a couple of pair of jeans and boots."

"Apparently."

Carol kept chuckling as she took a box out of Gregory's hands. "And there are four seasons to dress for."

"There's only two for men, warm and cold. Flynn's an exception."

"See? Now you're getting it. Oh, here comes Devin." A pair of headlights could be seen dancing over the ruts in the lane.

"Can you move my car out of the way please?" Carol handed Gregory her keys. She stood at the entrance to the kitchen and watched as Devin pulled up and got out of the truck. The two men shook hands and walked off to examine the stable project. Carol went off to organize the first load of boxes.

"HERE'S TO YOU, MADAM. I hear you were amazing. Guzzo and the team heard it all." Devin clinked his glass to Carol's. "He particularly liked the part where you pepper sprayed her and said it was for me and Scott."

"To be honest, I didn't know I had it in me." Carol sipped her wine appreciatively. "If someone had told me even two months ago that I would bring down a psychopathic murderer and arsonist, I would have checked what they were putting in their coffee. I don't mind some excitement in my life, but this was definitely extreme."

"Well, you saved my sorry butt and Scott's too."

Carol cut off a piece of the fragrant lasagna and ate it with gusto. "We haven't eaten since breakfast. I'm famished."

"Well, eat up, my dear." Devin's eyes smoldered as he gazed into Carol's eyes. "You and I have a long date night ahead if I have anything to say about it. I need to properly thank you for saving my life."

"You can thank me for it for the rest of my life if you like." She looked back at him and smiled, her eyes sparkling in the candlelight.

"That is certainly my plan."

Epilogue

"They're here!" Gregory opened the mud room door and let in a blast of cold air.

Carol, Devin, and Flynn got up from the kitchen table, put their coffee mugs in the sink, and went to the doorway to welcome their guests.

"Merry Christmas, everyone!" Jennifer came in first with an armload of gifts. Lana was behind her with a box of desserts. Ben and Mark brought up the rear with babies and baby gear.

"Jim and Ashley are out riding. I'm sure they'll be back soon. They must have heard the van." Carol let Jennifer put down her bags and then reached out to give her a warm hug.

"What's this I see?" Jennifer grabbed Carol's left hand. "Oh my. This looks like an heirloom."

Carol held up her hand and gently waved it as the diamonds and rubies sparkled in the sunlight streaming through the window. "It's Victorian. Flynn found it and told Devin to buy it. He knew I'd love it."

"Congratulations, Carol. You two will be very happy together." They hugged again. "When did he ask you?"

"Christmas morning. The box was in the Christmas tree when I came down." Carol laughed lightheartedly. "He said it's a gift, so you can't refuse it. What could I do? I had to accept."

"I see the new stable is finished already. That was fast."

"Gregory and Devin know a few people. When the word got out about the fire, a bunch of volunteers came forward to make sure the horses would have a warm stable as quickly as possible." Carol took the dessert box out of Lana's hands. "You go help Mark with the twins. Where's Danny?"

"He ran off to see the horses. Merry Christmas, Carol." Lana took off her hat and coat as Mark set down the two baby seats. "It's so good to be back here. I can't get over how beautiful and peaceful it is here."

"It won't be peaceful, once we're all in the house. Enjoy it while you can." Carol smiled and walked over to see the babies. "Hello, little darlings. I bet Santa Claus was really good to you two."

"More than you can imagine." Lana started undoing Angela's snowsuit. Carol got to work on Christopher's.

"Here come Ashley and Jim." Carol looked out the window with pride as her tall daughter and son rode into sight. "You'll have built-in babysitting for the next few days."

"Just being here is like a vacation. I don't know what's in the oven but it smells heavenly."

"Devin and Flynn have made a couple of their specialties. I've only been allowed to observe."

"Ben just told me he's going to come and speak at Syracuse in April after they get back from their trip." Ashley breezed into the house just ahead of her brother. "He got everything confirmed before the university shut down for the holidays."

"That's wonderful news, Ash." Carol's smile radiated her pleasure at the happiness on her daughter's face. "You must be so excited."

"I am. I can hardly wait to introduce him around. He's going to stay a couple of days at the Dean's house."

"And Jim has some news to share." Devin looked up from the counter where he was chopping cabbage.

"I do." Jim picked up Angela, who squirmed happily in his strong arms. "Devin has asked me to meet up with his partners to see if I'd make a suitable student intern for the summer. Get some on-the-job training."

"That would be excellent for you, Jim." Ben overheard the announcement as he stepped into the kitchen. "What's for dinner? This house smells incredible."

"Devin and I have been testing some of the recipes from the Thai cookbook Carol and Jennifer gave him. I think you'll like what we've cooked up." Flynn rinsed off his hands and gave the counter a quick wipe. "That's it for now."

"WHAT'S HAPPENING WITH THE WENDOVER HOUSE?" Ben and Devin stood in the solarium with cold beers in their hands. A light snow had begun to fall in the waning twilight.

"The basement took a lot of damage. We're going to have to replace some of the original support beams. They're pretty charred." Devin watched as Aero, Sabrina and Pablo got brushed down in front of the new stable after an afternoon of riding the young people over the trails.

"There's some major damage in the dining room and living room. I think we'll rip out the walls, floors and ceilings and start over. Re-do all the wiring, insulation and some plumbing at the same time." He took a pull on his beer. "I figure we can get the house in fighting trim by June or so.

"Is insurance covering?"

"Oh yes. It's a hefty price tag, too."

"What's the latest on Allison?"

"She's at Bridgewater undergoing another psychiatric evaluation. The first one was inconclusive. Her lawyer has pleaded her not guilty by reason of insanity. Apparently it's a rare defense and a very difficult one to prove beyond any doubt." Devin watched as Danny and Charlie cavorted with Mark. "I just hope they keep her there for the rest of her life."

"Amen to that. The world will be a lot safer with her behind bars."

Carol joined them with a glass of wine. She was smiling brightly. "Colin just called. An offer will be coming in on the condo tomorrow at close to full asking." Carol raised her glass and looked lovingly at Devin. "Here's to a new year and new beginnings, my love."

Next up in the Look to the Future Series: Road to Tomorrow (Fall 2012)

Andrea Garrett is trying to escape her abusive marriage. Fearing for her life, she leaves her two small children with her twin brother and flees her home the day before her husband is due to arrive back from a tour of duty. After falling asleep at the wheel and landing in a ditch, her life takes on a new direction when strangers step in and introduce her to a life she could only have imagined and one that could save her soul and give her children the future they deserve.

CPSIA information can be obtained at www.ICGtesting.com
Printed in the USA
LVOW080011090513

332905LV00001B/5/P

9 780987 930040